Praise for

Jones

This gripping romantic thriller is another stand out for Hill. Her compelling characters and well-scripted plot offer readers an immersive reading experience, one filled with tension, emotion, and unexpected twists. This is a must-read for anyone who loves romantic thrillers threaded with captivating mystery. It's sure to linger long after the last page.

-*Women Using Words*

Jones is an intriguing, well-crafted mystery novel with its clues methodically revealed right up to a satisfying ending.

-Sue M., *NetGalley*

The Apple Diary

Hill has always been known for captivating storylines and well-developed characters, so it should surprise no one that *The Apple Diary* is an enchanting, heartwarming story that will leave one wanting more. Readers will appreciate her intriguing storyline and immersive story world.

-*Women Using Words*

Hunter's Revenge

Hill brings it all together for Tori in book five of this series in ways only a skilled storyteller can. Readers will no doubt appreciate the depth she brings to Hunter's story. *Hunter's Revenge* is a first-rate piece of storytelling and I guarantee Hunter fans will not be disappointed.

-*Women Using Words*

As always, Hill does a fantastic job of weaving the reader through a multi-layered path into a beautiful meadow of a perfectly told story.

-Denise J., *NetGalley*

Such a great ending to one of this genre's most beloved series.
-Patricia B., *NetGalley*

I could wax on and on about this novel, but I won't. If you've yet to read this series, crack on with it now. It is brilliant.

-Natalie T., *NetGalley*

Timber Falls

Gerri Hill is the only lesfic writer I can think of who can write absolutely any genre, and consistently produce top-quality work. Romance, mystery, paranormal...*Timber Falls* is no exception.

-Karen C., *NetGalley*

I would say this is a typical Hill novel but only if you understand 'typical' to mean an outstanding story, intriguing characters, beautiful settings, and unparalleled writing.

-Della B., *NetGalley*

This book may well be the best book Gerri Hill has written in years. It has everything needed to keep her readers reading into the wee hours of the morning...

-Abbott F., *NetGalley*

The Great Charade

One of the big loves I had for this book, among other things, was it is so full of rich dialogue.

-Carol C., *NetGalley*

The Great Charade really is a heartwarming, romantic holiday book that I'm really glad I was able to read this season.

-Betty H., *NetGalley*

…this was a perfect Christmas book. Not only does it nail the Christmas theme, but the premise is also engaging from the very first page… I absolutely adored this Christmas novel and it's definitely one of my favourites from Gerri Hill.

-Natalie T., *NetGalley*

Red Tide at Heron Bay

Ms. Hill has certainly done it again. I was hooked from the beginning to the end. This is a murder, mystery, romance with loveable main characters who are fully developed and has great chemistry… You can actually picture yourself in the setting watching the story unfold. This is now one of my favorite books.

-Bonnie A., *NetGalley*

This is exactly why Gerri Hill is a master in suspense and crime and romance books! Sooo good! This book was a brilliant slow burn in both ways, the romance and the crime.

-Stephanie D., *NetGalley*

Another brilliant gripping crime thriller from Gerri Hill, couldn't put it down and read in one sitting!

-Claire E., *NetGalley*

Gerri Hill writes wonderful mysteries, and this is no exception. I know I'm reading something special when I can't put a book down.

-*The Lesbian Review*

The Stars at Night

The Stars at Night is a beautiful mountain romance that will transport you to a paradise. It's a story of self-discovery, family, and rural living. This romance was a budding romance that snuck-up and on two unsuspecting women who found themselves falling in love under the stars...It's a feel-good slow-burn romance that will make your heart melt.

-Les Rêveur

Hill is such a strong writer. She's able to move the plot along through the characters' dialogue and actions like a true boss. It's a masterclass in showing, not telling. The story unfolds at a languid pace which mirrors life in a small, mountain town, and her descriptions of the environment bring the world of the book alive.

-The Lesbian Review

Gillette Park

...is a phenomenal book! I wish I could give this more than five stars. Yes, there is a paranormal element, and a love story, and conflict, and danger. And it's all worth it. Thank you, Gerri Hill, for writing a brilliant masterpiece!

-Carolyn M., *NetGalley*

This book was just what I was hoping for and wickedly entertaining... If you are a Hill fan, grab this.

-Lex Kent's Reviews, *goodreads*

Gerri Hill has written another action-packed thriller. The writing is excellent and the characters engaging. Wow!

-Jenna F., *NetGalley*

LYON'S DEN

GERRI HILL

Other Bella Books by Gerri Hill

About the Author

Gerri Hill has forty-five published works, including the 2022 GCLS winner *The Great Charade* and the 2021 GCLS winner *Gillette Park*, the 2020 GCLS winner *After the Summer Rain*, the 2019 winner *The Neighbor*, the 2017 GCLS winner *Paradox Valley*, 2014 GCLS winner *The Midnight Moon*, 2011, 2012 and 2013 winners *Devil's Rock*, *Hell's Highway* and *Snow Falls*, as well as the 2013 Lambda finalist *At Seventeen*. Gerri lives in south-central Texas, only a few hours from the Gulf Coast, a place that has inspired many of her books. With her partner, Diane, they share their life with two Australian shepherds—Rylee and Mason—and a couple of furry felines.

For more, visit her website at gerrihill.com.

Bella Books, Inc.
P.O. Box 10543
Tallahassee, FL 32302

First Edition - 2025

Editor: Medora MacDougall
Cover Designer: Kayla Mancuso

ISBN: 978-1-64247-640-8

PUBLISHER'S NOTE

LYON'S DEN

GERRI HILL

BELLA BOOKS

CHAPTER ONE

Joni James stared at her boss, her perfectly plucked eyebrows drawn together in a sharp V. "Excuse me? *What?*"

Mr. Turnbull sat down and gave a fake smile. "What part didn't you understand?"

"Well, I actually stopped listening when I heard 'wilderness.'"

"It's an assignment, Joni. Like many before." He pointed at her and waved his hand in a circle. "What? I don't understand this look you have on your face."

She stood up quickly, pacing. A retreat? In the woods? For a freakin' *month*? Was he out of his mind?

"Look, not to be disrespectful, but…no. Absolutely *not* going. As you know, I was born and raised in Manhattan. I don't do woods. I certainly don't do wilderness. I prefer concrete under my feet." She pointed to herself. "I know I'm gay, but I'm not *that* kind of gay. I wear suits, I wear makeup. I wear lipstick." She smiled and shook her head. "I don't do the woods," she said again louder than before. "I'm sure you can find someone who loves the outdoors who would jump at this assignment."

"Of course I could. It's because you hate the woods that I want *you* to do it. You're perfect for this."

She looked past him to the view of downtown Denver. She brought her eyes higher, seeing the mountains in the distance. Mountains she had never ventured into. Mountains she had no *desire* to venture into. Why had she ever left Manhattan? Why had she moved out here?

Don't you remember? Her name was Elana, and you thought you were in love. Why in the hell hadn't she moved back east already?

She blew out her breath, then sat down again. "Okay. Explain it once more."

"It's a retreat for women. It's in Tin Cup, which is south in the Gunnison National Forest."

Forest. For god's sake, a fucking forest. She closed her eyes and rubbed her forehead but said nothing.

"I would like you to write an in-depth article on the place."

She raised an eyebrow. "Why me?"

"Because you'll hate it. And because my wife went there in September and came back a completely different person. I don't even know her anymore."

"Charlotte? The woman who does champagne brunch every single day went to the woods?" The woman was dripping in diamonds and furs. Why in the world would *she* go to a place like that?

"Yes. She *used* to do champagne brunch every day. She no longer drinks alcohol. She's cut her hair short and has taken up yoga. She's eating tofu now, if you can believe that."

She frowned, then her eyes widened as she had a brilliant idea. "But that's great! There you go! You already have your insight. You don't need *me*. You can write the article yourself based on your wife's experience," she said enthusiastically.

He stared at her for a long, quiet moment before he spoke. "She's filed for divorce."

"*What?* Charlotte?" She finally understood. "Oh my god. You want me to do a hit piece. And because I don't like the woods…"

"You're perfect for it. Yes, a hit piece. I want to *ruin* this place."

"Why do you think this place—"

"The Lyon's Den." He smirked. "What a silly name."

"Right. Why do you think this place—Lyon's Den—is the reason she wants a divorce?"

"Because it's a man-bashing place, I'm sure. Charlotte is like a stranger now." His eyes narrowed. "She lost nearly twenty pounds while she was there. She changed the way she dresses, the way she eats. She's got these new friends that she met there. She donated money to the Colorado Wilderness Conservancy of all places. And she's joined a hiking club! But she, like you, hates the woods! Or she used to. She's been brainwashed, I'm certain of it."

She was at a loss for words. Surely he didn't seriously expect her to spend a month out there just to write a hit piece. She could do that from her desk in her comfortable office chair.

"You're booked for the month of July. You might want to research it before you go. I'll email you all the correspondence I have from them." He tapped some papers on his desk. "I'll forward the info they sent me, but there's a waiver for you to sign. And from what I've learned, the owner doesn't give interviews. They know you're a journalist and know who you work for, but I don't think they're interested in publicity, so I don't know how much cooperation you'll get."

She again rubbed her forehead. She wondered how long it would take to find a new job if she simply quit and walked out. Or she could simply refuse the assignment. Would he fire her? If so, it could be her excuse to move back east. She sighed. *I wonder how much wine I have at home.*

CHAPTER TWO

"Are you serious? Why you? You hate the great outdoors!"

Joni opened up her laptop and plopped down on the sofa. "Because he's fucking insane, that's why."

Kimberly sat down beside her. "Does he not know you?"

Joni fake smiled at that. "That's why he picked me. He *wants* me to hate it there—which I will—and he wants me to write a hit piece on them."

She pulled up the website, going immediately to "About" and clicking there. "Ah. Now I know why it's called Lyon's Den. It's owned by Kendall Lyon."

Kimberly leaned closer. "Oh wow. She's cute."

Joni stared at the dark-haired woman who was smiling charmingly at the camera. Her short hair appeared to be windblown, and she was surrounded by trees. "You think so?"

Kimberly laughed. "Oh, that's right. You go for the more femme type." She patted her leg. "That's worked out great for you, hasn't it."

"I just haven't met the right one," she said in a clipped tone. She turned her attention back to the screen. "And yes, she's cute.

But her kind—no. Way too woodsy for me." She clicked out of that and went back to the main page. Her eyes widened. "Oh my god. Look at this! They're climbing fucking trees!"

"There's an obstacle course too. Looks like Ninja Warrior stuff. How fun!"

"Seriously?" she muttered. "Fun? Can you see me out there?"

Kimberly laughed. "No." She pointed to the top. "Click on the rules."

She did. Her eyes widened as she read. "Oh, hell no. No fucking way."

Kimberly nearly laughed hysterically as she read out loud. "No cell phone usage except during quiet time in your own room. No alcohol permitted on the premises." She laughed again. "If they had a rule for no cursing, then they'd hit all your vices," she teased.

Joni slammed the laptop closed. "That's fucking crazy. What's the purpose of these stupid rules?" She grabbed her phone and held it lovingly to her chest, then looked at the glass of wine sitting on the coffee table.

"What are you going to do?"

"Well, obviously there's only one thing I *can* do." She picked up the wine. "I'm going to have to quit my job."

CHAPTER THREE

Joni stopped her rental car at the entrance, a large metal gate standing open invitingly. Above the entrance was a large wooden beam, its ominous sign seeming to mock her.

LYON'S DEN RETREAT

"I must be insane."

Obviously, no, she had not quit her job at *Mountain Life Magazine*. And no amount of pleading—begging—had changed Turnbull's mind. She'd even written a quick article based on a perusal of the Lyon's Den website. She'd absolutely trashed the place; no one in their right mind would pay money to go there after she'd ripped them so thoroughly. He loved it. In fact, he said it was exactly what he wanted. However, to avoid any potential legal issues, he thought she needed to actually *go* to the place before trashing it. It was a minor detail, in her opinion, but he didn't agree. He wanted her "in the trenches" as he'd put it. He'd even ponied up the money to rent a Jeep Wrangler for the trip as the instructions said a "high clearance vehicle recommended."

So here she was, in the middle of freakin' nowhere, already feeling claustrophobic from the forest surrounding her. Yeah,

yeah, the views had been pretty, but she was not used to mountain driving and the trek across Cottonwood Pass had nearly done her in.

By the grace of god, the Jeep's navigation had gotten her to the tiny so-called town of Tin Cup over a boulder-laden road that had her bouncing around like a pinball. The directions that she'd printed out—as instructed—to navigate from there had left her clueless. After driving around in circles for nearly an hour, she'd ventured into the general store, seemingly the only business in town.

"I keep telling Kenni her directions are all wrong. Can't imagine anyone could find her place without my help." The very friendly man had shuffled out to the porch with her. "Go on up yonder there past the old church. Don't take that first left. That's not really a road, but that's where most go wrong and they end up at the old Stanford Mine. Most get lost on their way back down. No, you take that second road there. It's bumpy as hell, but you'll make it in that Jeep. Then you're going to take a right where the road forks. Stay on that for a good mile or two. You'll come to her place soon enough."

And here she was. About to enter the Lyon's Den. She glanced at the clock on the console. She had eleven minutes to spare. According to the very nice woman named Sky that she'd spoken with two days ago, unofficial check-in was any time after one o'clock but before four o'clock. At four was the official welcome and the meet and greet with the other participants. Then they would have their individual check-in and be assigned rooms. Dinner was at six sharp.

She gripped the steering wheel tighter, her eyes still glued to the sign. Then, with great effort, she made herself drive through the gates of hell. *Maybe it wouldn't be so bad*, she thought. She had at least gotten a new wardrobe out of the deal. Not that she would ever wear any of these clothes again. Turnbull had handed over his personal credit card and had sent Dana—an avid hiker—out shopping with her. She'd been horrified at the clothes that Dana had picked out, but they were going by the list that was on the website—jeans, hiking shorts, T-shirts, sweats, hiking boots, and the like. The only thing of hers that she packed were the silk pajamas she slept in.

The road spilled into a clearing and a huge lodge came into view. The parking area was on the left and it was nearly full. She didn't know if she was more surprised by the number of vehicles or the type of vehicles. There were the giant SUVs—Yukon, Expedition, Wagoneer, and Suburban. Smaller SUVs—Lexus and BMW. Then she spotted a Mercedes. What the hell kind of clients did this place cater to anyway?

She found a spot on the end and parked. Before she turned the engine off, she had a notion to pull away and leave. But no. How bad could it be? She killed the engine and, with a heavy sigh, opened the door.

She got out, her new boots crunching on the rocks. She ignored the fact that her feet hurt. The first thing that struck her was the smell. She breathed deeply. Vanilla? Butterscotch? The second thing she noticed was the quiet. She looked around, seeing no one and hearing nothing. She tilted her head. It was eerily quiet. Where was the traffic noise? Where was the familiar hum of the city? The breeze was blowing through the tree that she had parked under. There were birds—tiny little gray things—flitting about and tweeting at her. She looked up, watching them for a moment.

"Can I help you with your luggage?"

She jumped and nearly tripped in her haste to turn around. It was her. The Lyon woman. Her hair was as windblown as in the picture on her website, just begging to be tamed. Her eyes were dark and alert. There was a hint of a smile on her face, and Joni thought she was much more attractive in person.

"I…"

"You're the last one. I'm assuming you're Joni James. The reporter?" The woman flicked her wrist up, glancing at the big sports watch on her wrist. "Running late, I guess. You only have a few minutes to spare."

"Journalist," she corrected. "And yes, I'm late. Sorry. I got lost. The very nice gentleman at the general store got me back on track."

The woman nodded. "Jimmy. He says my directions suck."

She was about to agree when the woman pointed to the back of the Jeep she'd rented. While it wasn't the only Jeep there, she was parked next to a huge-ass Expedition that dwarfed it. Perhaps she should have asked Turnbull for something a little more luxurious to rent. Maybe then she wouldn't have felt like she was on a trampoline while driving.

"Luggage? I'll help. I don't want to get behind schedule. Everyone is already waiting."

"Yes. Okay. Thank you." Damn, but the woman was all business, wasn't she? She went back inside the vehicle and unlocked the back door.

"Three bags, huh? Missed that section where you'll have access to a washer and dryer?"

She gave a humorless smile. "I'm a heavy packer. Sorry." She hurried around the back, taking one of the bags. "I can get this one."

"Sure. Well, come on. We're running late."

The woman strode off, leaving her standing there holding her most precious bag. She went back to the front seat and grabbed the backpack that Dana had bought for her. It held her laptop and some other things that she would normally keep in her purse—a purse she'd left behind. She slung it over her shoulder, feeling completely out of place.

"What the hell am I doing here?" she murmured as she hurried to catch up with the Lyon woman.

CHAPTER FOUR

Kenni smiled broadly at the twenty women who were gathered in the dining room, which also served as the lecture hall—five round tables with four women sitting at each. She glanced over their faces, most showing excitement. She looked at the latecomer, Joni James. The journalist. She appeared to be more nervous than excited. Cute, though. Hazel eyes with a hint of green in them. Light-brown hair that barely brushed her shoulders. Parted on the side and swept across her forehead—she didn't seem like their normal clients. She was a bit too young, for one. Of course, she wasn't a real client. She was here to do a piece for some magazine. Well, it wasn't the first one, and she doubted it would be the last.

Sky cleared her throat beside her, and Kenni drew her gaze away from the lovely Joni James. She addressed the group.

"Welcome, everyone. I'm Kendall Lyon, your host for the next month. Most everyone calls me Kenni. You're going to love it here." She motioned to the women standing behind her. "Let me introduce you to the staff.

"My right hand, Sky Reynolds. She does a little of everything around here. I'd be lost without her."

Sky stepped forward, her blond hair cut stylishly for summer. She smiled broadly and gave a wave. "I've spoken with most of you on the phone. Welcome." She clapped her hands together enthusiastically. "I can't wait to get started."

"And this is Mindy Furbaugh," Kenni said, moving down the line. "She will lead our meditation classes and is also our expert yoga instructor."

"Hello, everyone."

"Next is Wanda. She plans our menus and supervises the kitchen staff." She paused. "She's everyone's honorary mother and tries to keep us all in line. Tough job."

"I try, honey."

Kenni turned to her right. "This is Karla Timpson. If you can't tell by looking at her, she'll be your trainer in the gym."

On cue, Karla flexed her biceps, getting applause in the process, as usual. "Can't wait to get started, ladies."

"And this is Jenn Klein. She is our outdoor enthusiast, and she has designed all of the obstacle courses and will lead our daily hikes."

"Hello, ladies," Jenn greeted with a wave. Her dark hair was pulled into its familiar ponytail, and she looked eager to get started.

Kenni walked closer to the group, going to stand between two tables. "If you've read through all the information that Sky has sent you, then you already have an idea of what your days will be like. Those of you who got here early have already had a chance to look around the grounds." She looked pointedly at Joni James, who had a rather bored expression on her face.

"Let's go over some of our rules and the reasons for them. First off, there are no TVs on the property. And cell phone usage is restricted to your room during your evening hours. I urge you to limit phone use. Stay off social media. Disconnect from the world while you're here. Get rid of the electronics in your life. Get away from all that noise. Free your mind," she said, repeating the same spiel she used with every new group. "You'll be surprised at how much clearer your brain will be. How focused you'll be on the world around you instead of what's on your screen. You'll spend most of your time in nature, out in the sunshine. By the end of your stay, I hope that you'll be much more interested in what is going on outside," she said, pointing to the windows, "rather than what is happening on your phone. Or what's in the news. Or what's happening on the other side of the world. All stressors. I want to teach you how to live a more quiet, slower life without all the unnecessary noise."

Someone raised a hand, and she moved closer, reading the name tag. *Sharon*.

"What if there's an emergency?"

"Such as?" Kenni asked.

"I mean, what if one of our family members needs to get in touch with us but we don't have our phones?"

"They can call our main line here. It's never been a problem, Sharon." She moved into the center of the tables. "Also, no alcohol is allowed here. Whether you're an occasional drinker, a weekend drinker, or a daily drinker, you will be amazed at how wonderful you'll feel after a month of abstaining. I hope you'll continue to abstain when you leave here. Alcohol is a toxin—a poison—and does nothing good for your body."

That was met with groans, as it usually was.

"Breakfast is at six each morning," she continued. "Lunch times are varied, depending on the plans for the day. And dinner is at six p.m. After dinner, you may want to go outside again and wander the grounds. Or you may want to take advantage of our game room. Cards, board games, and the like. Sounds boring to you now, I'm sure," she said, getting a few laughs from the ladies. "With all of the electronics in our lives…when's the last time you've played an old-fashioned board game?"

"Years," someone answered, and others agreed.

"Well, now's your chance," she said with a grin. "Each morning at breakfast, we'll go over the day's planned activities. We usually start the day with yoga. Nothing too intense. Very beginner. Something to loosen us up and get us prepared for the day. I'm a firm believer in circadian rhythms. Early morning sunshine sets your internal clock. I recommend that before breakfast you step outside and let the sun hit your face. You may also want to practice grounding—or earthing as some call it. Let your bare feet touch the ground. Hug a tree," she said with a smile. "Embrace nature."

She glanced at the women, seeing mostly blank stares. Joni James was looking at her as if she'd lost her mind. She was fairly certain not a one of these women had ever heard of grounding.

"Grounding normalizes your cortisol levels and reduces stress," she explained. "It has been proven to improve sleep, too. Take ten minutes and try it. I think you'll be surprised by the sense of calmness and serenity you feel." Again, more blank stares. She smiled at them. "I know it sounds a little crazy, but trust me, it works. But, if it's not your thing…" She shrugged. "After morning yoga," she continued, "Jenn will take us on a group hike. Not long. Usually about an hour to start."

That was met with more groans, and Jenn laughed. "After two weeks, you'll think that's only a warmup." She paused. "And it will be!"

"You will be broken up into five teams," Kenni continued. "We will have different competitions. Most will be on the obstacle course. There will be a daily scavenger hunt with clues to follow. Those are fun too. And we'll do a harder one each week. The winning team gets treated with a full-body massage the next day in place of the morning hike."

"Speaking of massages," Sky said on cue, "we have a mini spa area out behind the gym that has a sauna and a jacuzzi tub. You'll be able to do red-light therapy if that's your jam. Even the ice baths that I know some people enjoy." She laughed. "I'm not one of them!"

The group of ladies laughed as they usually did. Kenni wondered if they needed to update their routine. Was it getting stale? She waited, knowing that Karla would speak up next.

"After your gym workout and lifting sessions, you'll want to take advantage of the sauna and tub. But I do recommend the ice bath. It's great for you. Only thirty seconds to one minute will do wonders."

Kenni moved back to the front of the tables, smiling at the women. "I don't want to overwhelm you with all the details right now, so we'll wrap this up. Sky will pass along her famous wooden bowl. Grab a number out. We'll have five teams, like I said. Four members to a team. Then we will do your check-in and show you to your rooms. You'll have a little time to relax before dinner."

She turned to her staff, who were already going out into the lobby where everyone had stashed their luggage. They each took a team under their wings, except for Wanda, who solely managed the kitchen. Kenni always took Team Five. She turned her gaze back to Sky, who was moving among the women, holding the bowl out to each. The journalist, Joni James, reached into the bowl without much enthusiasm. She wondered why she was here. If she planned to write an article about them, Kenni hoped she didn't think she could skip out on all the activities.

Judging by her demeanor, though, that was exactly what the journalist had in mind. She smiled to herself. This could be fun. Or it could be a pain in the ass.

CHAPTER FIVE

Joni looked at the number she'd drawn—5. She crumpled it up, not really caring. This whole thing was *so* not her. She hated these team-building exercises. She'd interview some of the women who'd signed up for this torture session. Then she'd interview some of the staff, if she could. She'd take a few photos of the place. She'd hang out in her room. And if she was lucky, she'd write the damn article in less than a week and get the hell out of there and back down to civilization.

"Okay, grab your luggage and find your team leader," Kendall Lyon said. "She'll get you checked in and direct you to your rooms. After you get settled, come back out and enjoy a little time to introduce yourself to each other and get to know names. Then we'll have dinner and let you have some free time the rest of the evening. You can stay and chat more or go to the game room. Or go to your room and get to bed early. It'll be a full day tomorrow, so get your rest."

Joni rolled her eyes. God, the woman was like a drill sergeant. She shuffled out behind the others, wishing she were anywhere but here.

"What's your number?" Sky asked her as she went out into the lobby.

"Five."

"Oh, lucky you. Kenni is your leader." Sky pointed to the last table where three other women were already waiting. "There's your team! Go meet them!"

Joni managed to crack her face into a fake smile. "Great!" The smile disappeared as quickly as she'd forced it. Yeah, how lucky for her. The Lyon woman was her team leader. She sighed as she dragged her bags over with her. That might be good, though. Maybe she could interview her without her *knowing* that she was interviewing her. She might be able to glean some insight into the operation. So far, however, she thought Turnbull was off base. She didn't get the impression that it was a man-bashing group. Most, if not all the women appeared to be very upper-middle class or even more uppity than that. Like Charlotte Turnbull, they appeared to be wealthy women who apparently had too much time on their hands. She'd spotted gold and diamond watches, diamond earrings, huge obnoxious diamond rings. Most everyone was dressed in expensive clothes and had their hair professionally done and makeup applied to perfection. She had a hard time envisioning these women out there climbing fucking trees!

"Joni?"

She looked up, seeing the last of her team leaving to follow some of the others up the large staircase that was against the far wall. Kendall Lyon—Kenni—was waiting for her. She met her gaze and nodded, finally moving closer. She was surprised when the woman hoisted one of her bags onto the table and opened it.

"What do you think you're doing?" she asked sharply.

"Searching your bags."

"Whatever for?"

Kenni pulled out a bottle of wine. "This, for starters." She set the nice bottle of red aside, one of the blends she'd brought, next to a bottle of pinot grigio.

"Look, I'm just here to write a story. I don't think I need to adhere to all these silly rules you have."

The woman stared at her. "Silly? If you think they're silly and have no merit, perhaps you should request a refund and head back to Denver."

She didn't know what to say to that, other than, yeah, she'd like to head back to Denver. This whole setup here was so over the top, she felt like she was in a 1970s time warp and stuck in a commune of *not* like-minded women.

"No?"

Joni shook her head. "No. I don't think my boss would go for that."

"Right. Hard to do an article on us if you don't actually participate in things. So, I guess you're stuck with my silly rules."

To her horror, Kenni next picked up the bag she'd stuffed full of wine. She was surprised that the annoyance on the woman's face turned to amusement as she searched through the clothes that had been painstakingly wrapped around each bottle.

"Wow. Eight bottles in this bag alone." Then she fished inside a shoe. "Ah. And a corkscrew." The woman actually smiled at her. "You've won. Congratulations."

"Won?" She smiled too. "Does that mean I get to keep the wine?"

"No. That means that over the ten years that I've run this place, no one has tried to sneak in more than two bottles."

"Only two? Amateurs," she muttered.

She'd packed ten bottles and, yes, the Lyon woman found them all, as well as the cute little plastic wine glass she'd hidden in a side pocket.

"You're on the third floor. Room 33."

"I don't guess there's an elevator."

"No."

She blew out her breath. "Bellboy?"

"Afraid not. Feel free to make two trips."

Kenni turned away and left her standing there. All the other women had already gone up the stairs. And all of them had only two bags. In fact, most had one large bag and a smaller backpack. They had all apparently read—and adhered—to the *rules*. She looked at her three bags—which now weighed much less without wine—and the large backpack. *I hate this place.* She slung the backpack on her shoulder and picked up one of the bags and headed to the stairs. Yes, she would have to make two trips.

"I should have quit my job."

CHAPTER SIX

Kenni walked down the steps of her cabin, her moccasin-clad feet making little noise as she moved over the pine needles that littered the forest floor. The moon was high and bright as it shone through the trees, and she walked among them, her gaze going to the sky time and again.

For five months out of the year—May through September—she hosted twenty women for a month-long retreat. The program had evolved a lot in the ten years she'd been doing this, and the message had changed some too. Her clientele had certainly changed from those early years, that's for sure. She still didn't know why the rich and pampered women flocked to her. Because being pampered was the last thing they were going to be.

And maybe that was why they were drawn here. Most of the women were very intelligent and able-bodied, yet living a life where they were coddled and had most of their life decisions made for them, usually by the wealthy, domineering husbands that they'd married. Here, they would learn independence and perseverance. They would challenge their bodies to do things they'd never imagined. In one short month, their eating habits would change, their bodies would change, and their mindset would change.

She could already picture them in the morning. Six o'clock was much earlier than most were used to having breakfast. In fact, she guessed most would not normally be awake at that hour. But they would show up, all having taken the time to apply their makeup as they usually did. By the third day—or even the second—most would have completely ditched the makeup routine. After the first week, those whose hair was long and flowing would be tying it into ponytails. All of their status symbols—like their gold and diamonds—would be stripped away. Two weeks in, they would be more concerned with their team and winning the daily activities than worrying about how they looked. By the time the month was up, each would have transformed into a very different woman from the one who had arrived today.

Not all hung on to their new identity, of course. Some went back to their lives and reverted to their earlier selves. Yet some felt so inspired when they left here that they completely changed their lives—for the better she would like to think. Judging by the number of emails and letters she received from them, it was. Some divorced their overbearing husbands and got out of loveless marriages. Some started new careers. And some gave back to the community, volunteering when they'd never entertained the idea before.

For some reason, the image of Mr. Willet popped into her mind. He'd been the epitome of a domineering husband and father. She imagined he ran his household much as he did his company—with an iron fist. It was a shame his oldest son had slipped out from under his thumb. She sighed and pushed those old memories away. She didn't want to think about that night and the heartbreaking weeks afterward. No, she rarely thought of that night.

Instead, she walked on through the trees, seeing the lodge. All was dark and quiet...except for a lone room on the third floor. She smiled slightly and shook her head. Was it the journalist? Most likely. That made her wonder why in the world a magazine—

Mountain Life—wanted to write an article about them. Lyon's Den didn't do much advertising anymore. They didn't have to. Through their website and word of mouth, their monthly sessions were always sold out. In fact, next year's sessions were already booked, with only a couple of spots still available for next September.

Well, she didn't suppose it mattered. She wasn't going to deviate from their normal routine because a journalist was here doing a story. And she also wasn't going to cut the woman any slack. She'd signed up for a spot and she was now on a team. It wouldn't be fair to the others if Joni James got special treatment. That, in turn, made Kenni laugh out loud, remembering the ten bottles of wine she'd confiscated from her. Wine and the contraband that went with it. Yes, there was always someone who tried to sneak in a bottle or two. But ten? She laughed quietly as she made her way back to her cabin.

When she had bought this place, the lodge had already been there. It had been a summer church camp, built with a generous donation from one of their members. Unfortunately, the wealthy donor had passed away and his children had no interest in supporting the church. Their money dried up quickly, and they were forced to abandon the project. She and her grandmother had snatched up the lodge and the fifty acres it sat on, outbidding another buyer who had wanted to turn it into a fancy resort.

To be fair, it was her grandmother's idea to start the retreat. This type of endeavor had not occurred to her. She had simply wanted to take the money and forget all about that tragic night. But after many long discussions, her grandmother had convinced her that she could do something good with the money. She had enough capital to get started but still needed to secure a business loan for all the upgrades she needed. Pitching her idea for the retreat was met with skepticism by most loan officers. She kept trying, finally securing a loan at a higher interest rate in order to get the approval.

That was ten years ago. And in that time, the price they charged per month had doubled to nearly ten thousand, which was why their clientele had changed too. At first she'd been shocked by all the wealthy women who had started to come. How could she possibly help them? They had plenty of money for therapists to get them through any rough patches they may have. She soon realized that was the very reason they came to her.

The women with less income, those who saved for months or a year to be able to come there, only benefited as long as they were there. Once back in the real world, they didn't have the money to make changes in their lives, even if they wanted to. Well, some did, sure. But not most of them. The ladies who came now, though, didn't have that restriction. Those who came now left empowered and they had the money to redefine their lives if they chose to. And surprisingly, a large number of them did.

She climbed the steps back to her front porch, then turned again, taking one last glance at the moon. This little cabin was home for six months out of the year. Or more, if she could stretch it. At the end of September, when the last clients left, they closed up the lodge and the staff departed for their winter homes.

Wanda lived down the mountain in Gunnison with her daughter. Sky was from Miami and worked for her father's real estate company during the winters. Mindy traveled back to Los Angeles and worked at a yoga studio. Karla and Jenn were both from Denver. Jenn spent the ski season in Vail, and Karla was a personal trainer at a gym.

And her? While her grandmother had left Phoenix and retired in Flagstaff, she had settled in Santa Fe, although she didn't consider it home. She stayed right here until the snow came. Then she'd venture off the mountain and head south. Depending on the weather, she came back around the first of April, getting everything ready and organized for their first group of ladies on May 1.

It was a routine she was well used to by now. She much preferred the summers. She'd made a few friends in Santa Fe, but she wasn't there enough to nurture relationships. But up here? Yes, this was home now, and her staff had become not only good friends, but they were as close as family.

She stood still, listening to the quiet, listening to the darkness. She was aware of the contented smile on her face as she slipped back into her cabin.

CHAPTER SEVEN

A loud blaring noise made Joni sit up in bed, her heart pounding. "What the fuck?" She fumbled with her phone, but the sound was coming from the hallway. *Fire alarm?* But no. The sound stopped and she heard no screaming or running. She lay back down with a groan. Surely it was still the middle of the night. She picked up her phone again—5:31 stared back at her.

"Oh my god." That must have been that stupid alarm Sky had mentioned. Who got up this early? Who ate breakfast at six in the goddamn morning? She rolled over and closed her eyes again, hoping to fall back to sleep. Without her usual glass or three of wine last night, she'd still been wide awake at nearly midnight. Maybe she could snatch another hour before they missed her. But no. She heard the sounds of doors opening, heard voices in the hallway. The others were up and about. *Crazy-ass women.*

With another groan, she tossed the covers off and made herself get up. She had discovered last night while roaming the halls alone that there were three bathrooms on each floor. They were surprisingly large, with three showers and three toilets in each. She'd even wandered downstairs into the lobby for a bit but felt embarrassed for snooping around. Especially after she'd convinced herself that the Lyon woman surely had security cameras hidden about.

She stood there now in the middle of her tiny bedroom, eyes still closed. She yawned. Did she have time for a shower? That would at least help wake her up. She shuffled to the small dresser and grabbed her toiletry bag. She opened the door, then shielded her eyes against the bright, glaring hallway lights.

"Christ," she muttered.

"Oh, good morning. You're Joni, right?" said a cheerful voice in the hallway.

She blinked her eyes, then yawned, barely managing to cover her mouth somewhat politely. "Yes, Joni," she said hoarsely. She had no clue who the woman was.

"I'm Christine. We're on the same team."

"Uh-huh. Great." She motioned to the bathroom. "Shower."

"Oh." Christine looked at the diamond-studded watch on her wrist. "Better hurry. I don't think you're allowed to be late."

Allowed? She mentally rolled her eyes. What were they going to do? Kick her out of camp?

"I'll save you a seat," the overly friendly woman said as she hurried down the hallway to the stairs, her long blond hair flowing nearly down to her waist.

Joni guessed her to be late forties, maybe even fifty. Wasn't it time to cut that mane already? She sighed loudly. "Somebody shoot me."

Apparently she was the only one who needed a shower to wake up. The bathroom was blessedly empty. Despite her indifference to the rules, she did not linger in the shower. As she was brushing her teeth, the freakin' alarm went off again and she nearly choked on her toothbrush.

"What the *fuck*?" she murmured as she rinsed out her mouth. A glance at her phone told her she had three minutes. She shoved everything into her bag and nearly raced back to her room. She stood there stupidly. What the hell was she supposed to wear? She closed her eyes. What had Christine been wearing? She shook her head. She hadn't been awake enough to notice. She jerked on a pair of navy sweats and shoved her sockless feet into the new pair of running shoes. *Right! Running shoes! How funny!* She allowed a quick laugh. She hadn't run a day in her life.

She pulled out one of the new T-shirts that Dana had bought for her—nothing she would have ever picked for herself. She was as flat-chested as a runway model and rarely wore a bra. *Did I even bring any?* She slipped on the shirt, then grabbed her phone, and, with one look in the mirror, realized she had forgotten makeup.

It was 5:59. She ripped open her makeup bag and hastily applied moisturizer—6:00. "Oh, fuck it." She ran a hand through her still damp hair, shoved her phone in her pocket, and bolted for the door.

* * *

Kenni glanced at the list, noting the lone name not crossed off. She stared at the stairs, then shook her head. Karla elbowed her.

"Looks like one of your team is late."

"The journalist. Joni."

"Gonna be a problem?"

Kenni glanced at her. "She's the one who tried to sneak in the wine."

Karla laughed. "Oh. That one." She clapped her shoulder. "Glad she's on your team and not mine."

They both looked up at the running down the stairs. Kenni was shocked at the transformation of Joni James. Gone was the makeup. Gone was the styled hair. Gone was the expensive blouse and tight-fitting black jeans. In its place was fresh, clean skin, hand-tousled hair that was still damp, and baggy sweatpants with a loose-fitting T-shirt.

"Good morning," she managed as she stared at the lovely woman approaching. Then she remembered her purpose here and gave a slight scowl. "You're late, Ms. James."

Joni gave her an "I don't give a fuck" look—complete with an eye roll—and sauntered past them into the dining hall. Kenni couldn't keep the smile off her face.

"Oh, she's going to be fun," Karla teased.

"Yes, I think she is." She held up her cell phone. "Go on in, Karla. I'll run the first test."

That first test was calling everyone's cell phone. It was such a habit for most that they often forgot the rule of no phones, simply slipping it into a pocket without thinking. Inevitably she would find someone who had forgotten. And if she had to guess, Joni James would be that someone. She called all twenty numbers, saving Joni's for last. She stood in the doorway as it rang, the sound causing everyone to stop talking and look around for the offending phone.

Kenni nearly laughed as Joni tried to discreetly pull her cell out. She answered quietly.

"Hello."

"Ms. James, could I see you in the lobby please?"

She watched as Joni jerked her head up, meeting her gaze across the room. "Well, fuck," Joni mouthed at her.

The call disconnected, and Kenni turned away, unable to keep her laughter in any longer. She waited until Joni came out, then she closed the door to the dining room. She held her hand out.

Joni frowned. "What?"

"Your phone."

"What about it?"

"We went over this yesterday. Phones aren't allowed. Hand it over."

"So now what? You're confiscating it?"

"Yes, I am."

"Okay, no you're not. I cannot *live* without my phone."

Kenni sighed. "Of course you can."

"No! Really. I can't." She clutched her phone to her chest. "You can't take my phone. I won't let you."

"You can get it back tonight after dinner. If you feel like you need some of that nonsense that's on there, look at it then. In your room. Alone. But during the day, from six in the morning until after dinner, no cell phones."

"No. I'm sorry. I can't do it. I just can't do it." She held the phone up. "My *life* is on this phone."

Kenni rolled her eyes. "Oh, give me a break."

"It is!"

"Then you need to work on your life. And this is a great place to do that." She held her hand out again. "Now, give me the phone," she said slowly, enunciating each word clearly.

"No. I'm serious."

Kenni was losing the little patience she still clung to. "Okay. I'm serious too." She pointed toward the stairs. "Pack your bags. Go back to Denver. Use your precious phone to call your boss and let them know you got kicked out!"

They stared at each other, neither of them blinking. Joni's greenish-hazel eyes were shooting daggers at her. Kenni narrowed her eyes as well. Finally, Joni broke.

"Okay. You win. But this is inhumane treatment."

She laughed at that. "Inhumane? Wait until we climb up the giant pine tree. Then you might think inhumane." Her smile vanished and she held her hand out. "The phone."

Joni clutched her phone tighter. "All right. But I'm doing this under protest." She then slapped the phone in her hand. "There."

"Thank you. Now, was that so hard?"

Again, daggers. "Yes. Yes it was. When will I get it back?"

"It'll be in your room. Where it needs to stay."

Joni turned on her heels, mumbling "stupid goddamn rules" as she opened the dining room door.

Kenni was grinning as she went into her office. Joni James had a potty mouth, it seemed. And yeah, this was going to be fun.

CHAPTER EIGHT

While Joni admitted that the breakfast had been good, it was food she would never have eaten normally. Certainly not at six o'clock in the freakin' morning. The scrambled eggs tasted buttery. There was a choice of bacon or sausage patties. She took one slice of bacon. There were no options for toast or biscuits. No muffins either. Individual bowls of fruit were offered, and even though she knew she'd never be able to eat it all, she took a bowl—strawberries, grapes, and pineapple chunks. To her surprise, she finished off everything and wished she'd taken two pieces of bacon. She rarely bothered to eat breakfast, but when she did, it was something simple, like a packaged blueberry muffin that she might or might not heat in the microwave.

Now, though, they were gathered outside on a giant deck, each sitting on an exercise mat. The sun was slicing through the trees, and she squinted at it. She was certainly far too full to attempt any stupid yoga poses. Mindy, the instructor, was going over breathing techniques. She stopped listening and took that opportunity—while everyone's eyes were closed—to look around at the other women. She guessed their ages to be from midforties to midsixties. Most were wearing what she assumed was real yoga attire—mostly tights—but some had loose fitting pants on instead. None were wearing sweatpants like her as far as she could tell. All were barefoot, sporting perfect nails and polish. She looked down at her own toes, glad she'd taken the time for a pedicure last week. Since she was heading to the wilderness, she'd skipped her usual red and settled on a more neutral color.

"Joni? Are you having trouble with it?"

She jerked her head up, finding Mindy looking at her with raised eyebrows. "I'm sorry. What?"

She looked around then, seeing everyone sitting cross-legged with their arms resting on their thighs, hands turned upward. Most were also looking at her. *Oh god, are we going to start chanting or something?* With a sigh, she crossed her legs, the act reminding her she wasn't as flexible as she'd once been.

"Good," Mindy said. "Now, take a deep breath in through your nose. Visualize it and pull it deep into your lungs. Hold it. Now, let it out slowly. Once more. Deep breath. Remember to sit up straight. Pull it in. Hold it. Out slowly."

Okay, well, that did feel kinda relaxing, she conceded. At least there was no chanting. A few more deep breaths, then Mindy stood.

"Okay. Up, everyone. Now, who is familiar with yoga? Do any of you practice it?"

A few hands went up, and Joni rolled her eyes. Who had time to take yoga classes? Of course, she doubted that *any* of these women worked for a living.

"I used to do Pilates," one woman said.

"Good. Then you should have no problem with this. Okay, we're going to do the Mountain Pose. Stand very straight, arms at your sides, fingers pointing downward. Imagine a straight line from your head to your heels. I like to keep my feet closer together, but you may feel more comfortable with them separated more."

Joni mimicked Mindy's position, thinking that this wasn't so hard. Maybe she'd at least leave here with good posture.

"Lift your toes up, keeping your weight on your heels and try to lengthen your spine. Breathe deeply. Good. Now we're going to fall into Downward Facing Dog."

Everyone bent over and placed their hands on the mat as if they knew exactly what the hell a Downward Facing Dog was. With a sigh, Joni did the same.

"Keep your back straight. Your hands are for balance. You want your weight on your legs, not your hands. Arch your hips high. Now, don't stand on your toes. Press your heels down. You should feel a nice pull in your hamstrings."

Nice?

"Hold it. A little longer."

Joni was getting lightheaded.

"Okay, stand straight again. Walk it back up if you need. Once you learn the poses, you won't stand up, you'll simply move into the Warrior Pose. Watch me first to learn, then we'll move into it together. Now, from Downward Facing Dog, you'll bring your right leg up next to your hand, like this, bending your knee. Your left foot, you'll want to angle it a bit, like this, and bring the heel down to the mat. Keep your spine straight as you lift your torso, knee still bent. Extend your arms overhead, palms facing each other. Feel the energy all the way to your fingertips." Mindy held the pose for a moment, then stood up, smiling. "Easy. Now you try it."

Oh god. At least she wasn't the only one having trouble. She winced, feeling fairly certain she'd torn her hamstring when she brought her right leg up to her hands.

"Excellent. Keep your spine straight. Now rise up. Good. Arms overhead. Feel the energy."

"Energy, my ass," she murmured quietly.

And so it went. The Extended Side Angle, the Triangle Pose, the Reverse Warrior, the Garland Pose, the Pyramid Pose, and many others she could no longer remember. All she wanted to do was to sit down and rest, as she'd long forgotten not only the names but how to do the damn poses in the first place. Unfortunately, sitting meant more stretches and more stupid poses—the Cobra, the Bridge, the Cat-Cow—until she finally heard one she knew.

The Plank. By that time, she was completely spent and thankfully so were some others.

"I know this wasn't much," Mindy was saying, and Joni made eye contact with the woman next to her and they both raised their eyebrows in horror. That nearly made her laugh, exhausted as she was.

"After a week, you'll be able to do these in sequence and move easily between the poses. My hope is that after your month with us, you'll have fallen in love with yoga and will continue to practice it when you leave here. Find a class to go to and immerse yourself in it."

Yeah, right.

"Okay, ladies. I think Jenn is ready to lead you on a morning hike. Go ahead and put your hiking boots on, then grab a water bottle from her before you go."

Oh, good lord. A hike? She again looked at the woman next to her. "Are your legs as rubbery as mine?"

"I'll say. I'm Sarah Beth," the woman said in a rather thick Southern accent. "I've never done a single yoga pose in my entire life!"

"Me either. And I'm Joni." She got to her feet, suddenly feeling far older than her thirty-one years.

"Yes, I think everyone knows your name," she said with a laugh. "I heard you tried to sneak in ten bottles of wine."

"I did. The Lyon woman confiscated them. And my phone," she added.

"Honestly, I was glad to ditch my phone." She leaned closer. "I did miss my nightly cocktail, however."

Joni sighed. Yes, she'd missed her wine too.

"I'm looking forward to the hike, though. Being out in this cool weather is wonderful, isn't it? July in Dallas, I barely set foot outside. Where are you from, hon?"

"Denver. Originally from New York City—Manhattan."

"Really? Well, I'm originally from South Georgia, if you can't tell by my accent. Bill and I live in Dallas now, but I still twang a lot more than they do there."

Sarah Beth was a little overweight, but she wouldn't call her fat. Her hair was dark and cut in a bouncy bob style just below her chin. Her makeup appeared caked on.

"You're on Team Five, right?"

"Yes," Joni said as she slipped on the hiking boots she'd retrieved from her room earlier, knowing she looked absolutely hideous with boots and sweatpants. Of course, everyone else was still in their yoga attire and looked equally silly.

"That's great. I'm on Team Five too."

Oh, look, Joni...you've made a friend already. She followed Sarah Beth—a woman she would peg to be in her early forties—to where the others were gathered. Jenn, their hiking leader, handed them each a bottle of water. She was dressed in smart-looking khaki shorts and matching socks and boots.

"We're taking a short hike this morning. When we take longer hikes, you'll be issued a waist belt that will hold two water bottles. Tomorrow, after yoga, you'll be split up into two groups. While one goes to the gym, the other will hike, then you'll switch. You may want to take the time to change clothes after yoga. Today, though, we'll introduce you to the grounds here, and I'll point out some of the different trees. If we're lucky, we'll get to spot some birds, and I'll help you identify them." A big smile. "Ready, ladies?"

"Can't wait," Joni muttered quietly.

She found herself walking with Sarah Beth, but thankfully the hike—and perhaps the altitude—rendered Sarah Beth breathless and unable to chat. In fact, very few of the women were talking. It was then she reminded herself she was supposed to be interviewing them.

"So, what brings you up here?" she asked casually.

Sarah Beth glanced at her and smiled. "I needed some time away. Bill suggested I go back home to Momma to sort things out." She shook her head. "Momma loves Bill. There would be no talking to her."

"Oh? Marital problems?"

Sarah Beth waved her hand in the air. "I don't know. Bill says it's a midlife crisis. I'm forty-three." She shrugged. "I'm sick and tired of the country club. I'm sick and tired of hosting dinners." She paused. "Bill is in the oil and gas business. He's moved up to president of the company and he's not home much."

"You have kids?"

"One. He's nineteen and in college. Bill is grooming him for the business too."

"So you're suddenly alone?"

"Yes, alone. Oh, don't get me wrong, I have friends. And I do lunches and dinners often, but it's not the same as having a partner at home, you know." She smiled quickly. "I don't mean to complain. I never want for anything. Bill makes sure of that." She sighed rather loudly. "Just seems like something is missing."

"And this place resonated with you?"

"I'll admit I live a pretty pampered life, Joni. Now I do anyway. Certainly not when I was younger. I grew up on a farm with seven siblings. Never had my own room. Only had two bathrooms in the house, so there was a lot of sharing."

"How did you meet Bill?"

"We went to school together—he was a grade ahead of me. Then he got a football scholarship to Texas Tech in Lubbock. I followed him there." She laughed. "The terrain was a far cry from South Georgia, but let me tell you, oil wells and natural gas wells were everywhere. That's how Bill got into the business."

"And you?"

"No, no. I never worked. When Bill graduated, he already had a job lined up making more money than either of us could even comprehend," she said with a laugh. "We stayed in Lubbock for three years, then moved down to Odessa for a year. I don't mind saying, I was so thankful when the company moved us to Dallas. Been there ever since."

A loud squawking sound came from the trees, and they all looked up. A blueish black bird watched them.

"That's a Steller's jay," Jenn said to the group. "You'll notice them at the birdfeeders near the lodge. The tree he's in is a Douglas fir. Notice the pinecones. They call those 'mouse tails' that stick out from each scale. These trees are one of the easiest to identify the cones for. Legend has it that many, many years ago there was a forest fire in the mountains. Animals were running from the fire to escape the flames. But little mice couldn't outrun the fire. So, they asked the trees for help. These tall Douglas fir trees gave them shelter and allowed them to hide inside the cones and out of danger of the fire." Jenn smiled broadly. "The mice survived, and to this very day, if you look at the cones, you can still see the mice tails as they hide."

Joni reluctantly looked at the cones, seeing the "tails" as they peeked out. Sarah Beth picked one up from the ground.

"Look here! Isn't that cute? They do look like little tails."

"Yep," she said dryly.

The group walked on, and Sarah Beth dropped the cone. "I do miss the pine trees in Georgia."

Joni sighed. "I miss sidewalks."

CHAPTER NINE

Kenni watched the hikers file into the dining room, most of them with sweaty red faces and tousled hair. Makeup was smeared and not a hint of lipstick remained on a single woman. She nodded and inwardly smiled at their flushed faces.

"Each table is marked so find your team. Sky has printed out the itinerary for this afternoon. After lunch, you'll have a quick session in the gym, then we'll head out into the woods to take a look at one of the obstacle courses."

As predicted, her statement was met with groans. She smiled at them. "You're going to love it." She walked among the tables, her gaze finding Joni James. "How was the hike?"

"Long."

She laughed. "That's the shortest one you'll ever take." She turned to the group. "What lessons did we learn today, ladies?"

"What do you mean?" someone asked.

"If you had to start your morning routine over today, what would you do differently?"

"Run away."

Everyone—including her—laughed at Joni's reply.

"Surely it wasn't that bad." She turned to someone else. "Marsha? What would you do differently?"

"I would not bother with makeup, that's for sure."

"Excellent." Most everyone nodded at that. "What else? Anyone?"

"I'm not wearing my rings tomorrow," someone said.

"I would wear shorts. It was hot out there."

"Yes. Good. Remember, there is no one here you're trying to impress. You don't have to be properly dressed—or what you may consider to be proper—and have your makeup applied as usual and your hair fussed with. You need to wear functional clothing and be comfortable. That's why we gave you a list before you came. Since your yoga classes are early in the morning and it's still a little cool, bring a sweatshirt to slip on. Or wear sweats over your shorts so that you can take them off before the hike and before we start the day's activities. Of course, you can always run up to your room to change. Your choice."

She motioned to Sky, who came forward.

"Ladies, by now I'm sure you've met your team members. We will have our first test before lunch." Sky motioned to the papers on each table. "This will be a mini scavenger hunt. I hope you were paying attention to Jenn while on your hike. The lists there on your tables are the items you're to find. The first team to come back with all their items wins." Sky pointed to the whiteboard that hung on the back wall. "All wins get marked on the board, but some wins will also get you added prizes. Like extra time in the sauna or tub." She smiled. "Or ice cream after dinner. Things like that."

Kenni watched the faces of the women, feeling her gaze drawn back to Joni James. She could tell by the panicked look on her face that she had not been paying attention to Jenn earlier. A frown marred her features as she read over her list.

"Your team leaders will go out into the woods with you, so you won't be completely on your own," Kenni said, hoping to assure those few who looked terrified. "Okay, we're going to give you a short break. Since you'll be outside for the rest of the day,

I'd suggest you take this time to change into shorts or jeans since you'll be out in the woods." She glanced at the black sports watch on her wrist. "Ten minutes. Then we'll meet out on the deck." As everyone got up, she called, "Don't forget to take your lists with you."

"This is kinda fun," she heard someone say as they filed out of the room.

She found Jenn out in the lobby, and she went over to her. "How was the hike?"

"Everyone did pretty well. A few stragglers."

She raised her eyebrows. "Any of them on my team?"

"Two. Joni and Sarah Beth." She laughed. "No way your team wins this month."

"It's only the first day. Don't count your bonus money already."

That was the motivation for her staff—if their team won the month, they got an extra thousand bucks added to their salary. Her motivation for winning was not having to pay the thousand bucks. But yes, she probably did have her work cut out for her.

CHAPTER TEN

Joni plopped down on her bed, completely exhausted from the morning activities. Then her eyes popped open. *My phone.* She sat up, frantically looking around for it. Apparently the Lyon woman hadn't bothered to bring it up here yet.

"Figures."

With a sigh, she ripped off the sweatpants and put on one of the pairs of hiking shorts she'd bought. Her feet were absolutely killing her, and she rubbed her toes before putting her socks and hiking boots on again. It was a miracle she didn't have blisters. She heard the others in the hallway heading back downstairs, and she got up, wondering if this was what prison was like.

She was the last one down, and she found her teammates—Sarah Beth, Erin, and Christine—gathered around...around *her.* God, why did *she* have to be their team leader?

"There you are," Sarah Beth called, motioning her over.

"Glad you could join us," Kenni said quietly before walking to the edge of the deck and addressing the whole group. "Okay, ladies. The goal is for each team member to gather the items on her particular list. If you finish your list and another on your team has not, then you may help them. After all team members have completed their lists, hurry back here as fast as you can." She pointed at the large bell with its long hanging rope. "The first team to ring the bell wins."

"Here are your bags," Sky said, passing out mesh bags to each of them. "I would suggest you all head in opposite directions so that you don't get in each other's way." She gave them a big smile. "Team leaders ready?"

Kenni nodded. "Let's go!"

Joni stood there as her team darted off without her. *Oh, fuck.* She scampered after them, ignoring the Lyon woman, who followed her. When they got into the woods, the others were already picking stuff up. She glanced at her list. An Engleman spruce cone. *Was that the one with the damn mouse tail?*

A rock smaller than a quarter but bigger than a penny. Easy. She kicked at a few, then selected one and shoved it into her bag.

A piece of fungus? *What the hell? Fungus?*

A twig from a ponderosa pine. *Oh, for the love. What the hell was a ponderosa pine?*

"Need some help?"

She jerked around. "I can manage, thank you very much," she said, heading off to find Sarah Beth.

"I'm here to help you, you know."

She turned to the woman. "If I had my phone, I could look up what the hell a goddamn ponderosa pine was." She glanced at her list again. "And a piece of quartz."

"I see your mind must have wandered during your hike. Jenn pointed out all those things to you."

"I found one!" Christine yelled. "Yay!"

Joni rolled her eyes. "This is fucking stupid."

"What's stupid about it?"

Joni narrowed her eyes and glared at the woman. "What's stupid is that I didn't willingly sign up for all this shit! I hate the outdoors! I—"

"*What?*" She spread her hands. "How can you possibly hate this?"

"Where's my phone?" she demanded.

"It's in my office."

"You said you'd put it in my room."

A quick smile, one she wanted to slap off her face. "And I will. After dinner."

Joni narrowed her eyes. "I don't like you very much."

Another smile. "Yes, that's obvious." She motioned into the trees. "Better hurry."

"Come on, Joni! I already have four items," Sarah Beth called to her.

She stomped into the woods, following the others. Yes, her mind had wandered during the stupid hike. She'd been daydreaming of Starbucks and of sitting in her plush office chair in air-conditioned comfort.

She looked at her list again. Douglas fir cone. Her eyes widened. *Yes! The damn mice!* She looked around frantically, not seeing any cones with the stupid little mice hiding inside. *Shit!* She kicked absently at the cones she did see.

"What's wrong?"

She jerked her head up. "Are you following me or what?"

"I *am* your team leader. You appear to be the only one who needs help."

She sighed, then held the list up and pointed. "I know this one. Douglas fir. It has the damn little mice hiding in it. But none of these cones have it."

"Good. You paid attention to that story. So, if there aren't any mice cones here, what does that tell you?"

Joni stared at her. "Is this a test?"

The woman smiled. "Different trees drop different cones. If there are no cones here with the mice tails, then this probably isn't a Douglas fir tree. In fact, it's definitely not. It's an Engleman spruce."

"Look, she didn't tell us what a Douglas fir tree looked like. She just told us what the damn cones looked like." She waved a hand at the forest. "They all look alike! They're pine trees!"

The smile Kenni gave her was a bit smug. "They don't all look alike and they're not all pine trees. Spruce and fir too. But it reminds me of a John Muir quote. 'Between every two pines, there is a doorway to a new world.'" Kenni spread her hands out. "So very true, don't you think?"

Joni scowled. *What the hell is she talking about?*

"But back to this," Kenni said, pointing to her list. "I'll guess that when you were looking at the mice tail cones hanging on the tree, you weren't looking at the *tree*."

Joni took a step closer to the woman. "Why do you irritate me so?"

"Do I irritate you?"

"If I thought I was able to, I'd knock you to the ground and beat the shit out of you!"

Kendall Lyon laughed so heartily that she bent over at the waist. If only Joni knew a few karate moves, she was certain she could have taken her down already. Instead, she marched farther into the damn woods, looking for stupid mice hiding in fucking pinecones.

Needless to say, because of her, they were the last team to make it back to the deck, the bell having long ago rung to announce a winner. Even Sarah Beth had found all her items well before Joni had managed even three. Now her team members were looking at her accusingly. The other four teams had been back long enough for everyone to have downed a bottle of water already.

"Look, I didn't know what the hell quartz was. I thought it was pink. She said it was pink!"

"The granite is pink," Christine corrected, holding up the piece she'd found.

"Remember the pile of quartz rocks that Jenn pointed out to us on the hike? Those were like this big," Erin added, cupping her hands as if holding a melon. "Beautiful white color."

Joni closed her eyes, hoping to be teleported to Paris or perhaps London.

Sarah Beth patted her shoulder. "We'll do better next time."

Kenni Lyon sauntered over to them. "Last place, huh." She looked at them all, but her glance lingered on her. Joni threw up her arms.

"Okay, okay. Yes, it was my fault we lost. I'm sorry."

"I hope you all had fun," Sky said to the group. "Congrats to Team Four!" She clapped enthusiastically. "When you run the obstacle course this afternoon, another team—or maybe Team Four again—will have an opportunity to put a win on the board." She opened the double doors that led back inside. "Now after all that...it's lunch time!"

"Oh, thank god. I'm starving," Joni muttered as she hurried away from her team...and their disparaging eyes.

CHAPTER ELEVEN

Joni found herself near the front of the buffet line and she was nearly salivating. Who knew yoga, a hike, and a stupid scavenger hunt would be so strenuous. Her normal lunch of a tiny salad wouldn't even make a dent in her appetite today, although it looked like that was to be their meal. The giant bowl of salad—different lettuces, numerous greens, and purple cabbage—did look appetizing. She took the tongs and added a generous portion to her plate, then proceeded to top it with cucumbers, sprouts, chunky boiled eggs, pickled onions, and black olives. She paused, then added a scoop of shredded carrots. She topped all of that with a rich and creamy blue cheese dressing.

"You're Joni, right?"

She looked up, seeing the older woman behind the counter. Her gray hair was cut short, and she wore black-rimmed glasses. The honorary mother. *How does she know my name?*

"Yes, I'm Joni."

"I'm Wanda. Which do you prefer? We have chicken and salmon today. Or you can have some of both."

She looked over the two trays which appeared to be steaming hot. "Chicken, please." She held her salad out, and Wanda added a huge serving of chicken slices to her already full plate. "Thank you."

"Enjoy."

Her plate was piled to the brim and nearly falling off the sides, but she knew she'd probably eat every bite of it. She found the table marked for Team Five and sat down. She noticed that there were five chairs, not four. She sighed. That meant the Lyon woman would be eating with them.

She didn't know why the woman got on her nerves so. All her silly rules, maybe. Or the fact that she'd confiscated not only her wine but her phone too. Of course, she realized that she hadn't really missed the phone today. She hadn't had *time* to miss it. On a normal day, she would have used it a hundred times by now.

She looked around, wondering if she should be polite and wait for the others or simply dig in. The rumbling of her stomach made the decision for her. She actually moaned at the first mouthful. Who knew a positively loaded salad could make her moan with pleasure. Her normal lettuce and tomato salad paled in comparison to this monster she was about to devour.

Christine was the first to join her. Her long flowing blond hair was in disarray, and her face glistened with smeared makeup. Joni was now thankful that she'd been too late that morning to put on her usual makeup. She guessed tomorrow they would all skip it.

"Are you as hungry as I am?" Christine asked.

"Starving," she said as she shoved another forkful into her mouth.

Sarah Beth started eating before she even sat down. "Remind me not to skimp on breakfast tomorrow."

"I was thinking the same thing," Joni admitted as she stabbed a piece of chicken. She glanced around, seeing Kendall Lyon at the back of the buffet line. Their eyes met for a second before Joni looked away.

Erin sat down, and if possible, her plate seemed to be even more loaded than her own had been. "I've never been a breakfast eater. That will change tomorrow," she said before taking a bite. "I'm starving."

Erin was the oldest of their team, but Joni hadn't asked her age. Her hair was dyed a dark, nearly black color. She thought it made Erin look older, not younger. She was in her early sixties perhaps. Christine was the gregarious one; Joni figured she could find out about the others through her without having to come right out and ask ages and what the hell they were all doing here. Erin surprised her by asking the question she had not.

"How old are you, Joni?"

She finished chewing the bite she'd taken before speaking. "Thirty-one."

"Oh my. Kinda young to already be disillusioned with your life and wanting a change."

She raised an eyebrow. "Disillusioned? Is that why you're here?"

"Isn't that why everyone is here?"

Was it? She looked at the other two women at her table. Yes, she knew that was why Sarah Beth was there, but she didn't know Christine's story yet.

"I'm kinda at a crossroads in my life, both professionally and personally," she lied. "This place was recommended to me."

"Are you married?" Christine asked, glancing at her ringless fingers.

"No."

Erin nodded as she took a bite of the salmon. "My therapist suggested I come here. I found out my husband has a mistress, and I alternate between wanting to kill him or the young redhead I caught him with." She smiled. "Preferably him. The girl was all of twenty-one."

"How old is your husband?" Sarah Beth asked.

"Sixty-six."

This was met with eye rolls from the other two women.

"Now what draws a twenty-one-year-old woman to a man his age?" Christine asked in a sarcastic tone.

Joni watched in fascination as the three of them looked at each other, then burst out laughing.

"Money!" they said in unison and continued laughing.

She felt completely out of place as the three women continued smiling at their shared joke—one she was not included in. She was actually thankful when Kenni joined their group.

"How is lunch?" she asked as she sat down.

"Delicious," Sarah Beth said, getting nods from the others.

Kenni turned to her. "And yours?"

"Quite good. Of course, when you are starving to death, anything would be good."

"I do recall telling everyone to eat a hearty breakfast. Most everyone ignores me on the first day. Not the second, though."

Joni noticed that Kenni's salad was miniscule, and she had both chicken and salmon on top of it.

As if noticing the scrutiny, Kendall said, "I don't really like salads, but Wanda always insists I take some. I won't eat it."

"Is salad the normal lunch fare?" Joni asked.

"Only on light workout days like today."

She stared at her in disbelief. "That was considered light?"

That smug smile again. "Very. Activities increase daily."

"You have quite a difference in ages here. Can everyone handle it?"

It was Erin who laughed. "Are you talking about me, Joni? I may be over sixty, but I'm a monster on a treadmill. I run three miles every morning and then walk two each afternoon." She smiled. "Well, on those days I don't have lunch dates, that is. After a couple of martinis, I'm in no condition for an afternoon walk."

"We have a gym at the country club," Sarah Beth said.

"Ours too," Christine added. "I don't use it as much as I should."

Sarah Beth laughed. "I said we *have* one. I didn't say I used it!"

They all turned to look at Joni, including Kenni. She forced a tiny smile. "I don't actually do any type of exercise. Not really." *Yeah, like none.* "But I'm young, so hopefully I can keep up with you all."

"My hope is that when you leave here, you'll be so invigorated by all the activity that you'll keep it up." Kenni looked at the others. "Everyone. That's why you came here, wasn't it? To make some positive changes in your life?"

"I'm having a midlife crisis," Sarah Beth offered easily. "Or so my husband tells me."

"My therapist suggested this," Erin repeated. Then to Kenni, "My husband is having an affair, and I didn't handle it well."

"I *wish* my husband would have one," Christine said, and the others laughed. "We rarely talk. We rarely share meals anymore. We go through the motions of being married."

"Why are you still married then?" Joni asked, then held up her hand. "Sorry. Absolutely none of my business."

"It's become routine," Christine said. "We have three kids—they're grown now. Grandbabies will be coming soon. We have a huge house in an exclusive neighborhood."

"There are perks, even in a bad marriage," Erin said with a smile.

"Exactly," Christine said.

"I hope that after this month is up, you'll learn to put your own happiness ahead of any so-called perks you think you might need," Kenni said. "I know it's an often-used phrase, but life *is* short. Don't waste it by only halfway living."

The words were spoken seriously without even a hint of a smile on Kenni's face or in her eyes. It made Joni wonder if she spoke from experience. She watched her then, and yes, there was a glimmer of sadness in her dark eyes. Had Kendall Lyon lost someone?

"Making a change is hard, especially at my age," Erin said. "Sixty-two," she clarified.

Kenni nodded. "Mel Robbins said it's not because things are difficult that we don't dare…it's *because* we don't dare that things are difficult." She stabbed a piece of salmon, then paused before eating it. "Another often-used phrase is 'life's a journey.' There will always be bumps in the road, regardless of the path you take, Erin. There's a quote by Zig Ziglar—'the more difficult the road, the more beautiful the destination.' Of course, that's up to each of you to determine if that's really true or not."

Joni glanced at the others, wondering if they were absorbing Kenni's words. She wanted to dismiss them, thinking it was a little too deep for her. But the others were slowly nodding, apparently taking it all in. She looked at Kendall, who had resumed eating. Their eyes met and she noted that Kenni's still had a touch of sadness in hers. It made her beyond curious. And curiosity was a journalist's best friend.

CHAPTER TWELVE

Kenni absently listened to the chatter of the women as they hiked along the well-worn path to the easiest of the four obstacle courses. The acreage that the lodge sat on had been transformed over the years, the trails strategically planned to link up with all the courses. Most of the hiking they did was in the nearby national forest, though. Jenn had mapped out a trail that linked with an established forest trail. From there, they could take shorter loops or hike for hours before making their way back to the property. There were stream crossings and rock outcroppings to maneuver past, making for adventurous hiking.

"I won't be able to lift my arms tomorrow," she heard someone say.

"I know. Makes me realize how totally out of shape I am."

She smiled at the exchange, knowing that Karla had barely gotten them started in the gym. Twenty women at once was too many, but she'd given them a quick rundown on all the machines. Tomorrow they would break them up into two groups. While one did the gym, the other would hike. Then they would switch out, culminating with ice baths, jacuzzi, and saunas. All of that before lunch.

She would go easy on them this afternoon too. All the obstacle courses were challenging, but the one they would tackle today was an easy, beginner course. Jenn was along and would help her go over the strategy that the ladies should use while navigating the run. They would go through the course twice, with the second run a timed challenge. Then they would break up into two groups. Jenn would take one and she'd take the other. They would hike into the forest on a loop trail, meeting up at the overlook, a large outcropping of boulders with a lovely view of Mirror Lake far down below them.

When she came to the clearing, she moved to the side, letting the group file in ahead of her. Most were staring with open mouths at the assortment of ropes and swinging logs, the different sizes of stumps, the tires, and the net climbing wall. It was Joni James who spoke first.

"Good god. What the hell is all this shit?"

Kenni smiled at Joni's choice of words. "It is a very basic, very easy obstacle course. There are four on the property, and each week you will progress to the next level, hopefully. Not all groups make it to number four, however."

"They are a lot of fun," Jenn added. "You'll love it!"

Kenni walked over to one of the stumps and hopped on top. "Jenn will run you through the course first. Pay attention to her." She looked pointedly at Joni, who gave her an eye roll. "You'll get a chance to run through it one time to practice. Then you'll get into your teams, and we'll do a timed run. Fastest team to finish wins." She hopped off the stump and went to stand with the group. "Jenn...take it away."

"I'll go slow so you can see how it's done. On your first run-through, go slow too, to get the feel of it. But on your timed run, you'll want to hurry as fast as you can."

Kenni scanned the group, seeing all eyes on Jenn. She went first to the eight tires that were staggered in two rows, much like football players used.

"We call this the tire hop," Jenn said as she ran through it slowly, putting a foot in the center of each tire. "Now, grab the rope here to help balance as you move across the stumps." At the last stump, she stopped. "Here's the first big challenge. Hold your arms out to the side as you walk down the log. If you do this fast, you can make it in like three steps."

"You mean fall off in three steps," Sarah Beth said, and the others laughed.

"You'll be fine," Jenn said. "Now you'll do the swinging rope ladder." She climbed up easily. "Run across the bridge to the other side, then grab the rope and swing down to the next balance log. This log moves, as it's tethered by rope, but it's pretty steady. Go across like before, but use the guide rope to help balance if you need to." Jenn did just that, landing on the ground with grace.

"Now you'll have these three walls to scale, each one a little higher, but you should be able to climb over them." Again, Jenn moved over each wall with ease. "Now here's your final run—four more stumps, then climb the mesh wall…like this."

Jenn made it to the top of the mesh wall—only six feet high— then tumbled to the ground on the other side, raising her hands triumphantly. The group clapped, although the applause was a little subdued. Most had a look of fright on their faces.

"Okay, let's go," Kenni encouraged. "Take it as slow as you need to on this practice run. Get your bearings."

No one moved.

"Joni? Why don't you go first?"

"Oh, hell no."

Kenni smiled. "I think you're the youngest of the group. Show them how it's done."

Joni James scowled and shot daggers at her—daggers she was getting used to. She smiled broader. "Do Team Five proud!"

Joni mouthed an "I hate you" before stepping forward, causing Kenni to laugh. The other members of Team Five clapped enthusiastically.

"Go, Joni! Go, Joni!" Christine yelled.

Kenni stepped back, her eyes lingering on Joni James's legs as she stood next to the tire hop obstacle.

* * *

Joni moved as gracefully as she could through the tires, pleased with herself that she hadn't tripped. Then she took ahold of the rope, wondering how in the world she was going to be able to jump two feet up onto the stupid stump. She grabbed the rope tightly and instead of jumping, she climbed up, one foot at a time. There! She'd made it. Only four more to go. She stood frozen to the spot, however, unable to jump to the next stump. The Lyon woman walked over to her.

"Problem?"

The words that wanted to come out—*You're my fucking problem*—didn't seem appropriate with all the others gathered around them. So she spoke the truth. "I'm afraid I'll fall."

"It's eighteen inches high. I don't think it'll hurt if you do. Besides, they're practically walking distance apart. Just step onto the next stump."

"I'll remind you again. I don't do shit like this," she gritted out as quietly as she could.

Kenni smiled at her. "You signed up for it."

She scowled so hard she was certain her eyebrows were meeting. "Why are you so obnoxious?"

"Oh, for god's sake! They're not that far apart."

Kenni hopped up on the second stump, then took her hand. "Like this. Big step. You don't even need the rope. Take a step."

She nearly screamed as Kenni practically pulled her across the stumps. As she teetered on the last one, Kenni was already across the balance log and about to climb the stupid swinging rope ladder.

"Come on. Follow me."

Joni glanced behind her as Jenn was lining up the others. A woman she'd not met before was already running—*running*—through the tires. Oh, for the love! The woman would be on the stumps in a matter of seconds. So, she took the guide rope and stepped onto the balance log.

"Come on. Just walk across," Kenni said.

"If you're still up there on that fucking bridge when I get there, I'm going to push you off!" she threatened.

Kendall laughed. "Do you always cuss like a sailor?"

She watched in awe as Kenni nearly flew up the rope ladder and onto the bridge above them. "Four older brothers. Fuck was one of the first words I learned to say. My mother grounded Kyle for teaching it to me." She smiled, remembering when Kyle had told her that story, but she had no time to reminisce now. She was holding up the line as the woman behind her was right on her heels. *Show off*, she thought as she rolled her eyes.

She made it across the balance log rather easily and then clung to the swinging rope ladder. How the hell was she supposed to climb it when it wouldn't stay still? She looked up, finding Kenni watching her.

"Come on."

"It's moving."

"Yeah. That's the point."

She closed her eyes, picturing herself wrapping the rope around Kendall Lyon's neck and pushing her off the bridge. Oh, but that was awful, she silently scolded herself. She didn't want to *kill* the woman. Not literally. So, she took a deep breath and proceeded to climb the ladder that swung with her weight. Again, it looked far harder than it actually was. Of course, climbing *off* the stupid thing proved more difficult.

Kenni took her hand and pulled her onto the bridge, then smiled charmingly at her. "Please don't push me off."

Joni met her gaze, surprised that she was returning the smile. "Sorry I said that. And sorry that I pictured wrapping the rope around your neck before I pushed you."

Kenni laughed. "Okay, so I probably shouldn't turn my back on you. Come on."

She hurried across the bridge which, thankfully, had guardrails to hold on to. Kenni waited at the end, then took the rope and swung down to the next log beam. The one that moved. The rope swung back to her, and she grabbed it.

"I have no upper body strength," she warned.

"It's not that far."

I'm going to fall, she thought as she held on tightly to the rope and left the safety of the bridge. Her hands slipped and she screamed, but Kenni was there, grabbing her waist and guiding her onto the log.

"Easy now. Just walk across."

She did, albeit much slower than she had at the first log. She hopped down on the ground with a grin. "Thank you."

"Sure."

The three walls were next, and Kenni scampered over them easily. She, on the other hand, struggled with the first one, even though it was the smallest of the three. The woman behind her was breathing down her neck, reaching the wall at the same time. Joni only barely resisted the urge to push her off. Oh my, but when had she become so violent? First she wanted to hang Kendall from the bridge and now this lovely fifty-something woman was about to get walloped for no good reason.

"Come on, pick it up," Kenni called. She'd already made it over all three walls.

The other woman passed her, and Joni scowled at her. *Bitch!* Then she remembered how Jenn had scaled the walls, taking a running start and nearly hopping over, as did this woman who was at least twenty years older than she was. Goodness, but didn't she feel like a slug.

She was totally exhausted and out of breath after managing the third wall. The woman who had passed her was already across the last four stumps and she heard running behind her, signaling that another woman was about to pass her up too.

"Hurry!" Kenni said, waving her on.

"Hurry my ass," she murmured as she took the rope to help her across the stumps.

Then she stood staring at the mesh wall. It was daunting. It was at least twenty feet tall. It was—

"Climb it like you did the rope ladder. It's easy."

"How tall is it?"

"It's only six feet."

"*Six?* Are you sure? It looks higher than that."

Kenni looked behind her. "You're about to get passed up again. By Erin."

"Oh god. She's in her sixties! How is she beating me?"

"Come on, Joni," Erin said as she grabbed ahold of the mesh. "It looks easy enough."

She blew out her breath and grabbed the freaking mesh. As she climbed, her feet kept slipping through the openings and she had a vision of herself at the top, dangling upside down by her ankles and flailing about.

"You're doing great!"

That from Kenni, which made her scowl. She only barely kept in the torrent of curse words that wanted to spill out.

Another woman came up beside her. The woman had the nerve to *smile* at her. *Smile!*

"Hi! I'm Amy. Team Four."

"How nice," she managed as her foot plunged yet again through the mesh. She watched as the woman carefully maneuvered the wall.

Shit! I can do this, she thought. She needed to balance on the front of her foot, not the middle like she'd been doing. She finally pulled herself up to the top. No, it wasn't easy, and she was damn near exhausted. Then she panicked. *Now what?*

"Drop down," Kendall said.

"It's like twenty feet to the ground!"

"It's six feet and there's a cushion of straw."

"Yeah, well, it's too fucking far."

Amy was still sitting at the top. "I think we just kinda fall down. That's what Jenn did."

"Jenn is twenty years old!"

Kenni laughed. "She's thirty-three."

Amy ignored both of them and actually jumped. She fell when she landed, and Kendall was there to pick her up.

"Great job, Amy!"

"That was fun!"

Kenni looked up at her. "Coming?"

"Do I have to?"

"Yes."

She wiped her forehead. "I hate to be the bearer of bad news, but Team Five is going to lose again."

"I don't know. Erin did pretty well. And I see Sarah Beth running across the bridge."

She looked up and sure enough, Sarah Beth looked almost lithe as she took the rope and swung down to the moving log beam. That was enough to spur her on. She swung her legs over the top and, with her eyes closed, fell the twenty feet to the ground below. She barely registered falling as Kendall had her picked up and back on her feet again within a second of hitting the straw padding.

"Way to go!"

She stumbled out of the way, going to stand near Erin as they watched the others. Most everyone was better than she was, though she was childishly pleased to see a couple of them stumble. Maybe she wasn't the worst one there after all.

CHAPTER THIRTEEN

Joni sat down on the ground and leaned against a tree, watching as Kenni separated everyone into their teams in preparation for the second run. She was an attractive woman, she conceded. And she appeared to love her job, as she'd been actively engaged with nearly everyone. Of course, she was probably very uptight, considering all the *rules* she had. Stupid, silly rules, in her opinion. That was enough to overlook her attractiveness.

"To make this easier, we'll start with Team One," Kendall said. "Jenn will time each team. Once the first member gets through the tires and lands on the stumps, the second member can go and so on. When the last member crosses over the mesh wall, the timer stops." She looked around. "Any questions?"

"It's good being Team Five," Sarah Beth said. "That way we'll know what time we'll have to beat."

"Yeah, right," she said dryly. "I'll apologize now for us losing."

"I think you should go third," Christine suggested. "Erin first, then Sarah Beth. Then you. Then me."

"Why?"

"Well, you can't go first. Everyone will end up passing you up. And you can't go last. There'll be no one to push you."

She was the youngest of the group, by far. Should she be insulted by their plan? Probably so.

"Okay, let's get started!" Jenn yelled cheerfully. "Team One! Let's roll!"

Joni wanted to just check out because she was *so* not interested in this. She ignored them all by staring off into the trees. She pictured herself sitting at her favorite table—corner, by the window—sipping on a frozen margarita and chatting with Kimberly and Gloria and whoever else joined them for the twice-a-week happy hour. Sometimes four of them, sometimes six. Sometimes they would stay for dinner and sometimes they'd only share appetizers. Tuesdays and Thursdays were their normal days. Friday was saved for date night. That made her roll her eyes. More often than not, she either spent Friday night alone or she hit up one of her single friends for a movie or dinner.

Clapping and cheers brought her attention back to the here and now. Team One seemed to be running the course without difficulty, and two of them had already made it over the damn mesh wall.

"I don't think we're going to win," Christine said rather dryly.

Joni noticed that all three of her teammates were looking at her. "Look, I already apologized for us losing. I know I'm the worst."

Sarah Beth looked down at her, then patted her head. "You'll do fine, hon."

"That was great, ladies!" Kenni high-fived all four women on Team One. "You set a good pace."

"What was our time?"

Jenn held up her stopwatch. "Two minutes and forty-nine seconds. Which is great for a first time. And not to discount what you did, but by the time your month is up, you'll be doing this little course in about a minute and fifteen seconds."

"A minute?" someone said in awe.

Joni's eyes widened. "*Little* course? You mean they get worse?"

"This is the shortest and the easiest of the bunch," Kenni explained. "The hardest one will take you about thirteen minutes once you get the hang of it."

Joni, still sitting, met Kenni's gaze across the forest floor. She didn't know whether to laugh hysterically or cry. She wanted to jump up and yell at the others. *Wake up, people! They're trying to kill us!*" But no, she swallowed those words, even if she thought them to be true.

"Okay! Team Two. Let's go!"

By the time Team Four ran, Joni made herself get to her feet, knowing they were next. Team Two didn't come close to beating One's time. In fact, Joni thought that just maybe they could actually beat Team Two and not come in last. Team Three didn't beat them either. All the others were encouraging Team Four on, and she found herself tensing up as one of the women slipped off the moving log and landed on her ass. One of her teammates circled back to help her up and she got right back on the log. Joni clapped along with the others, then stopped as soon as she realized what she was doing. She reminded herself that she *hated* this kind of team stuff.

Even with the woman falling, Team Four beat the time by *three* seconds, which Jenn announced enthusiastically, and everyone appropriately cheered, even Team One. Sarah Beth took her arm, urging her along to the starting line. It was their turn.

"Team Five? Ready?"

"Let her rip," Erin said as she rubbed her hands together.

Sarah Beth was behind her, and Joni took the third spot, as instructed. She nearly started hyperventilating when Kenni yelled, "Go!"

Erin nimbly made it through the tires and onto the stumps. Sarah Beth took off as soon as Erin touched the first stump.

Oh god, oh god, oh god, she chanted silently to herself, watching as Sarah Beth cleared the last tire.

"Go!" Christine said with a firm push.

Blood was pounding in her ears, and she heard nothing of the others as they cheered them on. She was going too slow, she knew, but her concentration was solely on the tires so she wouldn't trip on the damn things and do a faceplant. She was already out of breath when she reached the stumps. She paused to grab the rope, then glanced behind her. Christine was already halfway through the tires.

"Come on, Joni!"

Instead of jumping on each log with both feet, she did what most of the others had done. One foot on each log, using the rope to balance herself. *I made it!* The balance log was next, and she felt Christine right on her heels. She glanced ahead, seeing Sarah Beth already across the bridge and onto the second moving log. Erin was already at the mesh wall.

"Let's go!" Christine yelled.

She held her hands out to her sides, balancing as she hurried across the log. The swinging rope ladder was next, and she grabbed it without thought, climbing up rather easily to the bridge. She had no time to savor her victory because Christine was pushing her.

"How did you do the ladder so fast?" she asked, gasping for breath.

"Let's go!"

She held the rope, closing her eyes for a second before swinging down to the moving log. She nearly lost her balance as the stupid thing lurched forward and she grabbed the rope to steady herself.

"Go!"

God, she was beginning to *hate* Christine. But she jumped off the log and ran to the three walls. She was rather pleased with herself as she scaled each one without mishap. Four more stumps awaited her, and she hopped up, stepping across each one before running to the mesh wall.

Christine reached it at the same time. "Come on. You're doing great! I think we're going to win!"

Remembering to use the front of her feet to climb, she made it to the top only a few seconds after Christine did. Of course, the twenty-foot drop made her pause.

"Jump!" Sarah Beth yelled.

Oh shit.

"Come on!"

She fell over the side and onto the straw below. Unlike the first time, Kenni wasn't there to help her up. She opened her eyes, staring into a spectacular blue sky. It was pretty. She supposed she was still alive.

"You did it!" Sarah Beth exclaimed.

Erin and Christine helped her up. "You did great," Christine said again.

"Did we win? Did we win?" Sarah Beth asked Jenn.

Jenn gave an apologetic smile. "No. But Team Three only beat you by a few seconds."

"So we came in like…fourth?"

"Yes. Everyone did so well," Jenn said, clapping again. "Team Four is the winner! Then Team One, Team Three, Team Five, and Team Two. Excellent, ladies!"

Joni was grinning. "How about that? We didn't lose!"

Erin stared at her. "We also didn't win."

Sarah Beth draped her arm around Joni's shoulders. "You need to get through the tires a little quicker next time. And the mesh wall. Just think. If you'd gotten to the top and fell over right away, that would have knocked off four or five seconds."

Kenni came over and nodded. "Yep. Team Three only beat you by four seconds."

Joni stared at her. "How much did we beat Team Two by?"

A quick smile. "Two seconds."

Joni groaned. "We were two seconds from being in last place."

And yes, it was her fault. They all knew it.

God, I hate this shit!

CHAPTER FOURTEEN

While she stood under the warm water—taking a rather lengthy shower—Joni was certain she'd never been more tired in her life. After the obstacle course, they'd been broken up into two groups and hiked to what Kenni had said was an overlook. She admitted that the view had been pretty. Some lake was down below, but she didn't remember the name. Truth was, she hadn't been paying much attention because her feet were killing her. She turned around and closed her eyes, letting the warm spray hit her back. Some of the others had opted for an ice bath and a sauna. She, however, couldn't contemplate doing *anything* other than taking a nice, long shower.

She finally made herself get out. Each of the three showers had a dressing area, tiny but at least private. She heard water running in another shower and knew she wasn't alone. She dried off and hung the towel on a hook. With a sigh, she looked at the drab cotton athletic shorts Dana had picked out for her. Light gray, dark gray, and navy. The ones she'd grabbed were the dark-gray pair. The T-shirt had some stupid mountain scene on it. She slipped on her panties and then the shorts. Before putting on the T-shirt, she opened her toiletry bag and took out the deodorant. She heard the outer door open.

"Joni? You still in here?"

She arched an eyebrow. *Who is that? Christine?* "Yes, just finishing," she answered.

"Okay. It's ten minutes until dinner. I'll wait for you to go down."

She rolled her eyes. "Be right out." *Damn, there is such a thing as too much togetherness, isn't there?*

She gathered her dirty clothes and shoved them into the lightweight gym bag Dana had insisted she get. Back out into the bathroom, another woman was at the sink, applying lotion to her face. Joni was about to walk past without speaking but remembered her as the one who had fallen off the moving log.

"Have you recovered from the obstacle course yet?"

The woman looked at her questioningly. "What do you mean?"

"Aren't you the one who fell from that crazy moving log beam?"

The woman laughed. "Oh, that. Yes, that was me. I've never been able to balance worth a damn. But it was fun."

Joni wanted to scowl but refrained from doing so. "Fun? Well, if you win, I guess it makes it bearable."

"Oh, I can't believe we won. When I fell, I thought for sure that would do us in, but Britney came back to help. I love this kind of stuff, don't you?"

She met her own eyes in the mirror instead of this woman's. She nearly laughed at the obvious forced smile she was wearing. "Just *love* it, yes," she lied. "I'm Joni, by the way."

"Anna. Nice to meet you."

"Yeah. Well, I guess it's nearly time for dinner. I'm starving."

"Oh, I know. And they say this will be the easiest day we'll have."

"Does it make you reconsider this retreat?"

"No, not at all. I knew what to expect. My neighbor came here last year. She was thoroughly impressed by the whole thing.

Couldn't stop raving about it for months. I simply had to come."
Anna laughed. "I will admit that I started going to the gym in
January to prepare for some of the activities."

"Really? Maybe that's what I should have done." She waved. "I
should go. See you later."

"Sure."

Well, she definitely wouldn't use Anna in her article. She
needed to find someone who hated it as much as she did. Maybe
after a few more days of this nonsense, she'd be able to weed out
those who wished they were anywhere but here. Like her.

Out in the hallway, she found Christine leaning against the
wall, waiting for her. Joni gave her a smile.

"Are the others already downstairs?"

"Yes."

She went to her door. "Thought I needed an escort?"

Christine shook her head. "Not at all. I just finished my own
shower, so I thought I'd wait for you."

Her statement—and her demeanor—seemed genuine, so Joni
tried not to be annoyed at her. She tossed her bag onto her bed
and was about to return when she saw her phone on the dresser.
My phone! She was about to go snatch it up and see what all she
missed today but the damn alarm in the hallway sounded. Christ,
whose idea was it for that obnoxious thing? Had to be Kenni's.

"Come on, Joni."

With a sigh, she turned away from her phone and went back
out, letting her door close behind her. This day had lasted for an
eternity. And it wasn't over yet.

"I am so hungry. Are you?"

Joni nodded. "I am. I haven't had this much activity since…
well, probably ever."

Christine laughed. "I know." She pointed at her face, which
looked clean and fresh. Her long blond hair was pulled into a
ponytail. "And I can't remember the last time I went out in
public—to dinner, no less—without makeup on."

Joni touched her own face. It hadn't even occurred to her to
put makeup on. "I'm so tired, I didn't even think about makeup,"
she admitted.

"You don't need makeup. You have nearly flawless skin. How old did you say you were? Thirty-ish?"

They walked down the second flight of stairs, and they could hear loud conversations from the dining room. She glanced at Christine quickly. "Thirty-one."

"Still a baby. I'm forty-seven. Hard to believe. I was your age only a few years ago it seems," she said with a laugh. "Like Kenni said at lunch, life is short. And it goes by fast."

"If you don't mind my asking, why are you here?"

Christine patted her arm. "I'll use Sarah Beth's excuse. I'm having a midlife crisis. Or maybe that's wishful thinking." She paused before going into the dining room. "I'm terribly unhappy in my life, Joni. There. I said it out loud to someone at last."

"Your life? Your marriage?"

"Yes. All of it."

"What are you hoping to change by being here?"

Christine just smiled at her. "Come on. Let's get some dinner. I'm starving."

CHAPTER FIFTEEN

Kenni moved to the front of the dining room, looking at the tables where everyone sat. The smell of dinner was wafting about, and she imagined that most of them were famished. It only took the first day for them to learn to eat properly.

"I'll make this quick since I know you're all probably a little hungry."

A mixture of nervous laughter, nods, and agreements came from the women. She looked at her Team Five. Even Joni was paying attention. That was a first.

"I know most of you have been told your whole life to eat low-fat foods, lean protein, and lots of fruits and veggies." Everyone nodded. She smiled. "Horrible advice. We women need fat for our hormone production. A totally low-fat diet plus exercise will wreck your adrenals and skyrocket your cortisol levels. That's too much stress for your body. So don't skimp on fat. Women also need protein, so don't skimp on that either. The reason we sent the questionnaires out before you got here was to see what most of you like and dislike. There are no vegans in this group, so I won't go into our meatless protein options, but there will be tofu available for those who enjoy it. I once again encourage you to eat a hearty breakfast. Besides eggs and bacon, there will also be ground beef patties if you prefer that to bacon or sausage. There will be no cereal or oatmeal. We're concentrating on protein and healthy fats. There'll also be fruit bowls each morning too. Take what you want, as much as you want."

Someone raised their hand. "I was told to avoid bacon because of the nitrates."

Kenni nodded. "Yes. We buy natural bacon with no nitrates or nitrites, and it's cured without sugar. But if you prefer not to eat it, there will be other choices, like I said. For this month, you will be eating a fairly low carbohydrate diet. There'll be no snacks, no junk food, no processed food. Ever. There will only be three meals, so please eat your fill. Don't be shy to go back for seconds. We are eating to fuel our bodies. Your daily activities will increase a little each day, so you don't want to be running on empty."

"Like now," Sarah Beth said with a laugh.

"I normally do keto," Angela said. "Been doing it for years."

"And how has that worked out for you?" Kenni asked, noting that she would place Angela in the overweight category.

"I lost weight at first. But…"

"Keto is very high fat, low protein. That's not what we're after here. We want high protein and moderate fat." She motioned behind her. "Wanda varies the meals but always has two and sometimes three different protein choices. Help yourself to whatever strikes your fancy. Now…let's eat!"

Everyone moved at once and after the initial pushing and shoving, they settled down to wait their turn. She went over to where Sky and the others stood.

"I think we wore them out today," Jenn said.

"They never listen when you tell them to eat a big breakfast," Karla added.

"They'll listen tomorrow," Mindy chimed in.

"Do you all have the activities already planned?" Kenni asked.

Sky laughed. "You ask us this every day. How many years have we been doing this?"

"Sorry. Habit."

"Well, after the morning hike and gym, I have another scavenger hunt lined up," Sky said. "I've already let Wanda know that lunch will be a little later tomorrow. So, while you've got them out hiking, I'll plant the clues. Nothing too elaborate."

"Leading them to the jacuzzi and sauna?"

"Right. Winning team gets an hour there. The other teams will go to the gym for cardio. Lunch after that."

"The losing teams are going to hate you," Karla laughed.

"I know."

"Okay. After lunch I want to split them up into the two groups again," Kenni said. "Jenn can lead a group, and I'll lead one. Let's take them on the forest loop and meet up at the beaver ponds."

"Beaver ponds? You normally save that for the second week."

"I think they can make it. Then let's swing back by the obstacle course and see if any team can beat their time from today."

"You trying to mix things up on us?" Jenn asked.

Kenni shrugged. "Maybe we're getting stale, doing the same thing each time, each day."

"But we've got it down pat," Karla said.

"Right. We do it without thinking. I think it loses its freshness, and we do a disservice to our clients."

Jenn nodded. "Okay. I can see that. So, what's the new plan then?"

"We can decide each morning. Let's not change that routine. Yoga, gym, and hike. But we can be flexible in the afternoons. And if Sky wants to do a more elaborate scavenger hunt before lunch, we can skip a morning hike here and there or do a quick thirty-minute hike on the trails near the lodge."

"Well, the benefit of having everything planned out and the same each time is that we don't ever get behind schedule," Karla said.

"I know that. But if we get behind schedule, it's not the end of the world."

Sky frowned. "Who are you and what have you done with our Kenni?"

Kenni laughed. "What? Too spontaneous?"

Jenn laughed too. "You've always been a stickler for having a plan and following it, right down to the minute. Like the alarms for mealtimes. Next thing you know, you'll be ditching that."

"If we didn't have the alarm in the morning, half of them wouldn't make breakfast. Especially the first few days."

"Okay. You're the boss."

"You want me to stick to my usual scavenger hunts or mix things up?" Sky asked.

"I guess stick to them. We don't want to get too crazy."

CHAPTER SIXTEEN

"This has been the longest day of my life," Joni complained as she leaned against the pillows on her bed. "And I'm supposed to be down there playing some stupid card game with my team."

"But wait. Go back to this obstacle course," Kimberly said.

She groaned. "It's embarrassing. I'm the youngest woman here—by far—and I'm also the *worst* one. Can you believe that?"

Kimberly laughed. "Yes, I can. I'm still trying to picture you on an obstacle course."

"Well, if I was allowed to take my phone with me, I'd film it for you. God, I *hate* this place."

"What are they feeding you?"

"Yeah, that's been the highlight of my day. And I'm eating like I'm pregnant or something. Never in my life have I been so hungry."

"So normal food or what?"

"Yes. We had a killer salad for lunch topped with chicken or salmon. Tonight's dinner was either beef, chicken, or tofu and veggie stir-fry over zucchini noodles—zoodles, they called them. I took chicken and beef although Christine said the tofu was good. I might try that at another meal. Oh, and believe it or not, I plan on a huge plate of bacon and eggs for breakfast."

"You? You barely eat a muffin most mornings."

"I have been *so* hungry. Now I know why Turnbull's wife lost twenty pounds while she was here."

"Is it like a boot camp?"

"I've never been to a boot camp, but yes, this is how I would picture it. It's like nonstop activities all fucking day long. Even after dinner, they encourage you to stay down and play board games or cards or something. Or take another freaking hike! Christ, it's like we're stuck in the dark ages. No TV! No Wi-Fi! I'm shocked there's even cell service. I wouldn't have put it past the Lyon woman to block cell signals up here."

"What's she like? Is she as cute as her picture?"

"Yes. Yes, she is. She's also obnoxious."

"How so?"

"She's got all these rules. And she's so…so irritating. She gets on my nerves."

"You have a lot of interaction with her?"

"Yeah, she's our freaking team leader."

Kimberly laughed. "Teams? You're on a *team*?"

"Team Five, thank you very much. We have challenges and shit like that. I hate that kind of stuff. And get this. We're supposed to go out each morning at sunrise and reset our circadian rhythm, whatever the hell that is. Oh. And try *grounding*. Like I'm going to go barefoot out here to touch the earth! And she actually said to hug a tree! She's one of those crazy nature freaks." She tilted her head, listening. "Oh my god! Are you pouring *wine*?"

"Yes. Why? Don't you have a glass?"

She groaned. "No. I don't."

"Why not? We packed ten bottles in your clothes."

"Yes, we did. And they search your bags, if you can believe that. My wine got confiscated."

"You're kidding?" Then Kimberly laughed. "Were you pissed?"

"You think? She also confiscated my phone because I broke *that* rule this morning." God, was it only that morning that Kenni had taken her phone? "I should go. I'm so exhausted. I could fall asleep right now."

"It's not even nine o'clock."

She yawned. "I know." She yawned again. "Sorry. But I've been awake since five-thirty this morning, and it's been literally nonstop all day."

"Why so early?"

"Oh, Kimberly. They have this…like a blaring fire alarm. It goes off to wake everybody. It goes off right before mealtimes too."

"Jesus, it's like you're in the military or something."

"Or something," she murmured. "I gotta go. God knows what torture they have planned for us tomorrow."

"I take it you haven't had a chance to start on your article then?"

"No. And if every day is like today, my only free time is after dinner. Like now. And I'm too exhausted to even look at my laptop, much less pull it out and attempt to write something."

"What about your plan to stay a few days, then bail?"

"Yeah. I don't know if that's possible. I mean, yes, it's possible. It's not like we're locked up in here or anything." She paused. "At least I don't think so. But I've had no time to interview anyone."

"I thought you were going to just make shit up."

"I was. I am. I guess. I mean, I already wrote the hit piece. I think after being here a few days, I could tweak that enough to make it real. That's probably what I'll do." She yawned once more. "Okay. I'll talk to you later, Kim. I just want to get under the covers and go to sleep."

"Okay, sure. Call me when you can."

"Thanks. Good night."

She put her phone down. She hadn't wanted to tell Kimberly that she was already in her silk pajamas and under the covers. She simply reached for the lamp and killed the light. She fell asleep almost instantly.

CHAPTER SEVENTEEN

"I swear, I pulled a muscle doing that Downtown Dog pose," Joni said as she rubbed the back of her leg.

Sarah Beth laughed. "Downward Facing Dog. I'm actually enjoying the yoga sessions. But yes, I was sore this morning too." She leaned closer to her. "Did you go out before breakfast for grounding?"

Joni smirked. "Yeah, right." Then she eyed her. "Did *you*?"

"I did. There were quite a few of us out there. Jenn was out too. She told us anything we touched that was connected to the earth would help. Like sitting on a boulder or touching a tree. But standing barefoot was best."

"And you did?"

"Yes. I actually felt really amazing afterward. I think I'll do it every morning."

Great. Sarah Beth has already been brainwashed and it's only the second day.

"Okay, Teams Four and Five will head to the gym while the other teams go with Jenn for the first hike. When they get back, we'll switch up," Kenni told the group. "If you need to go up to your room to change, you have five minutes." She clapped. "Let's go!"

Oh god, not the gym. She'd rather go on a hike than attempt all those crazy weight machines again. She looked down at her lightweight hiking boots, thinking they'd be perfectly fine for the gym too. Unlike yesterday, today she was in shorts instead of sweats. The morning was cool, but after going through the yoga poses—and surprisingly, she did remember most of them from the day before—she warmed up quickly.

"I noticed you had a full plate at breakfast."

She turned, finding Kenni coming up beside her as they headed along the trail to the gym. She nodded. "I heeded your warning this time. I don't think I could have fit even one more slice of bacon on my plate."

"How did you sleep?"

At that, she smiled. "I have no idea. I passed out and didn't wake until that fucking alarm rattled the walls at five thirty."

Kendall laughed. "It's a bit much, I know, but it's necessary. The first year we relied on everyone setting their own alarms. We learned quickly that most lack the discipline to actually get up instead of hitting snooze."

"How many years have you been doing this? I think you said ten when you confiscated my wine."

"Yes."

"And how does one get into this line of work? I mean, as a chosen career. What made you start this?" She glanced over at her. "I assume you started it. Or did you buy it from someone?"

Kendall gave her a thoughtful look. "Curious or is this a question for the article?"

Joni's eyebrows shot up. "I can't ask questions?"

"Sure. But I don't do interviews."

"Why is that?"

Kendall smiled at her. "I don't trust journalists. Well, I did once. Learned my lesson."

"What do you mean?"

"I mean, my words got twisted around and taken out of context. The article made it seem like we were a weight-loss clinic and that we ridiculed and belittled our clients if they couldn't keep up and didn't shed weight. It was nothing but a hit piece."

Joni swallowed nervously. "A…a hit piece? Are you sure?"

"Very sure."

"Did it hurt your business? Did women cancel?"

Kendall laughed. "Actually, the opposite. We suddenly had overweight women booking with us thinking it *was* a weight-loss clinic. We have since tweaked the website to make it clearer what our agenda is."

"Yes. To empower and to liberate."

"That's what you took out of it?"

"Well, I didn't really look at it all that much. My boss sent me here. Against my will, I might add. And I did go to your website. But I freaked the fuck out when I saw women climbing trees. That's about as far as I got."

Kendall laughed again. "So, you tried to sneak in wine to get you through it all?"

"Something like that."

"Have you told the others the reason you're here?"

She shook her head. "No. I don't think I will."

Kendall nodded. "I don't think you should either. That might put a damper on your teamwork. They are all here for legitimate reasons."

Legitimate reasons? Well, she supposed that was true. But technically she *was* there for a legit reason. It certainly wasn't something she would pay money to do.

"Why do they come?" she asked. At Kendall's quizzical look, she elaborated. "I mean, judging by the vehicles out front when I got here—and the cost of the monthly stay—these are all fairly well-to-do women, aren't they?"

"Mostly, yes."

"Then why do they come?"

"Meaning they should have plenty of money to hire a therapist if need be?" Kendall nodded. "Most of them have probably already been down that road."

"So, you're like a last-ditch effort?"

Kendall met her gaze. "What is it that you think we do here?"

"Honestly, I have no clue. Other than wearing us the fuck out every day so we sleep like the dead."

Kendall laughed. "I don't think I've ever heard the word 'fuck' as much as I have since you've been here."

"Sorry. I blame my brothers for my potty mouth."

"I don't find it offensive, if that's what you think."

"My mother does. To this day, she wonders where she went wrong."

The others were already standing out on the large deck that surrounded the gym. It wasn't like a gym you'd find in the city. Most of the benches and free weights were outside. The different weight machines were inside, as well as the elliptical machines and treadmills. Kendall left her and went up to the deck.

"Since we have a smaller group, you should all be able to hit every machine in there. But Karla will also go over some of the free weights out here with you. In the next few days, she'll be monitoring your fitness level and progress and making individual plans for you. Before we get started, though, we'll go through our first weigh-in and measurement profile."

She pointed to where Karla was waiting. "Sky and Mindy will help her out with that, so it won't take too long. We'll use a body scan scale to measure both body fat and visceral fat. It's not as accurate as if you'd done a DEXA scan, but it's pretty close. Sky will keep a record of it all, as well as your measurements. We'll do this once a week and again on your last day here. Hopefully you'll all see phenomenal progress."

Joni looked around at the women with her. Her team, of course, and also Team Four. Of the eight of them, she was the youngest. She didn't suppose there was anyone younger than forty on any of the teams. They all varied in body shapes and sizes. A few were overweight but not glaringly so. Most were a little on the fluffy side, carrying ten to twenty pounds extra. Actually, as she looked them over, none were what she'd call overly thin either, not even herself. Anna, the woman she'd spoken to after her shower yesterday, was probably the thinnest of the group.

"Weight loss is not our main goal, although most everyone will lose water weight from inflammation and also drop a few pounds of body fat. Our goal is muscle building and retention, which will change your body composition. As we age, women especially, we lose muscle mass. When you're younger, it's easier to maintain. But as we get older, if we're not diligently trying to build muscle or at least maintain what we have, we'll lose a little each year. After age fifty, you'll lose ten percent per year if you're inactive. After age sixty, if you do nothing to combat the loss, you'll have fifty to eighty percent less muscle than when you were in your twenties. If you see an elderly woman who is frail, that's exactly what happened to her. It's called sarcopenia." Kenni smiled. "And I don't want any of you to end up like that. So, we're trying to teach you to be active and to make an effort to at least keep what you've got. Eat sufficient protein and lift heavy weights. The old saying is true. Use it or lose it."

"Yes, but I don't want to be bulky," someone said.

Joni thought her name might have been Marsha, but she wasn't sure. Regardless, the woman was already on the bulky side, but with fat, not muscle.

"You're not going to get bulky, Marsha. I promise."

Ah, so it was *Marsha.*

"Women don't have the same hormones as men," Kenni continued. "Eating a lot of protein and working out diligently with a trainer would take you years to even begin to resemble a female bodybuilder. What we're aiming for here is a nice muscle definition in your biceps, your shoulders. We want to get your legs in shape. This is all about aging gracefully and being independent when you're older. We want you to be functional. We want you to be able to lift things—a heavy sack of dog food, for instance. We want you to be able to open a pickle jar when you're older. We want you to get up and out of a chair easily."

Joni frowned. Who couldn't get up and out of a chair?

"I know what you're thinking. 'I can already do that easily. I'm young.' Well, we have ranges here from forties to sixties." She paused. "And one thirtyish. But one day you'll be in your seventies, eighties, and, hopefully, nineties. You don't want to lose mobility.

You need to start now. You don't want to only age gracefully...you want to age *healthfully*."

Kenni pointed at Sky. "Let's do a test. How many of you can fold your arms across your chest, cross your ankles, and then sit down on the ground without using your hands? Sky, please demonstrate."

Joni watched as Sky did just that. Easily and gracefully.

"Now, get up without using your hands."

Sky also popped right back up.

"Who can do that? Or have you ever tried?"

No one had. *Why would they?*

"Joni?"

She looked at Kenni, trying not to panic. "What?" she said shakily.

"You're the youngest one in the group. Why don't you give it a try?"

"Me?"

"Yes."

She narrowed her eyes at Kenni. "Is that how it's going to be? Since I'm the youngest, I always get to be the guinea pig?"

Kenni simply smiled back at her in an almost flirty manner. *As if.* She turned away from the woman. She didn't care how attractive she was, and she didn't care that she needed an interview. She certainly wasn't going to flirt with her. She took a deep breath. Okay, she could do this. She stood still, then, against her will, her gaze slid back to Kenni, who nodded. She found herself holding on to her eyes as she folded her arms across her chest. She then crossed her ankles like Sky had done. But she couldn't move.

"Now sit down," Kendall coaxed gently.

"Yeah, well, I'm afraid I'm going to fall backwards."

"Give it a try."

She took another deep breath, then squatted. And she landed with a thud on her ass, but at least she did not tip backward. *Success!*

"Great! Now stand back up."

Instinct had her wanting to use her hands to brace herself. How was she going to use nothing but her legs. *Shit.* She swallowed, then tried to stand, using a rocking motion to get her weight on top of her feet.

"Harder than it looks, isn't it?"

Before "I fucking hate you" spewed from her mouth, she rolled to her side and used her hands to stand up again. She smiled sweetly at Kenni. "Fucking hard, yes."

The ladies around her laughed nervously, as if hoping Kenni wouldn't call on them next. But she did.

"Everyone, give it a try."

Joni covered her smile as Sarah Beth did what she had feared she would do—fall down onto her back. The exercise was done with varying forms of success on the way down. No one could get back up without using their hands, however. For that she was thankful.

Kenni didn't seem discouraged. "By the time you leave here, you'll be popping back up just like that," she said, snapping her fingers together. "Okay, Karla. They're all yours. Let's get their weights and measurements done, then get to work."

* * *

Joni was shocked by her weight. Eight pounds heavier than her last doctor's visit if she remembered correctly. Her body fat percentage was twenty-seven, which Sky said was in the normal range. But for her height—five foot seven—Sky said an optimal percentage would be between twenty and twenty-three, if she was going for that fit, athletic look. That didn't seem too far off until Sky told her she'd need to lose about fifteen pounds of fat and gain about seven pounds of muscle. And if she worked with a trainer once she left here and continued to eat high protein, she might reach that goal after four or five months of hard work.

Yeah, right.

Karla had given them a list of workouts for today. Team Four was doing legs. Team Five would do arms and backs. They would switch up tomorrow. The last fifteen minutes of their gym time would be spent either on a treadmill, elliptical, or stationary bike. And after all that, they would get to go on a freaking hike.

Most of the others were inside on the various weight machines so she went outside, thinking she'd do a few bicep curls without anyone watching. Christine had the same idea apparently, because she was already out there. To her surprise, so was Kenni. Her mouth dropped open as she took her shirt off. *Good lord.* From what she'd learned of body fat and muscle from Sky, Kenni was definitely below twenty percent. She stood rooted to the spot as Kenni lay flat on a bench, her thighs spread and her feet firmly on the deck. The muscles in her shoulders and biceps strained as she lifted the bar. *Good lord.*

Christine nudged her. "What a body."

"I'll say." She realized she was nearly drooling, and she shook herself, pulling her eyes away from Kenni's spread thighs. "I mean, yeah, something to strive for."

Christine lifted an eyebrow. "Are you okay?"

"She's attractive. But not my type."

Christine's other eyebrow lifted.

"I'm gay. I don't normally find women like her attractive."

"You're gay? Never would have guessed. You don't look gay."

"What does gay look like?"

Christine slowly turned toward Kenni. "I guess more like her. A little on the boyish side."

Joni watched as Kenni finished her set and sat up, the muscles of her stomach outlined as she stood. Her eyes were glued to her legs as she moved over to another bench, where a rather huge dumbbell sat. Kenni picked it up with ease, curling it to her chest in a rhythmic motion, her bicep popping with the movement. Disgusted with herself for staring, she turned away.

"I don't find boyish women attractive. At all," she said with emphasis.

Christine smiled at her. "Really? But you said earlier that she *was* attractive."

Joni waved a hand in the air. "She's cute, yes. But I mean I'm not attracted to women like that." She moved to the rows of dumbbells and picked up a small one. Five pounds.

"Karla said to start with ten pounds," Christine said beside her. "She said not to bother with the fives."

"Then why are they out here?"

"They're for floor exercises," Kenni stated as she put her dumbbell back.

Twenty-five pounds? Shit.

Kendall took the small five pounder from her hand. "Start with ten."

Joni averted her eyes. "Can you please put your shirt back on?"

"Why? This is workout attire. Karla has on the same thing."

She was proud of herself for not staring at the workout bra. Or more importantly, what it covered. She simply put the ten-pound weight back down and walked as nonchalantly as possible back into the gym. Yes, Karla was dressed similarly to Kenni. Karla lacked, however, the allure that Kenni seemed to have.

She pulled up short. *What the hell?* Allure? God, no. Kenni irritated her. Annoyed her to no end. There was *nothing* about Kendall Lyon that attracted her.

Nothing.

Then she paused, staring off into space. She did need to interview her, though. She did need to ask questions. What better way to get close to her than to pretend to have an interest in her. Could she possibly suffer through that to get her story?

She shook her head. No. That would be crazy. She didn't *like* the woman. Not really. How was she going to pretend that she did?

CHAPTER EIGHTEEN

Kenni was pleased by the anticipation she saw on everyone's faces as the teams prepared to run the obstacle course again. After the short hike and scavenger hunt—which Team Four won again—they'd had a break before lunch during which the winners took advantage of the jacuzzi and sauna. The losing teams did a half hour of cardio in the gym, then had a few minutes of downtime. After lunch there was the longer hike to the beaver ponds—which most were fascinated with after she explained how they were formed. Even Joni hadn't complained much about the hike.

She glanced over at her team now, smiling as they seemed to be going over strategy. She hoped they made a better effort than the last time. Well, that wasn't really fair. Sarah Beth, Erin, and Christine had all done fine. She let her gaze linger on Joni James. There was just something about her. She was getting far too much pleasure picking on her. Rarely did they have clients as young as Joni. And never anyone who didn't want to be there. Which made her question why she'd been given this assignment in the first place.

"Ready?" Jenn asked.

She turned her attention to the group, nodding. "Yes. We'll start at the bottom. Team Five? Ready?"

"Us?" Sarah Beth asked. "But—"

Kenni nodded. "You'll do fine. Let's go."

Her four team members went to the front of the line. As expected, Joni shot her a look.

"Do you hate us or what?"

Kenni smiled. "You're my favorite team. I don't hate you. Now try to beat yesterday's time."

As they did yesterday, Erin went first. The other teams were clapping and cheering as Erin nimbly traversed the tires. As soon as she hit the stumps, Sarah Beth took off after her. Joni was next in line, and she was nervously shaking her hands. Christine gave her a shove when Sarah Beth was on the stumps. Kenni found herself watching Joni's every move. For someone who avoided exercise, she had nice legs. Then her breath caught as Joni nearly tripped on the last tire. She kept her balance and hurried to the stumps.

Kenni moved along with her, offering encouragement as she made it to the balance log. "You're doing great!"

"Shut up!"

She smiled. "Hurry!"

Joni climbed the rope ladder and pulled herself onto the bridge. Christine was crossing the log and gaining on her. As if sensing this, Joni ran quickly across the bridge and grabbed the rope, not pausing at all as she dropped down to the moving log below.

"Good job!"

She glanced toward the mesh wall where Erin was already over. Sarah Beth was on the last four stumps. "Come on, Joni!"

To her surprise, Joni scaled the three small walls easily. She had a big grin on her face as she went toward the four remaining stumps. In the background Kenni could hear the other teams encouraging her too.

Unlike yesterday, Joni did not pause at the mesh wall. She grabbed ahold of it and started climbing. Christine was on the stumps now, but Joni never looked back. At the top of the wall, she hesitated only a fraction of a second, then with a tiny scream, fell onto the straw padding. Sarah Beth and Erin picked her up and only seconds later, Christine landed.

Kenni was grinning as much as they were as all four women laughed and danced.

"I did it! And you didn't pass me up!" Joni declared with a fist pump.

"You did great!" Sarah Beth said.

Kenni walked over to them. "Great job, ladies. Jenn? How was their time?"

"Wow! Sixteen seconds faster than yesterday."

Joni's smile faded. "That's all?"

"That's a lot," Kenni said. "That time would have easily won yesterday's competition."

"Yeah, but if *we* were faster, then they'll all be faster too."

"Maybe."

She turned back to the group. "Okay. Team Four! Let's go!"

* * *

Joni stood with her team, only half-heartedly cheering for Team Four. They'd won the thing yesterday. And they'd won the damn scavenger hunt earlier. She certainly didn't want them to win again. Like yesterday, Anna slipped on the moving balance log and fell to the ground. Britney wasn't close by, though, so she had to get back on herself. *Good*, she thought. *Maybe that'll slow them down.* She found herself holding on to Sarah Beth's arm as Marsha scaled the mesh wall, the last to fall.

"Were they faster than us?" she asked quietly.

"Hard to say."

"Great job, Team Four!" Jenn yelled. "Two minutes and fifty-one seconds." She grinned. "Team Five…you're still in the lead with two minutes and forty-nine seconds."

"Okay. Team Three. Let's go!" Kendall said, clapping her hands.

"I can't watch. I'm going to hyperventilate," Joni said as she fanned her face with her hands.

"I didn't think you cared about it," Erin said. "Or you didn't seem to yesterday."

Joni shot her a look that previously had been reserved for Kenni only. "Of course I care," she lied. "I'm the youngest one here. I don't want someone in her sixties—like you—to beat me."

Erin didn't seem offended in the least. "Honey, I can still run circles around you. I told you, I'm the treadmill queen."

Whatever.

But she found herself holding her breath each time Jenn rattled off the time. And amazingly, they were still in first place with only Team One left to run the course. She was biting her nails nervously, hoping someone would fall. Hoping a rope would snap. Hoping someone got their foot stuck in the mesh wall. She did a quick fist pump when someone did just that, taking precious seconds to untangle from the mesh.

Again, she grabbed Sarah Beth's arm, squeezing tightly.

"That hurt you at the wall, Shelly. Time is two minutes and fifty-six seconds." Jenn looked at her notes. "Team Five is the winner!"

Joni's eyes widened. "*What?* We won? We fucking *won?*" She jumped up and down with the others, all grinning like they'd won the Super Bowl or something. "We fucking won!"

"Great job, everyone," Kenni said. "Especially my Team Five!" She looked at her watch. "Let's take a leisurely walk back to the lodge. You'll have over an hour before dinner. Free time."

Joni moved up beside her, nudging her shoulder. "We won!"

Kenni smiled at her. "Yes. I hear you *fucking* won."

"So, I'm kinda getting into this," she said, surprising herself with the words. "I mean the competition stuff."

"But not the outdoors?"

They were at the back of the line, the other teams all intermingling and chatting and walking ahead of them.

"I grew up in Manhattan."

"Kansas?"

Joni laughed. "No. My parents never even took us to Central Park. I barely knew what a tree was."

"Then how did you end up in Denver?"

She sighed. "Her name was Elana. I was working for a fashion magazine at the time. To be honest, I hated that job. Elana was a software engineer and worked for J.P. Morgan. When she got transferred to Denver, she asked me to go with her."

"Recently?"

"No, no. I was twenty-three at the time. So, eight years ago. The point is, I have never embraced living in Denver. Or Colorado, for that matter. And the friends I hang out with are city people too." She waved at the forest. "We don't do this kind of stuff."

"Yet you're here on assignment?"

Joni chewed her lower lip. "My boss thought I'd be great for it. You know, someone coming in with no expectations and no clue about what really goes on here. I wouldn't be predisposed to either like or dislike it because I don't know what the hell we're doing here."

That was technically a lie. Yes, she had preconceived notions about the whole thing, and yes, she was inclined to dislike—*hate*— the place. Kendall Lyon didn't need to know that, however.

"So, you came here blind?"

"I told you, I jumped off your website when I saw them climbing trees," she said with a laugh. "I also threatened to quit my job." That, at least, was not a lie.

"That bad, huh?"

"Well, I wouldn't dare tell my boss or any of my friends, but it's kinda nice here. Quiet. Peaceful. That's not to say that I don't miss my phone."

"How long did you stay on it last night?"

"Enough to talk to Kimberly. She's my best friend. I barely made it through the conversation. I crashed."

"So, what about Elana?"

Joni frowned. "What about her?"

"She's not in the picture any longer?"

She waved that question away. "No. That barely lasted six months once we got here. But I had no place to go back to. I had let my apartment go. My parents had moved to Connecticut. My brothers are scattered all over the place. And I liked my job."

"Yet you have not embraced living here." Kendall smiled. "And you work for *Mountain Life*. Kinda ironic, isn't it? I'm assuming you write articles about living here in the mountains."

"Not necessarily me. Besides, there are cultural events to cover. And restaurants. That's my perk since I get to eat for free. I have a monthly column on the best places to eat."

"The magazine comes out monthly?"

"No. Well, the online edition does, yes. But we also have a printed publication. Quarterly."

"And so here you are."

"Here I am." She smiled at Kenni. "I know you said you don't do interviews, but do you think any of your staff would?"

Kendall stopped walking and she did too. There was a slight frown on Kendall's face.

"What kind of questions?"

"Oh, you know, just general questions."

"Can you elaborate?"

Ah. Protective. Was it because of her staff or her business? "They've been with you a while?"

"Sky and Jenn since the beginning. Wanda came our second year."

"I'm surprised. Your website said you only did five monthly sessions. Surely you can't pay them enough for a year's worth of salary."

"You're getting really close to that line, Joni."

"The 'you don't do interviews' line?"

"That's the one." Kenni started walking again. "Why did you and Elana break up?"

God, what's with the questions about Elana? "Saying she turned out to be psycho doesn't seem fair." She gave a quick laugh. "Although pretty accurate. She started getting tattoos and piercings. Like everywhere. And when I refused to get matching tattoos—and I'm talking like all over my body—she said I didn't love her. Which at that point, no, I did not. I didn't even *know* her anymore."

"No tattoos?"

"No. Actually, I'm terrified of needles and thought I'd pass out if I attempted one. And when I came to, I imagined some

Goth figure painted on my torso. Or my face. She had five or six face tattoos. Who does that?" Then she paused. "Do *you* have a tattoo?"

"Yes. One."

She nudged her playfully. "Can I see it?"

"That depends. Do you plan on seeing me naked?"

Joni was the one who stopped walking this time. Kendall had a smile on her face.

"Of course, there's always the sauna," Kenni said. "You might be able to sneak a peek then."

"Are you flirting with me?"

"You're one of our clients. I think that would be terribly unprofessional of me. Don't you?"

Joni tilted her head. "I haven't decided if I even like you." In fact, if she'd asked herself that yesterday, "no" would have been the resounding answer.

"Because I have silly rules, and I confiscated your wine?"

"That...and you're annoying."

Kendall laughed. "Annoying?"

Kenni walked on and Joni fell into step beside her again. "Have you always been into all this wooey nature stuff?"

"'Wooey nature stuff'? Not like now, no. I grew up in the city—Phoenix. After...well, after college there was a..." Kendall shook her head. "A rather traumatic event. Life-changing."

Kenni said nothing else and even though a hundred questions were swirling in her mind, Joni didn't ask them, sensing that whatever Kendall had been about to say was very personal. And obviously something she wasn't comfortable sharing with her. Before she could think of a more neutral topic to broach, Kendall walked away, nearly jogging to catch up with the others.

Joni watched her, wondering at her sudden withdrawal. One minute Kenni was flirting with her, kinda, and the next, she'd run away. Oh, well. She'd try again tomorrow.

CHAPTER NINETEEN

"And we freakin' won! Can you believe that?"

"Well, you sure sound excited," Kimberly said.

"Yes. Because I'm not the worst one after all. There are four obstacle courses, and this is the baby course, as they call it. And we did a treasure hunt thing before lunch. Sky hid these clues all around and it directed you to the sauna and jacuzzi tub. The winning team—it was not us—got some alone time there. I've yet to do either." She twisted a strand of hair. "Although Kenni said she'd show me her tattoo if we went to the sauna together."

"Really? What brought that on?"

"I was kinda flirting with her and she was kinda flirting with me."

"I thought she wasn't your type."

"Oh, she's not. But I thought I might be able to interview her then. You know, without her knowing it." She yawned. "There are worse things. I mean, yeah, she irritates me most of the time, but she's really cute. We were in the gym today and she was in a workout bra. I'm pretty sure I was drooling."

"How old is she?"

"I don't know. Mid-thirties, maybe."

Kimberly laughed. "I'm still trying to picture you in a gym."

"In the gym. On hiking trails. Running a damn obstacle course. Who knew I was this competitive?"

"So you're really getting into it? I mean, the whole thing?"

"To be honest, I don't even know what the purpose of this place is. I mean, why are all these women here? The three other women on my team are all having marital problems. Well, I shouldn't say that. Sarah Beth is having a midlife crisis, she said. But why are they here? What do they hope to accomplish?"

"Are there like, therapy sessions and stuff?"

"No. At least not so far and I haven't heard it mentioned. Turnbull is convinced it's a man-bashing event, but there's been no evidence of that. I mean, other than Kenni stating that if you're not happy in your life, change it, because life is short!" she said dramatically.

Kim laughed. "Well, I was on their website again, just to be nosy. It's all kinda vague, but their mission, it says, is to empower and liberate women to reach their full potential or something like that."

"I really think they can be that vague because a lot of their clients find out about this place from others. I guess that's why they don't have to advertise. And Kim, if we're basing this on income, I am by far the poorest woman here. Everyone is dripping in diamonds and gold. *Dripping!*"

"Yeah, I don't get it either. I can't believe people are going to change that much in a month."

"That was my thought too, but it's so different than what any of us are used to, I'm sure. There are five teams with four women each. We do yoga, gym, hiking. The obstacle course. We have yet to climb trees, thank god, but that's coming, I'm sure." She paused. "Remember me telling you about grounding?"

"Yes. Walking around barefoot and touching the earth."

"Well, I kinda promised Sarah Beth I'd do it with her in the morning."

Kim laughed. "Oh, please take a picture of that for me!"

"I'm doing it for research purposes only," she added quickly. "It's not like I'm going to hug a damn tree or anything!"

"Well, I'm actually impressed that you haven't run away yet."

She sighed. "I know. I'm actually kinda shocked myself."

CHAPTER TWENTY

Kenni walked along the path from her cabin to the lodge. She was pleasantly surprised to find ten or twelve of the women out among the trees, faces pointed toward the early morning sun. She didn't want to disturb them, so she moved into the forest, planning to circle around them. She stopped short, however, when she spotted Joni off by herself, one hand touching the bark of a large ponderosa pine. She let her gaze travel over her, smiling as she noted the bare feet on top of a bed of pine needles.

There had been hundreds of women visit the Lyon's Den Retreat over the years. This was the tenth year so nearly a thousand now. Yet not one of them had ever intrigued her as much as the lovely Joni James did. She was just feisty enough to be entertaining, and Kenni was quite amused by her potty mouth. She was also impressed by her spunk, despite her self-professed loathing of the outdoors.

She stood still, continuing to watch. Joni took a few more steps into the woods, pausing to finger the branches of a spruce tree. Her head was tilted as if contemplating what she was feeling.

This brought another smile to Kenni's face. Was she thinking all this "wooey" stuff might have some merit after all? Then, as if sensing her watching, Joni slowly turned. Their eyes met, and a quick smile formed on Joni's face. Kenni took that as an invitation to move closer.

"Are you spying on us?"

Kenni shook her head. "Not at all. I was on my way to the lodge for breakfast."

Joni took a deep breath and turned her face to the sun again. "Okay, so this does feel pretty good." She pointed to her feet. "And I'm barefoot."

"I see that."

Kenni sat down on the forest floor and leaned against a tree near her. She, too, took a deep breath of the fresh morning air. "I only started practicing grounding about five years ago," she offered. "I was skeptical at first too. But it really does keep your circadian rhythm synced and it's a great way to start the day."

Joni looked at her, then she sat down too. "What torture do you have planned for us today?"

Kenni laughed quietly. "Torture? Is that what you think of it?"

"I'm a little sore."

"From the gym or the hikes?"

"Probably the gym. As I said, I've never been into exercise or anything like that. My muscles are in shock, I'm sure." Joni raised an eyebrow. "You obviously work out a lot. Has that always been a passion of yours?"

"Not really. We didn't put the gym in until the third year. I simply took advantage of it."

"Are you seeing someone?"

The question took her by surprise. "Seeing someone?"

Joni pointed to her hands. "I haven't seen a ring, so I assume you're not married."

She raised an eyebrow. "Is this a question for your article?"

"Of course not. I was simply curious. I mean, what about the others? All of you are here, what? May through September?"

"I come up in April, as soon as the weather permits, and I stay until the last moment before the snows close the road up here. The others all leave when our last clients do."

"Okay. And this is kinda for my article, but what do they do the rest of the year?" Joni quickly held her hand up. "And I'm not talking salaries and stuff. I know you shut me down yesterday. But when they leave here, where do they go? What do they do?" Then she smiled. "Where do *you* go?"

"I have a place in Santa Fe," she said without thinking. "And I usually spend the holidays with my grandmother in Flagstaff." Before Joni could ask questions about that, she continued, "Sky goes to Florida. Her father owns a real estate company, and she works for him. She's divorced and dates some during the winter months, but she always comes back here."

"I guess you'd be lost without her."

"Yes. If any of them left it would be difficult for me, but Sky is without a doubt the most important. She loves working here, though. In fact, that's why she's divorced. Her husband demanded she quit her job."

"So she quit him instead," Joni finished for her. "What about the others?"

"The same. They all have winter jobs. Mindy goes to LA. Karla and Jenn go to Denver. Wanda lives with her daughter in Gunnison. Jenn is dating someone so I wouldn't be surprised if she leaves someday." She glanced at her watch. "We should go. We don't want to miss breakfast." Then she smiled. "You know, so you'll be ready for your torture sessions today."

"Did you just shut me down again?"

"Yes."

CHAPTER TWENTY-ONE

Joni stared up at the huge tree, trying to wrap her head around the tangled mass of ropes leading to its top. She slowly turned her head to look at Kenni.

"What the fuck is this?"

"Well, I know how much you were looking forward to climbing trees." Kenni moved closer to the ropes which were wrapped around the tree's trunk in a teepee fashion. "I know it looks daunting, but there's no way you'll fall unless you intentionally fling yourself backwards. The angle is not that severe." She grinned. "It's just high."

Joni looked at Sarah Beth, whose eyes had a nearly frantic look in them. She was sure hers did as well.

"Who wants to go first?"

Joni moved behind Sarah Beth. There was no way in hell she was going first. In fact, she was fairly certain she wasn't going to do it at all.

"Joni?"

Oh, for the love! She peeked around Sarah Beth and glared at Kenni. "Why me?"

Kenni smiled at her. "You're the youngest."

"Look, you can't keep playing that card! I'm not a damn guinea pig!"

Kenni came closer, still smiling. "I'll do it with you."

Christine nudged her. "Go on, Joni." Her voice lowered to a whisper. "You can have some alone time up there."

Joni turned her glare to Christine. "Really?"

Christine winked at her and pushed her forward. "Show us how it's done."

Joni gritted her teeth as she walked away from the group. "If I fall, I will make your life *hell*," she threatened Kenni.

"If you fall, you're likely to break something. Or worse." Again, a quick smile. "Remember that waiver you signed?"

"I didn't actually read it. My boss made me sign it."

Kenni moved to the edge of the ropes. "You can't sue me. No matter what. So you're better off not falling." She turned to the group. "It's similar to the mesh rope wall at the obstacle course, only with much thicker rope. You'll use it like a ladder, balancing your weight on your feet and using your hands to guide you up."

"How high is it?" asked Anna from Team Four.

"Not too tall. Forty-three feet and some change."

Not too tall? Joni nearly choked on her own breath. "I have a fear of heights," she said quickly. "I'm not doing it."

"This will cure your fear of heights," Kenni said easily. "And when you get to the top, you'll know what a squirrel feels like."

Some in the group gave nervous laughs, but most seemed to still be thunderstruck by the prospect of having to climb the tree. As was she.

"Do it just like the mesh wall. Only this is easier because it's a more gradual slope."

Joni swallowed, noticing the lump in her throat as she watched Kenni take several steps up. *Christ, I can't believe I'm about to do this.*

"Come on. Climb beside me."

"You know, I was just starting to warm up to you," Joni said as she took hold of the rope ladder.

"Oh yeah? And now?"

"And now I think you're a fucking crazy woman who's trying to kill me!"

"No way. Who would I banter with then?"

Joni had an absolute death grip on the rope, and she was only two feet off the ground. She made herself relax, remembering how quickly—and easily—she'd traversed the mesh wall yesterday. Kenni waited, letting her get up beside her. Their eyes met and Kenni nodded.

"Good. Slow and easy. One step at a time."

"Shut up."

Kenni laughed. "We'll try to climb this twice a week. On the last week you're here, you'll be surprised at how easy it'll be for you. You're a natural."

"Natural my ass," she murmured as she climbed up another rung.

"Always look up, not down," Kenni instructed. "If you want, I can get a little ahead of you and you can watch me. I've been told I have a nice ass."

"Oh my god! Obnoxious *and* conceited. You've outdone yourself."

However, one look down—they were maybe seven feet up— had her jerking her gaze upward again. And, yes, her eyes landed on Kenni's very nice ass as she climbed steadily higher. Nice ass *and* nice legs. She sighed, dragging her eyes away. Her muscles were sore from the gym, and she was thankful she'd only half-heartedly attempted the leg press. She doubted her thighs would hold up as it was. As she continued to climb, she was aware of the silence from the women down below. Were they collectively holding their breaths, thinking she'd surely fall to her death?

"How you doing?"

"My thighs hurt."

"That's good."

Joni paused to rest. "Why good?"

"That means you're using them and not your arms."

She almost was tempted to look down again, but she didn't. "How high are we now?"

"About halfway up. Nearly twenty feet or so." Kenni paused. "Look over here. You can make out the roof of the lodge. When we get to the top, you'll have a good view of it."

"Oh goody," she said dryly.

"You're doing great."

"Why do you *always* pick me to go first?"

Kenni looked down at her. "Because who else would I be able to have these stimulating conversations with?"

"Right."

After six or seven more steps, she froze. "Wait a minute? How the hell do we get off this thing once we're up there?"

"How do you think?"

"I was hoping by some mechanical means."

"Sorry, but no."

A gust of wind rustled the trees, and she felt the tall pine sway, causing the rope apparatus to move too. Her eyes widened and she rested fully against it, her hands gripping it so tightly, her fingers were turning white.

"Kenni...it's moving! It's fucking moving! We're going to fall!"

"It's okay."

Okay? She was paralyzed with fear, and it was so *not* okay. She realized she was suspended in the air, several feet from the trunk of the tree and still ten feet or more to the top where the branches started. That meant she was at least thirty feet off the ground. What if the rope broke apart? What if the whole damn tree toppled over? Her breath was coming quickly, and she squeezed her eyes shut trying to stave off the panic attack she was having.

"What's wrong?"

"What the fuck do you think is wrong?" she managed, still refusing to open her eyes.

"Come on, Joni. We're almost there."

"No."

"No? No what?"

"I'm not going any higher."

"It was just a little wind gust."

She opened her eyes, finding Kenni looking down at her. "What if...what if the tree falls?"

"The tree is not going to fall. I promise."

"What is the purpose of this?"

"Climbing the tree?"

"Yes. Is it to scare the shit out of your clients?"

Kenni laughed. "No. It's to show you that you can do something that scares you. That you can conquer your fears. It's a challenge. Life has many challenges and uncertainties. You face them. You don't hide from them."

She blew out her breath. "All right," she said quietly. "Don't look down," she reminded herself.

"Right. When you get to the top, then you can look down. You'll be amazed at the view."

"You'll be lucky if I don't throw up."

She relaxed the grip she had and reached up to take the next rung. The spacing probably wasn't even a foot apart. She moved up slowly and steadily, following Kenni's progress. She was feeling some of her anxiety lessen the closer they got to the top because it was closer to the tree as well. Kenni had reached the top and was casually standing on the rope and holding on to the nearest limb.

"This pine is well over a hundred years old. Their lifespan is five to six hundred years. Not going to fall anytime soon."

When she reached the top where Kenni was, she heard clapping and cheers from far down below. She waved at them and grinned. "I made it."

"Of course you did. You want to stand up and see the view?"

"Oh, hell no."

"You can see the lodge."

"Yeah. I've seen it from ground level."

Kenni moved down beside her. "Aren't you proud of yourself?"

"I'll answer that question when—*if*—we get back down to Earth."

"Please take a look around."

"Why?"

"Because it's lovely."

She saw Kenni take a deep, slow breath. When she spoke again, her voice was quiet, soft.

"Time spent amongst trees is never wasted time." Kenni smiled at her. "I believe Katrina Mayer wrote that. And we are certainly amongst the trees up here." She waved a hand about. "Some trees are taller than this one, but I chose it because it's got such a long trunk, and the limbs are up high. I always wonder if a long-ago fire or windstorm knocked the lower branches off."

Kenni seemed so at ease, so comfortable up here, that Joni dared to look around her. She felt her breath catch.

"My god, we're up high." She held on a little tighter. "But yes, it's beautiful." They were literally among the trees, and yes, she now knew what a squirrel felt like. And a bird. The wind was gentle, bringing the soft scent of the pine to her and she breathed deeply. She let her gaze travel past the trees around them to the high mountains beyond—mountains she normally saw from behind the window in her office. But she wasn't looking at them from a distance. No, she was actually *in* the mountains. She was up in a freakin' tree! None of her friends would ever believe this.

"You like?"

She turned to Kenni. "I love it. I'm on the top of a mountain in a fucking tree…and I love it." Then she chanced a look down below and gasped. "Holy shit! Look how high we are!" She tightened her grip even more, feeling a bit of vertigo as her stomach rolled.

"On top of the world."

"How long did it take us to get up here?"

Kenni glanced at her watch. "Only about six minutes."

"Really? I would have sworn a half hour at least."

Kenni shifted. "Now we go back down. It's much easier."

Before Joni even began to contemplate moving, Kenni was scampering like a cat down the rope rungs. "Wait! Don't leave me up here alone!"

"Well, come on then."

Fear gripped her again as she slowly followed Kenni down. However, it was much easier, and to her surprise, she felt quite nimble as she traversed the rope contraption. Before she knew it, she was only about six feet from the ground. She heard Christine cheering for her.

"You did it! Way to go!"

Kenni took her hand to help her off the rope, and her legs felt shaky once she stood up. She smiled at her. "Thanks."

"Good job." Then Kenni turned to the others. "Okay, ladies. Six at a time. I'll go up again with you."

No one stepped forward and Joni laughed. "Oh, sure. You were all clapping when I had to go up." She motioned to the rope. "Go on. If I can do it, you all can do it. But don't look down!"

She moved away from the group and sat down against a tree, surprised to find a smile on her face. She watched as six women— all of Team Four and two others—went to the rope. From this angle, it really did look like a teepee around the tree. She followed the length of it, still amazed she'd made it to the top without passing out. And without falling.

She turned her gaze to Kenni as she once again took the lead up the tree. She couldn't make out her words, but she imagined Kenni was encouraging them, much as she'd done to her. The other voices faded to the background, and she let her mind wander, surprised that she wasn't picturing herself back in the city. She let the sounds of the forest in—the breeze, the bird calls. A sense of peace settled over her and she let it. Why had she never liked the outdoors?

She'd come here to the Lyon's Den to write a hit piece on the place and, in essence, on Kendall Lyon herself. Unfortunately— or perhaps fortunately—she was being pulled in, taking the subtle lessons to heart. There were no man-bashing sessions, no lectures on making changes to one's life. No bullying. It wasn't a fat-loss clinic with hours and hours in the gym. No. Instead there was quiet, peaceful yoga to start the day. An early morning hike. A relatively easy gym session. The mornings were routine. The afternoons were not. Today for instance.

She looked back at the tree, seeing the others nearly at the top. Amy and Britney from Team Four were in the lead. Kenni was already holding on to a limb. Even from this distance, she could see the smile on her face, and she found herself smiling as well.

CHAPTER TWENTY-TWO

Kenni stood at the back of the dining hall, listening to the chatter of the women. They were all animated this evening, still talking about the tree they'd climbed. She looked to where Team Five sat, smiling as Christine was apparently giving an in-depth account of her ascent to the top of the tree. Involuntarily her gaze slid to Joni, who was listening intently to Christine's story.

"Are you not eating?"

She turned, finding Sky coming toward her. She nodded. "Wanda fixed something up for me. I had some calls to return."

Sky motioned to the group. "We all thought it was too soon for the tree, but they seem like they enjoyed it."

Yes, they normally climbed the tree late in the second week and then once again each week after. But she wanted to break up their routine and thought the tree would be a great place to start.

"They did fine."

"I heard from some on my team that you made Joni go up alone."

"Well, with me. Not exactly alone."

Sky nudged her. "You got a thing for her or something?"

Kenni arched an eyebrow. "A thing?"

"She's cute."

"She's a client."

"I don't believe there are any rules for that sort of thing. Besides, I did hear that she's gay. In case you didn't know."

"Is that right?"

"Something about the gym and you in your sports bra."

Kenni gave a fake smile. "Okay. Don't you need to go eat?"

Sky laughed. "Yes, I do. But there are no rules and she's cute. I'd go for it if I were you."

Sky left then, and Kenni glanced again at Table Five. Joni turned, meeting her gaze. With a sigh, Kenni headed in that direction.

"Why didn't you join us for dinner?" Joni asked.

"I had some work to do in the office. How was the meal?"

Joni laughed and motioned to the others. "Not even a green bean survived. We were ravenous."

Empty plates all around, yes. She nodded at Erin. "I heard through the grapevine that you can't wait to climb the tree again."

Erin smiled at her. "That was so invigorating. I'll admit, I was terrified at first. Watching Joni climb it, I was holding my breath the whole time. But it was fun. And after that, I'm not sure there's anything you could pull on us that would be more frightening."

"Well, not more frightening, no, but perhaps more challenging. I still have a couple of things up my sleeve." She glanced at her watch, noting that it was almost seven. "Wanda made a plate for me. I think I'll go find my dinner. See you all in the morning."

Later that night as she took her evening walk, she wondered about her desire to change things, to get out of their normal routine. They'd added things here and there over the years, but for the most part, it was all regimented and ran like a well-oiled machine. She and her staff knew their roles and played them well.

Why, now, was she wanting to mix things up? She knew all too well—as did her staff—that she did not do change well. She didn't need to see a therapist to know that it stemmed from that tragic night when everything had changed all at once. She knew it was her way of trying to control things now. Probably not healthy, but it had worked so far.

Yet here she was, making little spontaneous changes. Why? Was she in a rut? Stagnant? She nodded as she moved on into the trees, following a path she'd walked hundreds of times. Yes. Stagnant. Five monthly sessions a year and they rarely deviated from the routine. Year after year. Month after month. Day after day. The only thing that changed was the clients.

She stopped, pausing to stare skyward. The clients were the same too, weren't they? Mostly middle-aged women drifting about in their lives, disillusioned by their unhappy marriages. Many had married for money, not love, and now they were paying the price. Some had married for love only to find they were now living with a stranger. The women who came here were happy on the outside yet miserable on the inside.

That thought hit home. Was she describing herself? She allowed a few moments of contemplation, then shook her head. No. She wasn't miserable. She was just...

Lonely? Maybe. Unlike the others who all had friends and family to go back to in September, she ventured to Santa Fe, a town she'd basically picked on the map. Not too far from here and not too far from her grandmother. She had considered Flagstaff, where her grandmother lived. But she was afraid she'd be in the way. Her grandmother lived in a retirement community and had made new friends. Her days were filled with activities, and she didn't want to disrupt that.

She paused again. So, yeah, maybe she was miserable. She shook her head again. No. She wouldn't put that label on her. She was only...yeah, lonely.

She was on the path to the lodge, and she looked up, seeing all the rooms dark. It wasn't quite ten yet. She assumed they were all exhausted after their adventure today. She supposed tomorrow afternoon they'd go over to the second obstacle course.

She was about to turn around when she saw someone on the deck, standing in the shadows. Her arms were crossed, and she was staring into the trees—Joni. She wondered what she was doing out there. Couldn't sleep? She should have turned around and left her in peace, but she found herself moving closer as if drawn to her.

She stepped onto the deck, and Joni jerked her head around, gasping loud enough for her to hear.

"Jesus Christ! I thought you were a bear!"

"Sorry." She moved up beside her. "What are you doing?"

Joni shrugged. "Saying I was contemplating life seems far too dramatic." Then she smiled. "But I kinda was."

"Picturing yourself at the top of that tree?"

"I'm trying to figure out why I'm feeling content here and not missing my life back in the city." Joni turned to her. "I haven't even picked up my phone today. You were right about that. We get so involved with what's going on inside that damn little phone that we forget about what's all around us." She held her hands out, making a sweeping motion to the forest. "I never in a million years would have thought I would—*could*—enjoy this."

"Too tame?"

"Too quiet. Too still. Too…peaceful." Joni turned to her. "I was used to noise, to motion. To chaos. Always going somewhere, always on the move. I rarely spent time alone. Happy hours and dinners and parties. Hitting the clubs for music and dancing. Everything always seemed…loud and fast."

"Dancing, huh?"

Joni smiled. "I have two left feet, as they say. Or as my friend Kimberly says, I have as much rhythm as a broomstick." Joni took a step away, going to the edge of the deck. "What are you doing out here?"

"Evening walk."

"Didn't get enough hiking in today?" she teased.

Kenni laughed quietly. "That's work. This is therapy." A quote came to her, and she said it automatically. "'A walk in nature walks the soul back home.' Mary Davis, not my words. But I find them to be true."

"Do you have an endless supply of quotes?"

"I read a lot. Inspirational books, mostly. Positivity."

"Like self-help books?"

"Some could be construed that way, I guess."

Joni tilted her head thoughtfully. "Did you need to make changes? I mean, that's what those books are for, right? To change who you are? That's what this place is all about too, isn't it?"

The words that tumbled from her mouth shocked her. "My parents and younger sister were killed on their way home after my college graduation. By a drunk driver." She hadn't said those words out loud in so many years, she couldn't believe she'd spoken them now.

"I'm so sorry," Joni said quietly.

Kenni moved deeper into the shadows, away from her. "I had a great family. We were very close. Kayla was in the tenth grade. She had her whole life ahead of her. I was…angry. And I needed some positivity in my life."

She felt Joni move closer to her. "Do you not have anyone, Kenni?"

She looked over at her, hearing the quiet words and the soft sound of her name. "My grandmother lives in Flagstaff. She is the one who talked me into this place, really. I think she did it hoping that it would help me as much as our clients. Of course, it's evolved over the years."

"Is that why the ban on alcohol?"

"Not really. We're trying to preach health and fitness. Ending the day with wine or cocktails is counterproductive."

"Did you drink…before?"

"College, yes. In fact, we had a graduation party the night before. I got wasted. I was so hung over the day of graduation, I hardly remember it. My parents and Kayla took me out for a celebration dinner, and I was thinking the whole time that I just wanted them to leave so I could go home and crash." She pushed those memories—and the guilt—away. "But even if I hadn't had that traumatic life event, I still wouldn't allow it here. Alcohol dulls your senses. It changes your personality. I've found that people who don't drink are much more productive, more creative. That's not to say that I don't enjoy a glass of wine. Sometimes. I do." She moved away again. "I'm sorry I intruded on your quiet time. I'll see you in the morning."

"You don't have to leave."

"Yes, I do."

She turned and retraced her steps along the deck. Before she stepped off, however, Joni called to her.

"It was a good day, Kenni. Thank you for the tree experience."

She paused, looking back at her. "You're welcome. Good night."

CHAPTER TWENTY-THREE

Kenni had been conspicuously absent at breakfast, and Joni found she was having a hard time carrying on conversations with the others. Christine had been an absolute chatterbox, and thankfully Sarah Beth engaged her. Joni's concentration kept going to the door, wondering where Kenni was.

Now, as they finished up the morning yoga, she saw Jenn waiting in the wings. Still no sign of Kenni, though. Should she worry? Was it her place? Should she tell Jenn about their late-night conversation? No. That had been a private conversation. Perhaps Kenni overslept. But no. Kenni was probably up with the sunrise each morning so she could go out *grounding* or something. She shouldn't make light of it because she'd been out this morning herself. Although she'd been keeping a lookout for Kenni more than she'd been working on her circadian rhythm.

"Okay, Teams Four and Five, go ahead and head to the gym. I'll take the others on a hike. You have five minutes if you need to change," Jenn said.

Joni went up to her. "Hey, where's Kenni?"

Jenn gave her a quick smile. "Good morning, Joni. Kenni went to the second obstacle course. She wanted to make sure it was ready to run."

"Oh, goody. A new one." Although her tone was flippant, she was actually looking forward to it.

"Yes. We'll go there after lunch."

"Okay. See you then."

She walked over to the gym with her group. Team Four stayed in their group as well. They were all nice enough, but one look at the leaderboard showed that they'd won four contests so far. Her team had only won the obstacle course the other day. She was also looking forward to Sky's scavenger hunt before lunch. She had a feeling they might win this one.

"You're quiet this morning," Erin noted.

Joni smiled quickly at her. "Still recovering from yesterday," she lied. Actually, she wasn't sore at all this morning, surprisingly.

Erin stretched her arms overhead. "I'm very sore. I'm sure Karla will work the kinks out."

When they got to the gym, she spotted Kenni already on the deck in her now-familiar sports bra. She was lying on a bench doing what Joni had learned was a bench press. She was staring. Yes, she knew she was, but she simply couldn't pull her eyes away. Christine nudged her.

"Close your mouth. You're drooling."

Joni was certain she had a blush on her face. "She's not my type," she said before going inside.

"Uh-huh."

However, it was "arm" day for her team, so Karla sent them right back outside. Team Four had a leg workout inside. Kenni was still sprawled on the bench, but her head was turned toward her. Joni paused as their eyes met. She gave a hesitant smile, and Kenni returned it. So instead of grabbing a dumbbell, she went over to her.

"Hey."

"Good morning," Kenni greeted.

"Missed you at breakfast."

"Did you now?" Kenni sat up. "I had something to check out."

She nodded. "The obstacle course. I asked Jenn."

Kenni smiled. "So, you really *did* miss me."

"I did," she said honestly. "I told you, you're starting to grow on me." Then she grinned. "Planning another torture session for us?"

"Another challenge. I think you'll do fine."

She was about to walk away, but she stopped. "Everything okay?" she asked quietly.

Kenni nodded. "Yeah. I...I didn't sleep very well. Old memories. I don't dwell on that day too much. It always puts me in a funk if I do."

"I'm sorry."

"No need. I'm fine." She got up off the bench. "It's not something I talk about. Hardly ever, actually. I'm not really sure why I told you."

Joni was tempted to ask more questions. *Who hit your family? Were they killed too?* But she asked something else entirely.

"How old are you?"

Kenni's smile was a little bit flirty. "Why?"

"Why? Because I want to know."

"Why do you want to know?"

Joni put her hands on her hips. "Why are you being difficult? It's a simple question."

Kenni pointed to the bench she'd vacated. "You want to use this?"

Joni shook her head. "I don't think I can."

Kenni nodded. "Yes, you can. I'll take some weight off. It's a great upper body workout. You hit several different muscle groups at once. Your shoulders, your arms. Your chest."

Joni stared at her. "Really? My chest? You're going to go there?"

Kenni smiled. "What?"

"I know I have no boobs. You don't have to point it out."

Kenni laughed. "I in no way meant anything by that."

"I have the breasts of a ten-year-old. I don't think lifting weights is going to make them grow."

Kenni laughed again, then pointedly stared at her chest. "I *have* noticed, however, that you don't wear a bra. So, your breasts can't be *that* small."

Joni felt a hot blush light her face, and she simply turned on her heels and headed to the dumbbell rack where the others were. She shook her head. *Talking about breast sizes with the woman! My god, are we in high school?*

"You okay?"

She glared at Christine as she jerked up a ten-pound weight. "She's annoying."

"I thought you said she was attractive."

"Who thinks who is attractive?" Sarah Beth asked.

"Nobody," she quickly said as she attempted a bicep curl. Really, ten pounds was too much. It was—

"She thinks Kenni is attractive, but she claims she's not her type," Christine explained.

"Oh, for god's sake," she muttered.

Sarah Beth blinked at her. "You're gay?" she asked in a whisper. "Or one of the other letters?"

Joni couldn't help but laugh at her innocence. "Technically I would be the L of the letters, yes."

"Oh wow." Sarah Beth put her dumbbell down. "My hairdresser is gay. Bennie. He's so cute."

Joni held her hand up. "I don't really want to have this conversation. Okay?" She moved to walk away, thinking she'd try the pullup bar.

"But wait!" Sarah Beth and Christine both followed her. "You think Kenni is attractive? Is she gay too?"

She gave Sarah Beth a fake smile. "I don't know. Why don't you ask her?"

Kenni cleared her throat behind them, and Sarah Beth and Christine turned around. Joni was surprised that Sarah Beth sported a blush.

"Having trouble with your arm exercises, ladies?"

"No, no. We were about to…to…" Sarah Beth looked around, finally pointing to one of the benches. "There. We were about to do that thing."

Joni looked where she pointed, as did Kenni. Joni wasn't sure what the apparatus was, but she was pretty sure it wasn't for arms. At the amused expression on Kenni's face, she knew she'd guessed right.

"Well, maybe tomorrow on leg day, you can use it. Come try the bench press instead. I'll spot for you."

CHAPTER TWENTY-FOUR

Joni had been overconfident in thinking they'd win the scavenger hunt. Team Four beat them by less than a minute as she'd seen them running—*running*—through the woods to get to the bell first. Yeah, Team Four was starting to piss her off.

"If we do a timed session on this new obstacle course, maybe we'll win again," Sarah Beth said quietly.

"I'm telling you, if we had run like them after we found that last damn pinecone, we would have beaten them," Joni insisted.

They were in the woods on a new trail, heading to the second of four obstacle courses. Kenni and Jenn were leading the group, and conversations were sparse among the women. Most were walking with their own team, as was she and the rest of Team Five. She admitted that the first few days she'd not really paid much attention to her surroundings. Trees, rocks, and the like. It was far too woodsy. But now she found herself looking into the trees, noticing the differences between them—the needles, the bark, the canopy. She took a deep breath, savoring the fresh, clean air.

"Oh, look! A chipmunk!" Erin exclaimed.

Joni looked where she pointed, seeing the tiny creature dart into a hole under a rock.

"I see them in the mornings when I'm doing my grounding," Sarah Beth said.

"Are you actually doing that?" Erin asked.

"Yes. I like it. Joni's done it too."

Erin glanced at her. "Joni? I can't see you out there."

"Well, the concept is a little strange, and I find my mind wanders. But it is peaceful."

"You need to work on your meditation," Sarah Beth said. "Do the breathing exercises that Mindy taught us."

A flippant "Yeah, right," left her mouth before she could rein it in.

"I think she's hoping to run into Kenni," Christine chimed in with a laugh.

Joni scowled at her. "Will you stop with that? I told you, I'm not—"

"Attracted to her," Christine finished for her. "And I think you're lying. She's too cute for you not to be attracted to her."

"That's ridiculous."

"You never said, but are you dating someone?" Sarah Beth asked.

"I'm not, no."

"Well, then?"

Joni rolled her eyes. Why were these married, middle-aged women so interested in her sex life? She chose to ignore them, focusing her gaze on the clearing up ahead. Her eyes widened.

"Holy shit," she murmured. "We're going to die."

The obstacle course wasn't elaborate, but it still made the first one look like child's play. More tires, yes. No big deal. And more stumps, although these appeared to be taller. The log beams seemed to be twice as long, and she noted that neither of them was stationary. That's where the similarities ended. A rope ladder climbed over a huge, smooth boulder the size of a tank. Another teepee-type rope circled a tall pine, but it was the rope bridge at the top that linked to another tree that had her feeling faint. And there was no mesh wall. No, it was a tall, wooden wall with three ropes dangling from the top. It had to be thirty feet tall, and Kenni was out of her fucking mind if she thought she was going to attempt to climb it.

"Here we are, ladies," Kenni said. "This one will be a little more challenging than the other one, but I think you'll make it through just fine. The wall will be the hardest part."

As she looked over the group, Joni took that opportunity to hide behind Christine.

"Jenn will run through it once to give you an idea of how it works. Then we'll let everyone take a turn before we break up into teams."

Joni dared to peek around Christine as Jenn started, running through the tires with ease. The first two stumps were much taller than the others and even Jenn had to use the rope to get on top. She hopped over the remaining stumps easily, then again used the rope to get onto the moving log beam. This one wasn't tethered as firmly as the one at the other obstacle course, and Joni caught her breath as Jenn nearly fell. Then it was on to the rope that scaled the boulder, and Jenn made it look easy, disappearing on the back side and out of their view. She popped back up when she came to the teepee on the tree, and she scampered to the top, which, Joni was thankful to see, wasn't nearly as tall as the tree they'd climbed yesterday.

"Here's where you need to be careful," Kenni said. "It looks scary, but unless you actually fling yourself off, you won't fall. But the bridge is far from sturdy."

Joni clutched Christine's arm as Jenn slowed her pace, taking the rope bridge slowly to the other tree.

"I'm so going to fall," she muttered.

Jenn made it down the rope teepee on the other tree, then up onto another moving log beam. Then there was the giant wall. Jenn took a running start, then grabbed a rope and walked—*walked*—up the wall to the top, pulling herself along with the rope.

"No way in hell," she murmured.

Then Jenn straddled the top of the wall and waved at them before disappearing on the other side.

"Great, Jenn! Good job!"

Kenni came closer to the group and again Joni hid behind Christine.

"Who wants to go first?"

Joni nudged Christine. "You do it!"

"No!"

"Joni? Want to be my guinea pig again?"

"Oh, for god's sake!" She hung her head down, then sighed. "I do not want to be your damn guinea pig, no."

"Come on. It'll be fun," Kenni coaxed.

Sarah Beth nudged her. "Go on!"

"Yeah, come on, Joni! Show us how it's done!" Britney from Team Four shouted.

Joni cut her eyes at her. Yeah, she didn't like Team Four very much. Then she slid her gaze to Kenni, who was smiling at her. Damn it all, but she found herself returning the smile before she realized it.

"First of all, if I make it up the tree and across the rope bridge without killing myself, I'll never in a hundred years make it up that damn wall."

"You just walk up the wall. It's easy." Kenni turned to the others. "Who wants to be next? Once Joni makes it to the boulder, the next one should start. Jenn and I will help you as you go, if you need it."

Joni rubbed her hands together, hating that she was so nervous. She glanced over her shoulder, seeing everyone watching her. Some gave her reassuring smiles.

"Okay. Take your time. You're not racing now, just getting a feel for it." Kenni smiled quickly at her. "And I promise I'll catch you if you fall."

Joni raised her gaze to the rope bridge hung high between the two trees. "You mean you're not going up there with me?"

"Nope." She clapped her hands. "Let's go!"

She took a deep breath, then headed for the tires, hopping through them fairly quickly and without misstep. When she got to the stumps, she saw that they were indeed much higher.

"Grab the rope, hop up."

"There'll be no *hopping*," she managed to say as she pulled herself up with the rope. The stumps were not only taller, but they were smaller around. She nearly lost her balance on the first one.

"Hurry across them. It's much easier."

"Shut up!"

She held her arms out to her side, walking quickly over the stumps. Her attempt to get onto the moving log beam, however, was not successful. She fell on her ass. A collective gasp from the other women had her jumping quickly to her feet.

"You said you'd catch me."

"It's two feet off the ground," Kenni said with a laugh. "Use the rope to balance yourself."

"The log is moving too much."

"Move with it. Use the rope as you walk across."

Halfway across she fell again. Kenni picked her up. "That was pretty good. Try it again."

"Fucking...stupid..." she mumbled as she got back on the log.

"Don't look at your feet. Look ahead."

"Will you shut up! You're making me nervous. Especially now that I know you're *not* going to catch me."

But looking ahead did make it easier, and she was shocked that she'd made it to the other side without falling again.

"Great! Now over the boulder!"

She stood staring up at the top. "Christ, how far up is that?"

"Don't worry about it. You've got a rope to hold on to."

She paused at the rope, then turned to Kenni. "You're annoying."

"This morning you said you missed me," she reminded her.

"I was obviously delusional."

"Really? Well, I heard a rumor that you think I'm attractive."

Joni's eyes widened. "Who in the hell told you that?" she demanded.

"Can't say. Now hurry. You've got Melissa already on the log."

She turned around, watching as Melissa fell off the log too. *Good.* She grabbed the rope ladder that circled the top of the boulder and started climbing. It was surprisingly easy, and she went a little faster. However, when she got to the top she frowned. What had Jenn done?

"Spin around and go down backwards."

That was easier said than done, since there was nothing to hold on to but the rope ladder, and it looked like a hell of a long way down.

"I'll catch you if you fall."

Joni turned and glared at her. "Right. Like you caught me by the log! And I do *not* find you attractive!"

As she maneuvered her way down, she could feel Kenni's eyes on her. She ignored that feeling and sighed with relief when she reached the ground again.

"Let's go! To the trees!" Kenni ran ahead of her, stopping at the base of the teepee rope. "Just like you did yesterday. Be careful going across the bridge."

She had no apprehension going up the tree, and she knew it was because she was confident she could do it. Yesterday's lesson had apparently paid off. She followed the same rule—don't look down. It wasn't nearly as high up as yesterday, though. When she got to the bridge, she was relieved to see that there were small, wooden planks for footholds. At least she wouldn't have to be afraid of sticking her foot through the rope. She paused to look down then, seeing Kenni watching her intently. When their eyes met, she swore she felt butterflies in her stomach.

Don't be ridiculous.

She started across the bridge without thinking, then gasped and clung to the side ropes when the damn thing started swinging.

"You're okay," Kenni called up.

She kept her gaze forward, looking at the other tree. The bridge was relatively short, and she grabbed hold of the second teepee rope, then easily backed down it. She was out of breath when she got to the bottom, but Kenni was urging her toward the next obstacle—another damn moving log beam.

Without being told, she took the rope and climbed up, then gave a tiny scream as it lurched forward, but she did not fall. She laughed instead, then tiptoed across before jumping to the ground. Then she stopped in her tracks. The giant wall stared back at her.

"I can't do it."

"You haven't even tried," Kenni said reasonably.

She looked behind her, seeing others coming. Melissa had just made it down from the tree and two from Team Four were already at the bridge. She took a deep breath.

"Okay. What do I do?"

"Like this. Watch me."

Kenni took a running start, landing nearly halfway up the wall with her feet as she grabbed the rope. "Now you walk it up, pulling yourself with the rope, hand over fist." At the top Kenni straddled the wall. "I'll wait for you here."

She swallowed. "How high is it?"

"It's eight feet. Only two feet taller than yesterday."

"Only," she muttered under her breath. "What if I miss the rope?"

"Then you'll fall backward."

"Just so you know, this is a stupid game."

"You can do it."

She started running—*please don't fall, please don't fall*—and nearly tripped as she attempted to jump onto the wall with her feet and grab the rope at the same time. She landed at the base of the wall, but at least she had the rope. Then she started laughing.

"God, that was awful," she managed between laughs.

Kenni joined in. "Yeah, not quite the way it was drawn up."

Joni sobered and looked up. "Oh my god! You're like twenty feet up there!"

"Come up and join me. Melissa's right behind you."

There were three ropes on the wall, and she saw Melissa eyeing the one to her left. Melissa was probably in her fifties. *Well, fuck…I can do this.* She took a few steps back, then launched herself at the wall again. Her thighs were screaming at her as she slowly inched higher, moving her feet ever so slowly.

"Hand over fist," Kenni instructed. "Look at me. You're almost here."

"You're like ten feet away still!"

She felt Melissa hit the wall, and she gave a sigh of relief as she saw her slip off. With determination, she climbed the stupid-ass wall, if only so that she could get to the top and push Kenni over the other side!

"Great! Just a little more."

"You better run," she threatened.

"What do you mean?"

"When I get up there, I'm going to kick your ass!"

Kenni nearly howled with laughter.

"You think I'm kidding?"

"Yes. Because you need me to pull you over the top."

Joni realized she was completely exhausted, and there was no way she was going to be able to swing a leg over the top of the wall and pull herself over. "You're right. Get me over this fucking wall."

Kenni reached down, but instead of taking her hand, she grabbed her foot.

"What the hell are you doing?" Joni demanded as she teetered on one leg.

"Swing it over."

"You're insane! I'm going to fall!"

"Hold on to the rope."

Jenn had come up next to her, giving Melissa assistance. She had half a mind to ask her to push her over, but no, Kenni was tugging on her leg, about to break it.

"I do *not* bend that way!"

"You're doing great," Kenni said with a smile. "Now take one hand off the rope and grip the top of the wall."

"I can't believe no one has sued you yet!"

"You signed a waiver, remember?"

"Under duress and against my will," she shot back.

"Not my fault."

Amazingly, she found herself sitting on top of the wall next to Kenni. How had that happened?

"See? Piece of cake."

"Piece of cake, my ass." She looked down to the other side. "Oh, good god. We're supposed to *jump*?"

"Yep. I'll go first."

Kenni fell over the side and onto the layer of straw. The way she bounced, though, indicated there must be something there other than only straw. She got up, smiling.

"Come on."

Joni sighed, then looked over to where Melissa was about halfway up the wall. Behind them were five others waiting to try the damn thing. She was convinced not one of them would make it over. Well, maybe one of those showoffs from Team Four. With another sigh, she pushed off the wall and fell to the ground. And yes, it was soft and bouncy, and she didn't break a leg. Kenni helped her to her feet, then went around the wall to help the others.

Joni stepped to the side and found a tree to lean against. She slid down to the ground and pulled her knees to her chest, watching the others attempt the monstrous wall. Well, not really watching them, no. She was watching Kenni.

She sighed. This whole thing was *so* not going how she'd planned. Yes, she expected to hate it here. And yes, she thought she'd hang out a few days and head back home to write the hit piece. And yes, she assumed that she wouldn't give this place or the people here another thought once she left.

Yet here she was, competing as a member of a damn team, climbing fucking trees, and not giving a thought to going home or writing the hit piece. And on top of that, she couldn't seem to take her eyes off the annoyingly irritating woman who she so wanted to dislike.

Whatever in the world was wrong with her?

CHAPTER TWENTY-FIVE

Kenni didn't even pretend that she was taking her normal evening walk. For one thing, she rarely went toward the lodge. More often than not, she meandered through the trees, finding one of the hiking trails and losing herself that way for an hour or so. She was going to the lodge this evening, though, in the hopes that Joni might be outside again.

She wasn't certain what her fascination with the other woman was all about. She was cute, yes, but it wasn't just her looks. Maybe it was the toughness she'd shown in making it through the obstacle courses...the determination to climb the wall. Or maybe she simply liked her spunk. Liked the way she could laugh at herself, liked the way Joni bantered and teased with her. She smiled now, thinking of Joni's threat to "kick her ass" when she got to the top of the wall.

She stopped walking and looked up into the sky and sighed. Maybe it was all of that or maybe it was something as innocent as simply being attracted to the woman. She found herself smiling more, laughing more. She found herself looking forward to each day's activities, knowing she would be able to see—and talk to—Joni.

That in itself was an oddity for her. All the joy in her life had disappeared that fateful day when her family had been killed. She'd seen a therapist, she'd done grief counseling, and she'd let her grandmother console her. None of that had brought any joy back to her life. She ran a retreat for disgruntled women who were unhappy in their lives and wanted a change. With that, she could relate. Unfortunately, she never took the lessons to heart herself. She went through the motions year after year, pretending she was happy and content with her life. In reality, she had to admit, she was lonely, depressed, and still feeling sorry for herself.

And now, all of a sudden, those feelings were receding to the background because she enjoyed sparring and teasing with Joni James.

She nodded and walked on, knowing she was smiling. If Joni wasn't out on the deck, she'd keep going, make the loop, and return to her cabin. And she'd look forward to tomorrow. But as she got closer—and spotted someone standing near the edge—her anticipation grew. She paused in the shadows, watching. As if sensing her presence, Joni turned. Even in the darkness Kenni could see the smile on her face. She walked out of the shadows and stepped on the deck.

"Evening walk?" Joni asked.

She nodded. "You?"

Joni looked up. "I was admiring the stars. I don't think I've ever done that before."

"Yes, they're lovely up here."

"Are you into astronomy and stuff?"

She smiled. "No. Not really. I enjoy the stars on dark nights, but I love the moon more, I think."

Joni moved closer to her, resting one hand on the deck railing. "I really came out here hoping you might come by."

"Really?"

Joni held a hand up. "Just to visit. I'm *not* attracted to you. You're not my type."

She asked the obvious question. "And who is? Someone like Elana?"

Joni stared at her for a long moment before answering. "I guess maybe I don't even know anymore. I usually date women who are on the feminine side, who dress fashionably, wear makeup." She paused. "I never really clicked with any of them, though."

"So, you broke up with Elana, what? Eight years ago, you said. No one since?"

"I mean, yes, I date. Of course. Some longer than others." She sighed heavily. "I guess I'm in a rut." Joni took another step closer. "What about you?"

"What about me?"

"Who do you date?"

"For the few months I spend in Santa Fe, I go out occasionally. I date some." *Was that a lie?*

"*Who* do you date?" Joni asked again.

She tried to think back to the last real date she'd had, and nothing would come to her. She seemed to remember having dinner at a Mexican food place one time with...what was her name? She moved to the side, contemplating darting off into the woods to avoid the question. She wasn't quite sure why.

"I don't guess I date all that much," she admitted.

"Why not?"

"I don't know, really," she said honestly. "I guess I'm tired from the summer and look at those few winter months as recuperating." She knew that was a lie, but she didn't know how to explain to Joni that she had little interest in dating and meeting new people.

Joni tilted her head, watching her, and Kenni felt like she was looking inside her for the truth.

"Is that your excuse?"

Kenni gave an embarrassed smile. "Yes."

"Do you enjoy being alone?"

"I'm rarely alone. Especially here."

Joni studied her again. "Being in the physical presence of others wasn't what I meant by the question."

Yes, she knew that, of course. Was she afraid to answer her? Was she afraid to admit it?

"No. I don't enjoy being alone." She leaned on the railing and stared into the darkness. "I don't date, though. I don't want to get involved with someone."

"Because?" Joni prompted quietly.

She shrugged but said nothing.

"Afraid? Afraid you'll fall in love, and they'll leave you?"

She turned her head slowly to look at Joni. Of course it was the truth. The look on Joni's face told her that Joni also knew it was the truth. She didn't say anything, though. She just gave a slight nod and turned back to the forest. No, she didn't want to love anyone. She didn't want to have her heart ripped out again. It was much safer this way.

Joni came up beside her, close enough that their arms were touching. "So, what tortures do you have planned for tomorrow?"

She smiled quickly, thankful Joni had changed the subject. "More tortures? Was it that bad today?"

"Well, considering we came in third place on the timed run, it wasn't so bad. But that damn wall is a bitch."

Kenni laughed. "Yes, it is. But no obstacle course tomorrow. We're actually taking an extended hike in the afternoon. We're going down to Mirror Lake. It's gorgeous. You'll understand how it got its name once you see it." She turned to face her. "There's a loop trail. We'll split into two groups and make it a challenge."

"I've seen the lake from up high and we're going *down*? That'll be fun. It's the hike back up that I dread."

"Yes. It'll be a great workout."

"If you're going to split us up into two groups, would you make sure that Team Four is not with us?"

"Don't get along with them?"

"Yes, they're fine. But they piss me off."

"Because they win?"

Joni laughed. "Yes. I hate them."

"Then I'll see what I can do."

"Thank you. And I guess I should head inside and get my rest."

"Probably so." She moved away. "Good night, Joni. Sweet dreams." She stepped off the deck and headed into the trees. She heard Joni's quiet voice call after her.

"Good night, Kenni."

CHAPTER TWENTY-SIX

"I know I haven't called. I'm sorry." Joni plopped down on her bed sideways as she cradled the phone. "It's been a crazy week."

"I can't believe you're still there!" Kimberly said with a laugh.

"I know. I have a hard time believing it myself." She stared at the ceiling and smiled. "I'm glad you called. I kinda need to talk."

"What's going on?"

"Well, first of all, I'm actually having a really fun time here."

"You're kidding?"

"No." She sat up. "Kim, I'm going on hikes. I'm going to the gym. I'm climbing fucking trees!" she said with a laugh. "And I like the stupid scavenger hunts, for god's sake!"

"So, you've been body snatched or what?"

"Well…something." She lay back down again. "I've got a huge crush on Kenni." There. She'd said it out loud. It was crazy, but true. She was thirty-one years old, and she had a damn stupid crush.

"Kenni? The owner of the place?"

"Yes. It's insane, isn't it?"

"Well, I've seen her picture on the website. She's cute."

"Right. But she's all boyish and woodsy and not anyone I would ever date."

"She didn't look boyish in the picture."

She sighed. "And she certainly doesn't look boyish in her sports bra and shorts, but she is."

"Okay, but let's go back to the crush part. You had said earlier that you were going to flirt with her to try to get some information out of her for your article."

"I haven't even thought about the damn article. I haven't gotten my laptop out of my bag yet. I forget I even have a phone. It's, like, who *am* I?"

"My, but you *have* been body snatched," Kim said with a laugh.

"It's so crazy. I'm attracted to her. But she's annoying and most of the time I want to throttle her. But then, we've been having these quiet moments alone—like earlier tonight—and she shows her vulnerable side, and I want to hug her." She rolled toward the wall and stared at it. "What's wrong with me?"

"Why does something have to be wrong? You have a crush on her. What's wrong with that?"

"Well, for one, I'm too old to have a crush on someone. Especially someone like her who I would never date in real life. Besides that, I'm only here for three more weeks. Then I'll never see her again. It's pointless."

"It's pointless having a crush? Or it's pointless following up on it?"

She sat up quickly. "Oh my god! You think I want to have a *romance* with her? Like sex and stuff? Don't be ridiculous!"

"Then why are we having this conversation?"

She ran a hand through her hair. "Because I've obviously lost my mind. I think Turnbull was right. They *do* brainwash you here. I'm hugging freaking trees now!" She stood up. "I've got to go to bed. I'm exhausted and talking out of my head." She paused. "And don't tell anyone about my crush."

Kimberly laughed. "Okay. I promise I won't talk about you at our next happy hour. Do you miss them, by the way?"

Of course she did. Didn't she? She hadn't given them a thought either, it seems. It was almost like she was living in an alternate universe. But she lied.

"I do. I can't wait to join you all again. Tell everyone hello for me."

"Will do. Talk to you later."

Instead of bothering with her silk pajamas, she simply pulled off her clothes and got under the covers. She punched her pillow a few times, then lay down with a heavy sigh. Yes, they were surely brainwashing her. Maybe some sort of telepathic wave or something. She smiled at her thoughts and closed her eyes. That didn't prevent an image of Kenni popping into her mind. Yes, that sports bra looked *really* good on her.

CHAPTER TWENTY-SEVEN

It was one of those cloudless, windless days where you could hear every sound in the forest. They were already well into the second week, and Kenni leaned against the deck railing, soaking up the late-morning sun and listening. She heard the calls of birds as they came to one of the feeders. She heard a squirrel scolding from high in a tree. And she heard the muffled voices of the women as they hurried through the woods on their scavenger hunt. She smiled quickly as she thought of Joni's parting shot as she led Team Five away. "No fucking way I'm letting Team Four beat us today!"

Two weeks in and everyone had settled in their routines by now. The morning yoga sessions were reduced to not much more than a quick warmup and stretching before the gym and hike. The daily scavenger hunt was getting longer. Their afternoons were always spent in the forest, either running an obstacle course or taking a longer hike into the canyon—sometimes both.

Gone was the makeup and fixed hair. Long gone was the jewelry. She could see in their faces how much they'd changed already. They were more relaxed, more confident, and more content. Nearly everyone sported smiles on their faces now. All had embraced the competition and teamwork—especially Joni. That surprised her. After the first couple of days, she'd been convinced that Joni would be a no-show when it came to teamwork. That turned out to be very wrong. She glanced at the board that hung under the bell. Yes, Team Five had had several wins lately and was now in second place.

"Counting your winnings?"

She turned, seeing Jenn coming out to join her. She smiled at her and nodded. "Despite the rocky beginnings, I think my team will overtake yours in a couple of days."

"Yeah, never would have believed it." Jenn looked a bit nervous and motioned her over to the edge of the deck. "I need to talk to you."

"Of course." Jenn seemed so serious, Kenni wondered if something was wrong. "What is it?"

"I don't know how to say this other than to just say it." She paused. "I'm...I'm getting married."

Kenni stared at her for a long moment, then grinned. "That's great! Congratulations." She went closer and pulled her into a hug. "I'm assuming it's Matt."

Jenn laughed. "Yes. Matt. We kinda talked about it over the winter, but I didn't think I was ready."

"And?"

"And we had a really nice talk last night." Jenn squeezed her arm. "You know I love it here and love working for you. But—"

"But this will be your last summer?"

Jenn met her gaze and nodded. "Yes. I'm sorry, Kenni. I—"

"No, no. Hell, you're getting married! We all know what happened to Sky's marriage. I wouldn't dare suggest that you keep working here."

Jenn laughed. "I know." She squeezed her arm again. "It'll be like leaving my family, though. You and the others, well, we're a good team. I'll miss it here. But I'm thirty-three years old and Matt and I want to have a baby. So, the time is right for me to move on."

"I completely understand. I knew this day would come eventually, Jenn. We're going to miss you being here too, but we'll get by."

"Thanks, Kenni. I haven't told the others yet. I guess I should find Sky and let her know."

She nodded. Jenn wasn't the first to leave and she wouldn't be the last. Of her current staff, she figured Sky was the only one who was safe to stay on indefinitely.

She turned around to face the woods, her thoughts scrambling. Was Jenn leaving a sign of some sort? Was it time for her to think about moving on too? For that matter, what the hell was she even still doing here? Was she helping anyone? Was she using this retreat as an excuse to escape her own life? Was she—

"Oh my god! Are we *first?*"

She turned, automatically smiling as Joni and her team ran up onto the deck. She nodded. "You are. Ring the bell."

"Hell yes!" Joni said with a fist pump. "Sarah Beth…ring that damn thing! Ring it loud!"

Kenni laughed and pushed her earlier thoughts of self-doubt away. Team Five was happy and smiling, which made her happy too. She found herself being pulled by Joni's eyes and she didn't shy away. She walked over to her, giving a high five, reveling in the true joy she found there.

"You found the pink rocks?"

Joni put her hands on her hips. "It would have been nice to know that there was a stream nearby. How have you kept that from us?"

"Because it's not anywhere near the obstacle courses or the hiking trails. And if I'd told you about it, it wouldn't have been much of a challenge today."

"There was a cabin back there. Is that yours?"

"It is."

"How do you cross the stream? I mean, you could probably jump across, but do you?"

"No. There's a small footbridge. The stream will dry up, though, in a month or so. It's fed by snowmelt."

Joni tilted her head, studying her. "What's wrong?"

She raised her eyebrows. "What makes you think something is wrong?"

"I don't know. You look—"

Her words were cut off as Team Four ran up, then they all stopped at once, disappointment on their faces.

"Yeah, we beat your ass! Again!" Joni teased them.

"It took us forever to find the stream," Anna said. "I think we only found it because Team Two was heading that way."

"Let's see…you had blue rocks?" Kenni asked.

"Yes. And where we were at the stream, there were yellow rocks only so that took a while."

The other three teams were coming up together, knowing that they weren't going to win the day's scavenger hunt. They were chatting and smiling, and she assumed they'd enjoyed the adventure, nonetheless.

"Good job, everyone!" she said enthusiastically. "The winning team—Team Five—will head to the gym. Your prize for the win is a full-body massage and sauna. A spa in Gunnison sends two ladies up for us. They're waiting for you."

"A massage?" Joni groaned with pleasure. "Yes!"

Kenni glanced at her watch. "Be back in forty-five minutes for lunch." Team Five nearly ran off the deck. "The rest of you have free time until lunch. Do as you please."

"The old me would have opted for a nap," Britney said. "The new me wants to go back out into the woods."

Some of the others laughed, as did Kenni. "Well, I would advise you to take it easy. We're going to run the obstacle course this afternoon."

They all dispersed, and Kenni was left standing there alone. Her gaze went in the direction of the gym, but she refrained from following Team Five. With a sigh, she went inside.

CHAPTER TWENTY-EIGHT

After dinner, Joni did what she'd been doing nearly every evening and made her way out to the big deck. She could hear the conversations and laughter coming from the women who were playing board games, something she had yet to be tempted to do. No, she'd rather have some alone time with Kenni. As was the norm, the deck was empty, and Kenni wasn't there yet. Of course, there was no guarantee she'd come at all. It wasn't like they had a standing date or anything. They didn't, no, but she suspected that Kenni enjoyed their visits as much as she did, considering she had been coming over every night.

She'd stopped trying to figure out her attraction to Kenni. She blamed it on the environment around her. She was in the woods, far away from her normal life. It stood to reason that she'd gravitate to someone who was the complete opposite of who she normally dated.

"Right," she murmured to herself.

Or she could use the excuse that she was fishing for information for an article she'd given little—or no—thought to since she'd been there. She'd been too busy playing and climbing trees and being a part of a team. Who knew she'd love it so?

But still, there was that nagging attraction that she didn't know what to do with. She didn't know how to handle it or where to put it. A part of her wanted to throw caution to the wind and... well, let it take her where it may. She knew it wasn't a one-sided attraction. She could see that in Kenni's eyes, could tell by the way she treated her, the teasing and banter, and yes, the subtle flirting. It was kinda nice, she admitted. Kenni was cute and fun and likeable. Yes, out with the others, she was engaging and gregarious. Yet, in the evenings when they visited, she got another impression of her. Kenni was quiet and subdued, and sometimes a cloud of sadness hovered over her. Sometimes she—

"Hey."

The quiet voice made her turn, a smile already on her face before she even found Kenni. Instead of coming up on the deck like she usually did, Kenni stayed in the trees.

"Hey yourself," she answered.

"Feel like a walk?"

She clamped down on the flippant remark she was about to utter because they had already walked *miles* today. So, she nodded and went toward her.

"I'm up for a walk, sure," she said easily.

The light from the back windows shined out, enough so she could tell that Kenni's dark hair was still damp from her shower. She followed closely to her as they made their way from the lodge. She wondered how she could even see where they were going. She got her answer a few seconds later when a tiny flashlight came on. Instead of going where they normally went during the scavenger hunts, Kenni led them around the lodge and toward the parking lot. She went past that too and came upon a sitting area. There were two benches made out of log beams and another two spots with large tree stumps. In the center was a firepit of some sort.

"I didn't even know this place was here."

Kenni turned the light off. "Because you didn't explore around the first couple of days. If we happen to have a damp, rainy day, we'll sometimes get a big fire going out here."

She sat on one of the benches, and Joni hesitated. Should she join her or take another seat?

"There's room for you," Kenni offered.

By the tone of her voice, she sensed that Kenni was, well, a little down. She certainly wasn't her normal teasing and pleasant self. Something she'd picked up on earlier that morning too. She sat down close to her, close enough that they were touching. She nudged her shoulder.

"What's wrong?"

"Why do you think something's wrong?"

"I just do. Is it because Jenn is leaving?"

Kenni turned to her. "You heard?"

Joni laughed. "You get twenty women together, there's going to be gossip."

"Yeah, I suppose so." She sighed. "I'm feeling kinda out of sorts, I guess. Jenn leaving is part of it, yes. I've been, well, questioning my purpose."

"Your purpose?"

Kenni motioned around them. "Here. This place. Questioning if I'm making a difference, if I'm helping anyone or only taking their money."

She frowned. "What brought that on? Surely not just Jenn."

"What do you think about it all? All of this."

"What do you mean?"

"You've been here about two weeks. What do you make of it? What gossip have you heard?"

"From the ladies? Well, just from my team, I've heard both Christine and Erin say they are ready to make changes once they get home. Meaning with their marriage. Now, Sarah Beth has not said that, but I don't think she's here because of her husband."

"Midlife crisis, yes."

"How does that make you feel knowing that some of these women will leave here and file for divorce?"

"You think I'm encouraging it?"

"Not by your words, no. And that's what's really crazy. You don't do any counseling. There's no man-bashing or anything. The most lecturing you've done is about food and fitness."

"A lot of the women who come here are not happy in their marriages or in their lives. You already know that. Most are afraid to make changes. Like that very first dinner we had with the team. Erin and Christine both said there were perks, even in a bad marriage."

Joni nodded. "Right. So, what prods them to finally make a change?" Kenni smiled at her, and Joni laughed. "Don't say it's because they feel empowered or liberated, as your website promises."

"But that's exactly what it is. They are climbing fucking trees, as you would say."

Joni laughed. "Yes, *physical* things. But what does that have to do with emotional?"

"You don't think they're related? You don't think their confidence grows in all things? They are doing things they never thought they could do. Or even *should* do. We're giving them the freedom to make their own choices. Even in something as simple as eating. Why do you think we have so many choices? It lets them choose what they want for themselves."

"Yeah, but we don't get to choose everything. Like the daily activities. We don't get to choose what to do."

"Don't you?"

"Do we?"

"Of course. You don't have to run the obstacle courses. You didn't have to climb the tree."

"Oh my god! You mean we didn't *have* to do all that?"

"No." Kenni smiled at her. "But you chose to do it."

Joni shook her head. "Oh, now you tell me."

"Yeah, but don't tell anyone else."

Joni nudged her again. "Why do all this, Kenni? What compelled you to want to help these women?"

"Well, it wasn't really *these* women. Not the wealthy and pampered. When we first started, we targeted more middle-class women. We soon learned that as much as they might *want* to make changes to their lives, very few could afford to leave their husbands and go off on their own. Lyon's Den only served to reinforce how unhappy they were."

"Okay, but *why*, Kenni? Why are you trying to push them to make changes?"

Kenni stood up and walked away from her. "Doing research for your article?"

"No, of course not. I haven't given the article much thought."

Kenni turned around to face her. "The guy who killed my family was the son of a very wealthy man. A man with a lot of political connections. He pulled enough strings that there were no charges brought against his son."

Joni's eyes widened. "But he was drunk."

"Yes. Drunk and speeding. He got what amounted to a slap on the wrist. My grandmother and I filed a civil lawsuit against the kid. I got to see firsthand how his father treated his wife and children. They were nothing but puppets. The wife was obviously remorseful. I could see that in her eyes, but she cowered before him. The son was used to daddy protecting him and he was pretty much indifferent to the whole thing. Anyway, we ended up getting some press finally, and there were newspaper articles and stuff. The husband didn't want all the bad publicity he was getting, and he finally settled."

Kenni sat down beside her again. "He was an overbearing bastard and thought he was being gracious to us by settling out of court. He told me I should be ashamed to be monetizing my family's death."

"Oh my god! I hope you told him off!"

"I wanted to punch him in the face. My grandmother wanted to bust his balls."

Joni laughed, then sobered. "Sorry."

"No, it's okay. But the wife came to see me. It was a month or so later. Like I said, she was genuinely remorseful, and I knew her apology was sincere. It made little difference to me, though. But it was that look in her eyes—that defeated, beatdown, *helpless* look—that I remember. She had more money than she could spend in two lifetimes, yet she was so very unhappy."

"That's what made you want to do this?"

"Yes. Maybe if she wasn't beatdown, wasn't helpless, she could have taught her son better." Kenni turned to her. "It's kinda stupid, I know."

"It's not stupid. You're obviously successful. From what I've gathered, you don't even have to advertise much, if at all."

"We are more successful than I ever could have imagined, yes." Kenni folded her hands together. "I just don't know why I'm still doing it."

"Are you not getting any satisfaction out of it? Do you not enjoy it any longer?"

Kenni smiled at her. "I've enjoyed this particular month much more than others."

Joni smiled back at her. "Because?"

Kenni looked away from her. "I don't have friends, really. My staff. We're close. I don't ever make friends with any of the clients, though. I leave here and go to Santa Fe and…"

"And what?" she asked quietly.

Kenni let out a deep breath. "And do nothing. Count down the days, months until I return. Visit my grandmother a couple of times." Kenni looked at her again. "I…I get lonely."

"Lonely for company? Lonely for someone's touch?"

"Yes. Both."

Joni felt a tug on her heart at the softly spoken words. She leaned closer, pressing against her shoulder. "Was that hard to admit?"

"Yes." Kenni smiled. "I must consider you a friend if I'm sharing feelings."

"I have a handful of good friends. I have a best friend. But…I get lonely too." She pressed harder against her. "I don't know that I've ever realized that before."

"Do you date a lot?"

Joni sighed. "I suppose. Lots of first dates, at least."

"Why is that?"

"Kimberly—she's my best friend—says that I'm either unrealistic about my expectations or that I need to broaden my search." She laughed. "Meaning I choose the wrong women to date." She sighed again. "She may be right."

"About which?"

"Both." She chewed her lower lip, wondering where this conversation was going. "That's why I'm feeling a little disjointed now."

"How so?"

She paused only a second. "I'm attracted to you." She closed her eyes and shook her head. Had she *really* admitted that to her?

"But you said the other day you *weren't* attracted to me," Kenni reminded her.

"I lied."

"Okay, just so we're on the same page…you *are* attracted to me now?"

"I just said I was!" she nearly snapped. "God knows why," she added under her breath. "You're not my type. I'm fairly certain I'm not *your* type."

"What would my type be?"

"You know, all woodsy and stuff. Like you. That's not me. I wear makeup. I dress up. I'm not an outdoorsy person. I—"

"I haven't seen you with makeup on since you walked into the lodge that first afternoon."

She narrowed her eyes. "You're completely missing the point."

"Am I?"

"Yes! What? Do you think I've changed? Because I haven't," she said firmly. "When I get out of here, I'm going back to who I am."

"Why?"

"Why? What kind of question is that? I wear makeup. I—" She stopped talking when Kenni took her hand and inspected it.

"No long nails. No polish. Just natural. Just you. Why then do you cover your natural beauty with makeup?" Kenni leaned closer. "Because you're absolutely gorgeous without it."

She swallowed. "You…you think so?"

"I do."

They were still holding hands, and she squeezed Kenni's a little tighter, wondering what in the world they were doing. She didn't have to wonder long, however. Kenni leaned closer, kissing her ever so lightly on the lips. That spark—that ever-elusive spark that she'd only dared to dream about—tickled her from her lips down to her toes.

She felt herself squeezing harder on Kenni's hand, not knowing if she was holding on for dear life or silently begging for her to kiss her again. A real kiss. A long, hot, passionate kiss that would surely make her moan. She found herself leaning closer and her eyes closed dreamily when she met Kenni's lips again.

Yes, she did moan, and she didn't care in the least. One hand still clutched Kenni's as the other rested on Kenni's thigh. Her mouth moved with Kenni's, and she was certain her eyes were rolling back in her head. *Delirious.* She didn't know what that felt like, but most certainly this was it. Wasn't it? Because she was melting. Right there on the wooden bench, beneath the canopy of trees that only partially blocked the stars...she was melting.

But Kenni pulled away as Joni had feared she would. Their kiss didn't end with them stripping off their clothes and making love on the forest floor in a frantic lust. No. That was for the movies—or a silly romance book. Things like that didn't happen to her.

"That was probably way unprofessional of me," Kenni said quietly. "But I won't apologize for doing it."

Joni leaned away from Kenni, trying to regain some semblance of her former self. The one who made herself up carefully before going out, the one who would *never* be attracted to someone like Kendall Lyon. Unfortunately, her mind was too jumbled to cooperate, and she wondered if she was having an out-of-body episode or something. Because even though she knew she was there, sitting on the bench next to Kenni—melting—she wasn't *really* there. Was she?

"Joni? Are you okay?"

Joni looked at her then. "I'm...I'm not sure."

Kenni tilted her head. "So, I should apologize then?"

Joni smiled at her. "Apologize for stopping?"

Kenni smiled back at her. "I didn't want to stop."

"Then why the hell did you?"

Kenni stood and pulled her up. "Come on. Let's get you back."

She blew out a frustrated breath. Would it be forward of her to beg Kenni to take her to her cabin? She nodded. *Yes. My god,* they'd had a couple of kisses. Now she wanted to go to bed with her? *Well, yes.* She shook her head. *No, don't be ridiculous! It was one freakin' kiss!* She closed her eyes and shook her head again. *Stop it!*

"Are you having a conversation with yourself?"

Joni jerked her head up. "Of course not!" She laughed nervously. "That would be crazy."

Kenni laughed. "Come on. Busy day tomorrow."

"Every day is a busy day." She fell into step beside her. "What torture should I dream about? Climbing trees?"

"Nope. Rappelling into the canyon."

"The canyon by the overlook?"

"Yep."

"No way. No fucking way."

"Yes way."

"Okay, say I did make it down alive. How do you propose I get out of the canyon?"

"It'll be a surprise."

"If you think I'm climbing back *up*, you're out of your fucking mind," she said louder than she intended.

Kenni laughed but said nothing.

"I'm serious," Joni said as she elbowed her. "God, you're already irritating me again. I can't believe we kissed."

"Believe it."

Joni walked quietly beside her, then paused when they got to the deck. "When's the last time you've kissed someone?"

Kenni's face was bathed in light that was coming from the back windows. She arched an eyebrow. "Why? Do you think I'm out of practice?"

"No. That's not what I meant." She shrugged, not sure why she'd even asked the question.

"Let's see. Last winter…" Kenni shook her head. "No, two winters now, I guess. I had a date. We went to dinner. Then a movie. And I kissed her at her car before we said goodbye."

Joni met her gaze. "First and only date?"

"Yes."

"Why? You didn't like her?"

"I liked her fine." Kenni stepped back into the shadows. "Good night, Joni. Thanks for the walk. And the talk." Then she smiled. "And especially that second kiss," she added quietly.

Joni watched her walk away, staring into the trees long after she'd disappeared into the night. Yes, they'd kissed. And yes, she'd felt her toes curl from it. Now what? Now what were they going to do?

She suddenly felt unsure of herself. Unsure of who she even was. She had denied it, of course, but yes, she had changed in these two short weeks. Two weeks that had been jam-packed full of crazy activities that had now become her daily norm. She was doing yoga and hugging trees. She looked forward to hiking. She looked forward to running the obstacle courses. She loved the competition. She would even say she loved her teammates. And no, she hadn't even thought about putting on makeup. And apparently Kenni thought she looked perfectly fine without it.

"Gorgeous."

Yes, Kenni had called her gorgeous. She smiled at that and turned on her heels, heading back inside. A busy day tomorrow and she was tired. But instead of dreaming of rappelling into the canyon, she was fairly certain that her dreams would be filled with kissing.

A lot of kissing. Maybe even *more* than kissing.

She climbed the stairs slowly, still shaking her head.

You've lost your damn mind.

CHAPTER TWENTY-NINE

"I'm not your goddamn guinea pig!"

Kenni tried not to laugh as Joni's eyes shot daggers at her. "You're not? Who should I pick then?"

"Anybody! Someone from Team Four, preferably."

This caused everyone to laugh, even Team Four, who had won the scavenger hunt before lunch. She arched an eyebrow.

"You're a little cranky today."

Joni gave her a fake smile. "Maybe I slept poorly."

"Have dreams, did you?"

"Not of you," she said under her breath, even though that was a lie.

"Well, a quick rappel off the side here should liven things up. What do you say?"

"I am not jumping off the side of this fucking mountain," Joni said slowly, enunciating each word succinctly. "I don't care what you say!"

"Come on. I'll show you how."

"Did you not hear me?"

She took Joni's hand and led her over to where the harnesses were. Some of the others in the groups started clapping, and Joni turned around and flipped them off. Kenni laughed loudly.

"See? This is you. Right here, right now. This is your authentic self."

"And it would be different if I was dressed up and wearing makeup? You think I couldn't still shoot them the bird?"

"Would you?"

"Yes." Joni smiled a little. "Maybe."

She nodded. "Yeah. You probably would." Then she lowered her voice. "I like you better this way."

Joni held her hand up. "You can try to sweet-talk me all you want, I'm still not jumping off this cliff."

"Come here. Let me show you. We're not actually going down into the canyon." She led her closer to the edge. "See?"

"Oh my god! You want me to drop down onto that skinny little ledge there? Have you lost your mind? It's like a hundred feet down!"

"It's thirty-two feet. That's all. And the ledge is bigger than it looks. And you won't have to climb back up. There's a very nice hiking trail you can take." She pointed past them. "Comes up over there."

"Why do you always make me go first?"

"Because I like you. I'd never be able to have these stimulating conversations with anyone else."

Joni rolled her eyes.

Kenni motioned for Karla. "Karla is actually going down first. She'll assist you on your landing and show you where the hiking trail is. And Jenn will meet you on the trail, so you don't get lost." She smiled. "Wouldn't want you slipping and falling off the edge."

"I can't believe I kissed you," Joni muttered.

Kenni winked at her. "But you did."

While Karla was helping Joni into her harness, Kenni went back over to the group. "Okay, it's a thirty-two-foot drop, but you're going to be perfectly safe. Your anchor rope is tied to that big pine over there. We'll all watch Karla go down and show you how it's done. You'll hike back up on a trail along the ridge. Jenn will assist you there." Most of the ladies looked at her with wide eyes. "Any questions?"

"Has anyone ever fallen?"

She smiled and shook her head. "Not a one. We did have someone make it down in record time, though. But you'll be wearing a backup rope so if your hands slip and you start rappelling too fast, I'll be up here to slow you down." She pulled out her gloves from her back pocket and held them up. "Don't forget to put your gloves on."

* * *

Joni told herself that she'd climbed the damn tree without an incident. And she'd managed the swinging bridge without falling. She was kicking ass on the obstacle courses too. So surely she could handle this...this drop down over a hundred feet into a steep, dark, rocky canyon. She got lightheaded thinking about it, and she turned, finding Kenni watching her. She narrowed her eyes and gave the best scowl she could manage. Kenni smiled sweetly at her in return.

"Okay, we're going to take it slow," Karla said. "There are footholds to land on—some of the larger rocks. You want a good balance between your legs and your arms."

Most everyone in the group had come closer to watch as Karla causally and gracefully walked backward off the edge of the fucking cliff and lowered herself down into hell, using a swinging motion to land against the rocks before pushing off again and going lower. She landed lightly on the ledge far, far down below and waved up at them. Joni felt her stomach turn over.

"See how easy that was," Kenni said. "When you get to the bottom, take your harness off and I'll pull it back up."

She did that now, pulling up the rope with the harness dangling from it. Kenni passed the harness on, giving it to Amy from Team Four. Joni then stood paralyzed as Kenni attached the rope to one of the buckles on her harness. Her eyes followed her movements as Kenni attached another rope to the other side.

"This is the rope that I'll be holding on to," she explained.

"Shouldn't we have practiced this first?" Joni asked.

"This is practice."

"Oh my god! You really *do* plan to have us go all the way down into the canyon?"

"Maybe. Just not today." Kenni turned to the others. "Ladies, it's very secure. What we're doing is called fixed-line rappelling." She picked up the thick rope that was tied to the large pine. "This is our anchor. The second rope I'll call a brake, which is what I'll be holding. It will act like a pulley system. If you start slipping or falling, I'll be your brake." Kenni came over to her and picked up the rope that had been attached to one of the buckles. She took her hand and placed the rope there. "Close your hand around it. Like Karla did, you relax your hand and let the rope slide through it as you lower. Your other hand is on the upper rope."

Joni shook her head. "I'm not strong enough. I'll—"

"I've got your brake," Kenni reminded her.

"Let me just say that I'm really glad Joni is the guinea pig," Sarah Beth said with a nervous laugh. "Because if she falls, I ain't doing it!"

"Thanks a lot," Joni murmured dryly.

"It's only thirty-two feet. You'll be down before you know it," Kenni said.

Joni gave her a fake smile. "Yeah, that's my worry."

"I won't let you fall. Promise." Kenni looked over the edge at Karla. "Ready?"

"Drop 'em down," she called back up.

Kenni laughed. "She didn't mean that literally, of course."

Joni was too nervous to even reply to that. She stood numbly by as Kenni turned her around, her back now to the edge of the cliff she was supposed to sail off from. Good god, what in the *hell* was she doing up here?

"You ready?"

"No, I am not ready to die," she choked out.

"You'll be fine. Now, hold on to the rope like I showed you. Use your other hand to feed it. And remember, I've got the brake."

She took a deep breath and squeezed her eyes shut. *Oh god, oh god, oh god.*

"Open your eyes. It's much easier that way."

She did, but she was too nervous to even attempt to glare at her. "I'm…I'm so scared," she said instead.

Kenni gave her a reassuring smile, a smile that was reflected in her eyes as well. "I've got you. I won't let you go. Trust me."

Joni held on to her eyes for a moment longer, then nodded. "Okay. Then let's get this shit over with."

Nervous laughter from the group made her feel a little less scared. Hell, she was the youngest of them all. It stood to reason that she should be the damn guinea pig.

"Okay. Slowly walk backward. Keep your feet on the rocks."

She took a deep breath. "And you won't let me fall?"

"I won't let you fall."

After all of that, it was almost anticlimactic when she finally let herself go. Because after five or six feet, she quickly realized that Kenni was doing all the work. She let the rope slack, and she didn't drop like a rock. In fact, she would go so far as to guess that the so-called anchor rope she was using was only a decoy. She didn't know if she was happy about that or pissed off that Kenni had gotten her scared for nothing. But she did as instructed and kept her feet against the canyon wall, bouncing slightly as she got lower. In no time at all, Karla was there, grabbing first her feet, then her legs and guiding her down to the ledge.

"Here you are. All safe."

"Yeah. I am. And I'm so going to kick her ass when I get back to the top."

Karla's eyes widened. "What's wrong?"

"There is no way in hell I could have done that. *She* was the one lowering me down!"

Karla laughed then. "Did you really think she'd let you all rappel down this wall without any training?"

"Well, I thought she'd lost her damn mind, yes."

She stood still while Karla unhooked the ropes, then she stepped out of the harness. She made the mistake of looking down past the ledge. Her eyes widened and she had a sense of vertigo.

"Oh my god!" She took a step back and hugged the wall. "We are on a tiny freakin' ledge thousands of feet in the air!"

"Only a couple of hundred feet. But yeah, you don't want to fall from here."

"This whole thing has taken years off my life."

Karla laughed. "It's something you won't soon forget, I hope." She pointed to her right. "Head that way. You'll find Jenn back there where the trail starts. She'll show you how to get out of here."

Joni took tiny, tentative steps along the ledge, keeping her gaze straight ahead, not even once glancing down into the deep darkness of the canyon. When the ledge started narrowing, she nearly panicked. How was she going to get to Jenn? She looked behind her. Should she go back?

"Over here, Joni!"

She looked up ahead, nearly crying with relief when she saw Jenn wave to her. "Can I make it? It's kinda narrow," she said hesitantly.

"Yes. Stay against the rock wall. There's a guardrail at the corner."

Only a few more steps and the ledge widened again. And yes, there was a manmade guardrail—wooden logs nailed together in a makeshift railing. It didn't look secure in the least; she didn't dare touch it for fear it would crumble and send her careening over the side. Jenn came out to meet her.

"You can use the railing for balance."

Joni shook her head. "I don't think so. It looks wobbly."

"No, not at all." To prove her point, Jenn leaned against it. "It's got a brace on the back side that's screwed into the rocks. You should have seen Kenni dangling off the side when she was trying to install that. It took us three days to build this little thing."

She dared to move closer, tentatively reaching out to the railing. Sure enough, it didn't budge when she touched it. She peered over the side, imagining Kenni hanging by a rope there. She got dizzy as she looked far down into the canyon, thinking there was no way in *hell* she would have attempted that.

"You made it down okay? No slips?"

She flicked her eyes at Jenn. "After I realized that Kenni was the one lowering me, my heart palpitations stopped. Couldn't she have told us before the drop that we weren't the ones actually in control?"

Jenn smiled at her and moved around the corner of the rock wall. Beyond that was nearly a staircase of rocks as it climbed gradually back up and into the trees. It was quite lovely, but she doubted it was all natural. As she started climbing up, she changed her mind. There was just enough imperfection to be Mother Nature's doing and not Kenni's.

"Oh, and, Joni, when you get to the top, please stay there away from the others. Wait until everyone gets through."

She nodded. "Don't want me warning the others that this is all for show?"

"Exactly."

CHAPTER THIRTY

"I was so scared, I almost peed my pants!" Sarah Beth exclaimed as they walked back toward the lodge. "I was about six feet down when my hand slipped. I swear, my heart jumped into my throat, and I thought I was a goner!"

The others on her team laughed, with Erin giving her own recount.

"I lost the rope the minute I went over the side. I screamed so loud I'm sure the others thought I was falling to my death!"

"Yeah, well, I was one of the last ones to go," Christine said. "I was shaking with fear by the time it was my turn. I was so scared, I didn't dare let go of the rope. It wasn't until I was almost to the ledge that I realized I was exerting little effort."

They all seemed to look at her. "What about you, Joni? You haven't said how your trip down was."

"About the same as yours. Of course, when it dawned on me that Kenni was actually the one lowering me, I wanted to climb back up and kick her ass for scaring me half to death!" she said with a laugh. "Because, as I told Karla, that took *years* off my life!"

"Well, I'm sure there is a lesson in this, as everything else seems to be," Erin said. "I can't for the life of me figure out what it is, though."

Yes, that was the first thing she was going to talk to Kenni about. What the hell was the purpose of that terrifying exercise? She didn't have long to wonder as it turned out. When they got back to the lodge, Kenni brought them all onto the large deck at the back. Joni noted that most everyone was gathered within their own teams.

Kenni spread her arms out and smiled. "So, how do you feel after that?"

There was a moment of silence as everyone looked at each other. It was Sarah Beth who spoke first.

"That scared the shit out of me."

Everyone seemed to nod at once.

Kenni nodded too. "I suppose so."

"My life flashed before my eyes," Britney from Team Four said.

Kenni nodded again. "But how did you feel?"

Joni frowned, as did Britney. Britney looked around at the others before speaking. "Feel? I...I was scared."

Again, everyone nodded and murmured their agreement. It was at that moment that Joni realized the purpose of the exercise. Yes, they were scared. Some terrified, as she had been. But they'd done it anyway. God knows why, but they'd done it.

"You were scared," Kenni said calmly. "Yet you trusted *me*. You trusted the process. You trusted *yourself*." She moved among them. "It took courage for all of you to go over the side of that cliff. Courage and trust. And every single one of you did it." She spread her arms out. "And you know why?"

No one spoke, yet every one of them was looking intently at Kenni, hanging on her words, Joni included. Kenni gave them another reassuring smile.

"You did it because you *believed* you could do it! It's as simple as that. You're strong and you can do *anything* you want to do. Anything you set your mind to. Whether it's out here or back in your real life. You can do whatever you want to," she said again.

"As Sir Edmund Hillary said, 'It's not the mountain we conquer, it's ourselves.' And today you did that. Because you are in control of *you*."

Joni wasn't looking at the others to see their reactions to those words. No, she was looking at Kenni. She loved her strength, her confidence. The way she carried herself, the way she spoke. She didn't look away when Kenni turned to her, capturing her eyes. No, she held them steady, feeling a little of that same melting sensation she'd felt last night. Last night when they kissed. Kenni was thinking of their kiss, too. The darkening of her eyes gave her away. Joni had a horrifying urge to go to her, to beg her to kiss her again, completely unmindful of the others around them. Of course she couldn't do that, so she pulled her gaze from Kenni, feigning interest in the pinecone she still held. *When did I pick that up?*

Kenni gave her a rather sweet smile, then went back to the front of the group. "Forty-five minutes until dinner. Free time for you so do as you like. If I'm not mistaken, I believe Wanda has pork chops on the menu this evening. Eat your fill, then get your rest. Tomorrow we'll go to the third obstacle course and get acquainted with it. No climbing trees this time."

Kenni left them and Joni moved with the others, not knowing what she wanted to do. Some were heading inside, saying they wanted a shower. Team Four all headed out into the woods, chatting quietly among themselves. Planning strategy for tomorrow's contests, no doubt.

"I'm going to shower," Sarah Beth told her. "Then I'm going to eat about four pork chops. I'm starving."

Christine pulled out her blue hair scrunchy, letting her ponytail come free. She ran her fingers through it a few times, then tied it back up a little neater than before. "Sometimes I just want to cut this off short."

"Why don't you?" Erin asked.

"My husband won't hear of it." As soon as she said the words, she seemed to consider them. She smiled. "But do I care what he prefers? It's *my* hair, not his!"

Joni clapped enthusiastically. "Yes! Cut that mess off!"

"I think I just may do that. To use your favorite word, fuck him!"

Joni was still smiling when the others walked off. That was probably easy for Christine to say since she didn't really like her husband or her marriage. Then again, when she got back home, she'd most likely reconsider. Oh well. It didn't matter to her in the least.

She turned around, eyeing the doors to the dining hall. She wanted to shower too, but she'd rather seek out Kenni. So, she went into the lodge in search of her. The dining room was empty other than the ladies who were setting up for dinner. She went through the double doors and into the lobby. It, too, was empty. She turned to where the offices were, but all the doors were closed.

With a disappointed sigh, she headed to the stairs. Kenni had probably already gone to her cabin. For as stressful an afternoon as it had been for them, Kenni was the one doing all the work. She was probably exhausted. She paused at the bottom of the stairs and looked behind her once more, then slowly made her way up.

She needed to get over this silly—crazy—attraction she had for her. She had known Kenni all of two weeks. And in another two weeks, she would leave this place and go back to the city and resume her *real* life. She would probably look back on this month and wonder why she'd ever been attracted to Kendall Lyon in the first place.

Of course, when she got back to her real life, she would also be back at her real job. How in the world was she going to write a hit piece about this? If she wrote an honest and true depiction of Lyon's Den Retreat, it would no doubt be glowing. She loved the place. She loved the staff. She loved the camaraderie. She loved the subtle messages that were sent. They weren't beaten over the head with lectures and counseling. Quite the opposite. Other than little nudges from Kenni now and then—like today after the rappelling exercise—they were left to figure out the lessons on their own. She loved it all.

So, how could she possibly write a hit piece about it?

CHAPTER THIRTY-ONE

Joni was disappointed that Kenni hadn't shown up for dinner. She leaned on the railing of the deck, thinking surely she'd come by on her walk. But as the minutes ticked by, she wondered if perhaps Kenni was avoiding her. But why? Because they'd kissed? No. Kenni was the one who had initiated that. Besides, it wasn't like she'd offered resistance. She'd wanted Kenni to kiss her, crazy as that was. Kenni was all wrong for her, and she had no business being attracted to her in the first place. Plus, she would be leaving in two weeks anyway. Why in the world would she want to become involved with her? Just to have sex?

She smiled at that thought. Well, it had been a while. The smile faded. It had been a long while, yes. So long, in fact, that she could possibly call herself celibate. She rolled her eyes, but it was the truth. She could have sex if she wanted to. It wasn't like she was abstaining for any particular reason.

She sighed. She didn't have sex because most of her dates were one and done and, as she'd told Kenni the other night, she was in a rut. A very long, deep rut. And the kiss last night told her that

Kenni could drag her out of that rut—and into bed—in a matter of seconds. Is that what she wanted?

"Yeah…pretty much," she admitted quietly.

She glanced at her watch. It was more than thirty minutes past Kenni's normal time to come over. She looked into the trees. Dare she venture over to Kenni's cabin?

* * *

Kenni sat on her porch steps, holding a mug of hot tea that she'd added honey to. Most nights up this high, the air would have a chill to it. But this evening, after a rather warm day, it was still pleasant enough for shorts.

She took a sip of tea, then placed the mug down beside her. Pulling her knees up to her chest, she wrapped her arms around them and rested her chin there. She was tired, but restless. She hadn't joined the others for dinner, taking a plate with her instead and eating here alone. And she'd intentionally skipped her evening walk. Why? Well, she knew why. She was avoiding being alone with Joni. Avoiding Joni.

It was the kiss. The kiss that made her want more. Much more. That hadn't happened to her in a very long time. Whether or not Joni would be receptive—and the look they'd shared on the deck earlier told her that she might be—she didn't think it was a very good idea to pursue it. Joni was only here for a couple more weeks. What would be the point of a very short-lived affair? It would serve no purpose other than to remind her of how lonely her life was.

In two weeks, this group—and Joni—would leave and another twenty ladies would take their place. September would follow and before long, the staff would pack up and they'd say their goodbyes. She'd be left here alone until the snows came. Surprisingly, she felt less lonely here by herself than during the summer months when the place was buzzing with activities. But the snow would soon push her down to Santa Fe. It was a familiar routine, but for some reason, the prospect of it all wasn't appealing. That's because her loneliness seemed to grow—not abate—over the winter months.

Every year it seemed to grow stronger. She usually dismissed it, wading through the last few weeks as time crawled by at a snail's pace. She admitted that it had been extremely tough last winter to keep depression at bay. She'd visited her grandmother more than usual, but even that didn't help much. It was a reminder that her grandmother had a full life that she enjoyed. She, on the other hand, was only going through the motions.

Maybe this would be the year that she stayed over the winter. She had the space at the lodge to stock up on food to last months. The large walk-in freezer held months' worth now as it was. She could easily have a load of firewood delivered. Would she chance staying here and being snowed in for a few months? Could she hide from her loneliness here? Did it really make a difference where she was?

She heard a twig snap, and she looked out into the darkness, seeing a shadowy figure in the trees. She wasn't really surprised. Joni had probably been waiting on the lodge deck for her, and she came looking when she didn't show. Didn't show for dinner and didn't show for her evening walk. Because she was avoiding her.

When Joni stepped out of the shadows, she couldn't avoid her any longer. There was just enough moonlight to make out her features. Her hair was messy and natural, evidence that she'd washed it and let it dry as it may. She was wearing baggy shorts and a sweatshirt, and she looked so relaxed and fresh and carefree that Kenni just wanted to embrace that, embrace her. She did no such thing, though. She sat there stupidly, waiting. Joni was the first to speak.

"Did you stay away on purpose?"

Should she answer truthfully or lie? She nodded. "You scare me…so I was avoiding you, yes."

Joni came closer, her voice still quiet. "I scare you?"

"Yes."

"Because you want to kiss me?"

Kenni smiled. "More than just kiss, Joni."

Joni was smiling too as she reached down and took her hand, pulling her to her feet. She went willingly, despite her reservations. The look in Joni's eyes gave her no choice. Still, she couldn't move closer. Her feet seemed to be glued to the ground. It was Joni who—still holding her hand—moved closer. So close that their bodies nearly touched. Their mouths were but inches apart, and she could hear her booming heartbeat, could feel each quick beat against her breasts, could feel her body trembling.

"I'm out of my mind," Joni murmured. "Because I want more too."

She didn't have time to reply. Joni moved the few inches that separated them, and she moaned as her mouth opened, meeting Joni's tongue in a torrid kiss. Should they stop? Should they talk?

No. Joni's hands had already snaked under her shirt and she found her hands doing the same.

"Can we go inside? Please?" Joni whispered against her mouth.

There were so many things she wanted to ask her. Her mind was twirling with a hundred thoughts bouncing around. But she pushed them all away. Because Joni wanted to go inside. Joni wanted more than a kiss. Joni's hands were cupping her breasts.

"God, I don't know what it is about you," Joni said against her mouth, "but you drive me crazy."

No, she was pretty sure it was Joni driving *her* crazy. She took her hands from under her shirt and led her up the steps and into her cabin. She didn't stop to consider what they were about to do. She went directly into her bedroom. The lamp was already on beside the bed. She dropped Joni's hand, intending to pull her sweatshirt off, but Joni's hands were already tugging at her own T-shirt. Shirts were removed and tossed aside without care. She hadn't put a bra on after her shower, and as usual, Joni wore none either.

They stared at each other for a long moment, then Joni smiled. "Part of me wants to go fast. And part of me wants to go really, really slow."

Kenni smiled too and took her hands, holding them down against her side as she leaned closer. "How about we do both?"

CHAPTER THIRTY-TWO

Joni was fairly certain she had been transported into the perfect paradise of Utopia. She was floating on a cloud of bliss as warm hands and a wet mouth rendered her powerless to even open her eyes. Oh, they'd gone fast, yes. She hardly remembered anything other than calling out to some higher deity as she'd climaxed. Her hand had been between Kenni's thighs at the time, and their orgasms had been almost simultaneous.

But now? Now she lay back, languishing in the slow burn as Kenni's tongue spun around her nipple. She wasn't sure if she was moaning or purring, and she simply didn't care which—she was enjoying Kenni's unhurried lovemaking too much.

"I'm melting," she murmured.

Kenni pulled away from her breast, lifting her head. "Does that mean you want me to hurry?"

"No. I love this. It's like…like you're painting me. Like your lips are…" She trailed off as Kenni's mouth kissed below her breast this time. She moaned deeply when Kenni's lips nibbled against her stomach, making her ache for more. Her hips automatically shifted, her thighs parting as Kenni nuzzled the hollow of her hip. She reached down, running her fingers through Kenni's hair, urging her lower.

She didn't know if it was the heat of the moment, but in that split second when Kenni's mouth moved over her and found her wetness, she couldn't recall a single lover that she'd had before who had made her writhe like this. Her hips arched up as her breath hissed from her mouth. Her clit was being devoured and she felt herself grasping the sheets as if afraid she'd fall into a dark abyss. The end came far too fast, and she actually felt herself convulsing from the pleasure of her orgasm. She knew her thighs were clamped tight around Kenni's head, but she couldn't seem to let go as Kenni drew the last gasp from her.

"Dear god," she murmured as she finally relaxed, releasing Kenni from the hold she'd had on her. "Damn, but you're good at that."

"You think so?"

She tried to open her eyes but couldn't. "I'm a pile of goo right now." She felt Kenni smile against her skin as she kissed along her side, up to her breast.

"Goo? Is that a good thing?"

Joni's eyes opened a fraction, and she found Kenni looking at her, a smile on her face. She smiled back and closed her eyes again. "I'm trying to think of something witty to say, but my brain is mush."

Kenni moved up beside her. "Let's rest for a minute."

She didn't want to rest. There were too many things she wanted to do still, but Kenni pulled the sheet over them, and she couldn't help but snuggle next to her. Yes, maybe they'd rest for a few minutes. Then she'd pick up where they'd left off. Then later, she'd sneak back to the lodge, and hopefully no one would have noticed her absence.

Now, though, she pressed close to Kenni, her face burrowed against her neck, her eyes still closed. She let her hand slide across Kenni's hip, lightly caressing her before stilling it again. She took a deep breath, feeling such contentment at that moment she hardly recognized it. When was the last time she'd felt this sense of peace after making love with someone?

Ever?

CHAPTER THIRTY-THREE

Joni moved through the yoga poses with ease, surprised she could now do them without thought. Because her mind was definitely *not* on yoga this morning. Mindy's voice drifted to the background as they transitioned to the Reverse Warrior pose.

She'd made it back to her room exactly fifteen seconds before the alarm shook the walls. She'd still been leaning against the door when it sounded, and she'd broken out into a fit of giggles at how close she'd been to being caught. She had quickly changed clothes and gone out into the hallway, mixing with the others as if nothing was out of the ordinary. No one seemed to notice that she was freshly showered. Or if they had, maybe they thought she'd gotten up early.

Oh, she'd gotten up early, all right. It had been close to four when she'd collapsed—completely spent—on Kenni's bed. She must have fallen asleep instantly because it seemed only seconds passed before Kenni woke her at five. She had moaned and complained and had adamantly refused to wake up.

"No. I can't move. You've ruined me."

"It's five. Time to get back to the lodge before someone misses you."

"No. I don't want to."

"Come on. Busy day today. New obstacle course."

Her eyes had opened, and she'd glared at her. "Are you serious? You expect me to run a damn obstacle course today? After getting no sleep?"

Kenni had smiled at her, then kissed her soundly. "Yes, I do. Let's shower."

She smiled now, letting scenes from their shower replay themselves in her mind. Yeah, it had positively been the best shower she'd ever had in her life. Then they had dressed, and Kenni had led them along the path to the lodge, daylight already showing in the sky. At 5:28, they'd tiptoed quietly into the lodge, both smiling with their shared secret. A quick kiss, then Kenni had motioned her up the stairs. She'd been breathless when she'd finally made the third floor, and she crept as silently as she could to her door…with only mere seconds to spare.

"Okay, ladies, That's it for this morning," Mindy announced. "There is no gym today. I think today's obstacle course will take the place of your gym session. Teams Four and Five, you have a hike with Kenni. The rest will go with Jenn. You'll meet up at the obstacle course before lunch. I will see you there."

"Why no gym?" Amy asked.

"The obstacle course has a lot of upper body work." Then Mindy smiled. "I'll be there to watch this one. It's my favorite of all the courses. It's so much fun."

What the hell did that mean? And what was that sneaky little smile on her face about? Well, they would find out soon enough. She was actually thankful to skip the gym. After her mostly sleepless night, a mindless hike would be welcome. A smile lit her face before she could stop it, however. Sleepless, yes, but she'd do it all over again. Why in the world had she ever thought that Kenni wasn't her type?

Sarah Beth came up beside her. "I heard from Britney, who heard from Sky, that the new obstacle course has a lot of new things to do. Like scary things."

She arched an eyebrow. "Scary things?"

"Yeah. Like some sort of swing on a roller track that you have to hang on to with your hands. Then there's a water tank or something that we have to swing over." Sarah Beth laughed. "I hope Kenni makes you go first again."

"I don't doubt that she will. I am her damn guinea pig, apparently."

Her heart jumped nervously into her throat when Kenni sauntered over to them. She was wearing her normal hiking shorts and boots, but this morning Joni let her gaze linger on those exposed legs, remembering them wrapped around her last night. She felt a flush on her face, and she pulled her eyes from her legs, traveling up her body instead, taking in the dark-blue T-shirt before landing on her face. Kenni was smiling at the group, not looking directly at her. She took that opportunity to let her gaze roam over her body again, remembering exactly what it looked like without clothes covering it. Yes, she remembered what Kenni's body looked like, how soft and smooth her skin was, how perfect her breasts were, how deliciously—

Sarah Beth elbowed her. "Told you so."

She blinked stupidly at her. "Huh?"

"The water thing."

She turned her focus back to Kenni, finally realizing that she'd been speaking.

"It'll be hard, I won't lie," Kenni was saying. "And most of you will not make it across the water. But don't worry. We have towels." She clapped her hands together. "Let's get started. Jenn, take your group on the upper trail. We'll take the one along the creek. Meet you at the obstacle course."

Team Four, as usual, took the lead behind Kenni. Joni absently started walking when the others did, but her focus was on Kenni, and she moved a little to her right to get a better view.

"I've been thinking about you and Kenni."

Joni jerked her head around, staring at Erin. "What about us?"

"You know, the gay thing."

She rolled her eyes. "Really?"

"Yes. I think you should make a play for her."

"A *play*?"

"Joni insists that Kenni is not her type," Christine chimed in. "I think they would be cute together."

"Oh, me too," Sarah Beth added.

She held her hands up. "Please stop. Kenni and I have...have become friends. That's it. Friends. Nothing else."

"Then why do you drool when you look at her?" Christine asked with a smirk.

"Oh, for god's sake, I do not drool!"

"You only have two weeks left," Erin continued. "If I were you, I'd—"

"Exactly! Two weeks. What could possibly happen in two weeks?"

"Well, I wasn't talking about a relationship or anything," Erin said. "I was just talking about sex."

"Me, too!" Christine said with a laugh.

"Oh my god! I will not talk about sex with you three married straight women! I will not!" she said with emphasis. Thankfully, no one commented, and they were quiet for the longest time. That is, until Sarah Beth spoke.

"What is it exactly that two women do together? I don't know a thing about gay sex."

Joni stared into the sky, knowing she wouldn't be too disappointed if a lightning bolt shot down and struck her right then. But no such luck.

"I mean, do you use, like, sex toys and stuff? Well, I guess you kinda have to since..."

Joni looked at Sarah Beth with both eyebrows raised. Sarah Beth looked back at her expectantly. There was no teasing expression on her face. It was completely serious, and she almost felt guilty for not indulging her questions with honest answers. Almost. Instead, she gave a forced, fake smile.

"Google it."

* * *

Joni stared at the cables that appeared to be hanging precariously from tree limbs. Then she slid her gaze to Kenni, giving her a "Don't you dare make me go first" look. The smile Kenni returned said that, yes, she *would* make her go first. She wanted to be annoyed with her, she really did. But their lovemaking was still too fresh in her mind, and she still had a bit of that sickly giddy feeling that she couldn't shake. Actually, she didn't want to shake it.

"Jenn will run through it first. This one is fairly short, so take your time. We'll probably practice three or four times before we do any challenges." Kenni moved into the middle of the course. "Some of the things you're already used to—the moving balance beams, the stumps." She pointed to a rope bridge that was only about four feet off the ground, secured between two large boulders. "The bridge is a little different because there are no planks to step on, so that'll be a bit more challenging."

"Get to the water already!" someone called from the back of the group.

Kenni laughed and walked over to a large, oblong-shaped tank that had been buried in the ground. The water glistened invitingly. Overhead were cables stretched taut between the trees.

"Here is your water obstacle." Kenni squatted down and dipped a hand inside, sloshing the water around. "It's three feet deep and twelve feet long." She stood back up. "It's a nice warm day. The water will be cool."

Most everyone laughed, knowing what she meant by that. Joni had no doubt that she'd be the first one to experience a dunking.

"Jenn will show you how it's done. Watch carefully." Then Kenni turned her gaze to her. "Joni? Want to be the first of the group to run it?"

"No."

Kenni smiled at her. "It'll be fun."

Joni pointed at the water tank. "I don't think falling into the water will be all that much fun."

"Sure, it will. Come over here with me. We'll watch Jenn run it, then I'll assist you as we go."

She felt Christine give her a push from behind, and she reluctantly moved forward. Kenni gave her a subtle wink which had absolutely no effect on her. *If we hadn't just slept together, I'd tell her to fuck off!* She gritted her teeth instead and gave a low growl. Kenni laughed quietly beside her.

"Thank you."

"I hate you."

"Really? I didn't get that impression last night." Kenni's voice lowered even more. "Or this morning in the shower."

Joni squared her shoulders. "I was obviously out of my mind."

"Okay, ladies," Jenn said as she stood ready to run. "I'll go slower than normal. This one kinda zigzags, and there are two parts to the overhead cable system. The first part is very short, and you'll use it to get over the pit, as we call it. Don't worry if you fall. It's padded with straw and rubber, like behind the walls when you jumped."

Joni watched as Jenn grabbed the familiar rope to get onto the stumps and then the moving log. Beyond that was a rope mesh thing that was about two feet off the ground. Jenn hit her knees, then crawled under the mesh on her belly to the other side. Once there, she got back up, then stepped onto a large rock. From there, she reached overhead and grabbed a black pipe that was attached to the track. She pushed off and sailed over the pit of death and dropped gracefully past it.

"I'm going to fall."

"Probably."

She glared at Kenni but said nothing.

Jenn was up on another boulder where the rope bridge was strung up. It swung wildly with her weight, and she found herself clutching Kenni's arm, sure Jenn was going to fall through. In four quick steps, she was on the other side and climbing off the rocks. More stumps and another moving log beam were next. Jenn climbed up to a small platform then and again took hold of the pipe that would supposedly carry her over the water. The track was a slight decline, and she pushed off the platform, again sailing easily over the water tank and landing with grace on the pile of straw beyond it. Jenn pumped her fist in victory, and everyone clapped.

"See? Easy," Kenni said to her.

"I'm not even going to reply to that," she said testily.

Kenni guided her over to the stumps, then turned to the others. "It's a nice, short course, but a little more challenging. This is a good test to see how much your strength has increased. I know we've only been in the gym a couple of weeks, but I can tell you're all getting stronger. However, conquering this course requires mental strength as well. I don't expect that many of you—if any— will make it through the first time. Or even the second. But that's not meant to discourage you. It's to motivate you."

"Let's go, Joni!" Sarah Beth yelled. "Prove her wrong!"

She nodded. "Okay. Let's go."

Kenni nodded too. "Remember, there's no rush. Just getting a feel for it."

Joni grabbed the rope and jumped up onto the first stump. She marveled at how easily she could maneuver them now. She moved to the log beam, holding her hands out to balance herself, then jumped down without using the rope. She paused at the mesh for only a second, then got down on the ground and crawled under it, feeling pine needles and rocks scraping her arms and legs as she moved. Though it was only about five feet long, she rolled to her back when she made it out and stared up into the sky.

Then Kenni stood over her. "Problem?"

"No. Resting." Then she smiled. "I didn't get much sleep last night."

"No?"

"Not that I remember." Kenni held her hand out, and Joni took it, letting herself be pulled up. She met Kenni's gaze. "Did you sleep much?"

Kenni smiled, then laughed. "Not that I remember."

She let go of her hand. "Okay...the death pit is next."

Kenni moved with her to the rocks. "Grab the bar. Hold on tight."

Joni reached up and took the bar. It wasn't a pipe but hard plastic. "Now what?"

"Push off and try to make it across the pit."

She took a deep breath. She could do this. It wasn't that far. She counted silently to three, then pushed off. She screamed when, not even halfway across, her hands lost their grip and she plunged down into the pit. She screamed again as she sunk down several feet below ground. Yes, indeed it was a death pit.

Kenni stood looking down on her. "You okay?"

"I keep wishing I knew some karate moves or something."

"Why's that?"

"So that when I get out of here, I could kick your ass!"

Kenni laughed. "I've fallen here before. It doesn't hurt in the least."

"No, but it scared the crap out of me. You could have warned me it was two feet deep." She held her hand up, silently asking for assistance. Kenni took it and pulled her out. She looked over to the group of women who were watching them. Some were smiling and some looked frightened. She gave a thumbs-up. "I'm okay," she called to them.

"Want to try it again?"

"No. I need to save my strength for the goddamn water thing."

"Okay. On to the bridge."

The bridge was harder than it looked, and it took her some time to get her bearings, walking gingerly across the rope so as not to slip through it. It wasn't as long as the bridges on the other two courses, and she hopped down from the boulder easily when she made it across.

She went to the remaining stumps and log beam, passing over those obstacles with ease. Then she stopped, staring up at the platform and cable, then looking over at the enormous water tank. There was no way she'd be able to hold herself long enough to make it across. No way.

"This one will actually be easier since you'll be going downhill."

Joni looked at her blankly. "What the hell is the purpose of this stupid thing?"

"The purpose?"

"Yeah. What lesson are we supposed to learn today?"

"Maybe it's simply a test of your strength."

"I'm going to fail that test then."

Kenni nodded. "Yes. If you think you'll fail, you will. That's why I said it's as much mental as physical. You have to believe you can make it rather than believe you'll fall into the water."

"Yes, that's all well and good, but I'm not strong enough. I know I'm not. I couldn't make it over the little pit thing. I know I won't make it over thirty feet or whatever it is."

Kenni stared into her eyes, then nodded. "Richard Bach described your thinking perfectly. 'Argue for your limitations and, sure enough, they're yours.'"

Joni swallowed, then nodded. "I'm being negative and self-doubting."

"Yes. And remember, if you fail this time, it doesn't mean that you'll fail the next time. It's only when you stop trying that you fail for good."

"You're right. I hate it, but yes, you're right." She offered a small smile. "I hope I don't drown."

"Fear not! I'll do mouth-to-mouth resuscitation," Kenni said with a wink.

Kenni stepped back and Joni gripped the bar, reminding herself to hold on to it much tighter than she did when going over the pit. She looked around, seeing all eyes on her. She squared her shoulders and took a deep breath. As before, she counted to three, then pushed off.

And as before, her hands couldn't hold her, and she felt herself slipping. "Oh god!"

The cold water was a shock to her system, and she came up sputtering, her arms waving wildly as she tried to stand.

"You did great!"

She stared at Kenni, then took a swing at her. Kenni deftly stepped out of her reach.

"Look. You almost made it," Kenni said reasonably. "Another three or four feet and you would have cleared the water."

"I can't believe I slept with you," she muttered as she climbed out of the water. "What in the hell was I thinking?"

"Well…you said that I drive you crazy. Remember?"

"And that is certainly not a lie." She wiped the water from her face, then grabbed Kenni's arm, playfully threatening to push her into the water.

She heard the others laughing as Kenni easily sidestepped her, almost causing her to fall in again. Kenni pulled her out of harm's way, her smiling eyes making her knees weak. She forgot all about how soaked she was as that now familiar "melting" feeling overtook her. *Damn the woman.*

Jenn tossed a towel at her, and she dried her face and hair. Her boots were waterlogged, and they squished as she walked back over to the others.

"How was the water?" Christine asked.

"Oh, I guess you'll find out soon enough," she said.

"Do you think we'll all fall in?"

"I'm going to say yes."

Kenni came over to them. "Okay, who wants to go next?"

There were no volunteers. Not even from Team Four.

"Anyone? Come on now. If Joni can do it…everyone can do it. How about…Anna?"

Joni heard murmurings from the others, then Anna came out of the group. "Okay. I'll go."

Everyone was watching intently as Anna started the course. Joni moved away a bit, going to stand fully in the sunshine, hoping to dry her clothes a little. She didn't know why. Kenni had already said they'd run it twice. She had a good view, and she was holding her breath as Anna went over the death pit. Unlike her, Anna made it to the other side without falling, and she grudgingly cheered along with the others. She was happy to see that it took Anna much longer to cross the rope bridge than her, though. Kenni was going along with her, offering encouragement. At the platform, Anna grabbed the rubber pipe and hardly hesitated at all before pushing off. She had been overconfident, however, and she plunged into the water barely three feet into her ride. Joni nodded to herself. *Yeah, not so damn easy, is it?*

By the time everyone had run through the course once—and every single one of them had taken a dunking—Kenni called a halt to the activity. A glance at her watch told her it was almost noon already.

"That took longer than I thought," Kenni said. "We'll run it again tomorrow. But now, I'm guessing you're ready to get out of those wet clothes."

"I'm almost dry already," Marsha said.

Joni nodded. Yes, so was she.

"Well, we'll have a short day. After lunch, we have only two activities. We're going to climb the big tree again. Then we'll go back to the very first obstacle course and see how many of you can beat your best time. Winning team gets ice cream after dinner. The rest of you will have free time. The sauna and hot tub would be my choice."

The smartasses from Team Four cheered. "I hope it's chocolate!" Amy said. "That's my favorite! The rest of you have fun in the sauna!"

Joni looked at Christine. "We're going to kick their ass."

CHAPTER THIRTY-FOUR

Joni was so excited to have ice cream that she had two huge bowls of it—one was chocolate with nuts and the other plain vanilla. Team Five had crushed it on the obstacle course, and while she didn't want to brag—well, not much—she had been flying over the course and had even passed up Erin at the mesh wall. She had been the one urging Christine to hurry, and Christine had sailed over the wall without even pausing at the top. They beat Team Four by a whopping thirteen seconds.

And now, while her team and some of the others were in the dining hall playing board games and visiting, she was sneaking out onto the deck. It was still early, not yet eight. She heard voices from around the corner and found three women sitting on the steps, chatting. Damn. She went in the opposite direction, around the side to where Kenni had taken her out to the sitting area. The place where they'd first kissed.

She was sneaking because she and Kenni had a secret date tonight. Well, not really a date, no. She was sneaking over to have sex. Again. She wasn't sure how she felt about that. Granted, last night was fabulous, but what were they doing? And why?

She rolled her eyes. *Why? Because you're crazy attracted to her. Duh.*

She wasn't going to go down that road again to try to figure out why. There was just something about the woman that, well, made her melt. Who was she to deny it? No, she wanted to bask in it.

When she got to the small stream, she could see the lights from Kenni's cabin. With athleticism she didn't possess two weeks ago, she easily hopped across the water. She was fitter, more agile, and certainly more flexible. She'd noticed that last night in bed. She smiled then as she hurried up the steps.

She didn't need to knock. Kenni was waiting for her.

"You're late."

"I had to sneak around and take the long way." She handed Kenni the small flashlight that she'd given her earlier. "Thanks for that."

Kenni raised an eyebrow. "How much ice cream did you eat?"

She laughed. "Two bowls. If I hadn't had plans with you, I might have had three."

Kenni took her hand and led her toward the sofa, not the bedroom. It was her turn to raise an eyebrow.

"I thought maybe we should talk or something," Kenni explained.

"Talk?"

"No?"

"No." She moved closer and wrapped her arms around Kenni's shoulders. "No talk. Kiss."

Kenni obliged, a long, lingering, heated kiss that made her head spin. And right on cue, she felt herself melting. Oh, what a glorious feeling that was. It was with weak knees that she went into the bedroom with Kenni. She fell onto the bed, pulling Kenni down with her.

"You drive me crazy."

"Is that a good thing?"

She didn't mind that they were both still clothed. She spread her thighs, and Kenni settled between them. Their kiss was hot and wet and mostly tongues, and it simply drove her mad. She arched her hips up, feeling Kenni press hard against her.

Yes, it was a good kind of crazy.

CHAPTER THIRTY-FIVE

Kenni leaned against the tree, still holding Joni in her arms. They had ten minutes before the 5:30 alarm.

"I love the way you kiss," Joni murmured against her mouth. "You have the softest lips."

"When you run the obstacle course today, will you say you can't believe we slept together again?"

Joni pulled back and smiled at her. "I wanted to push you into the water."

"I know. You had that evil glint in your beautiful eyes."

"Do you think my eyes are beautiful?"

"I think everything about you is beautiful."

Joni closed her eyes and leaned closer, kissing her with a smoldering passion that made her want to get impossibly close to her. She pulled her as tight as she dared.

"God, I could make love with you again," Joni whispered. "Right here."

"No time."

"If we get caught, we could say we were out grounding or earthing or whatever you call it."

"Why are we trying so hard to hide this?"

Joni frowned at her. "I didn't think you wanted anyone to know."

She shrugged. "I didn't want any of the others to think I was playing favorites or anything."

Joni laughed. "You make me go first every damn time! How is that playing favorites? Besides, my team keeps telling me that I should make a play for you. Even though Sarah Beth has no clue about two women having sex." She laughed. "She wanted me to explain it to her. I told her to Google it!"

Kenni laughed. "God, I'm glad I wasn't there for *that* conversation."

Joni pulled out of her arms. "I guess I should go in. I had a lovely night, Kenni. Thank you."

"Me, too."

"See you at breakfast?"

"Yep."

Joni turned to leave, then came back quickly, kissing her once again. And once again, she pulled Joni tight against her, feeling a surge of…of *something* as she drew out the kiss. When Joni turned this time, she didn't stop and Kenni watched her leave, staying until she went inside the back door. Then she let out a heavy breath and stared up into the morning sky.

What was it that she felt when she was with Joni? She was afraid to name it, afraid to examine it. Afraid to think that it was anything other than an uncontrollable lust. One thing was for certain, though. Joni made her feel alive. And that wasn't something she'd felt in a very long time.

CHAPTER THIRTY-SIX

The ringing of her phone startled her. She had come up to her room to change before lunch. The scavenger hunt had taken them to the stream today, and she'd slipped in. Her boots weren't overly wet, but she wanted dry socks. Of course, this would be the third day in a row for them to run the obstacle course. Since she had yet to master sailing over the water, she thought she might as well have left her wet socks on; she was sure to take a dunking again.

She went over to the small dresser where her phone now lived. Most days she forgot she even had a phone. She hadn't spoken to Kimberly in a while, and she assumed it would be her. But no. Her eyes widened in surprise, and she briefly contemplated not answering.

"Mr. Turnbull. What a surprise," she managed.

"Joni? Where the hell are you?"

She drew her brows together. "Umm…stuck in a lodge out in the middle of nowhere. Remember?"

"You haven't checked in. I was worried about you."

"I'm sorry. I didn't think you expected me to call."

"How's the article coming along?"

She bit her lip. "I've…I've got an outline," she lied. "But really, there is very little downtime. The hall alarm goes off at 5:30 each morning and it's go, go, go all day until, well, bedtime and then I'm exhausted." *Especially this last week*, she added silently.

"When do you leave there?"

Her shoulders sagged. "Ten more days."

"Well, I'll need your article the week after you get back. I want to publish it in this month's online edition. And in the quarterly print publication in September, of course."

"Okay, sure. But…" She hesitated. "There's really not a man-bashing thing going on here. You know, like you assumed. In fact, none at all. Nothing like that."

"I really don't care, Joni. I just need the article. And I can't wait to send it personally to this Lyon woman. I'm living in a goddamn apartment. Charlotte kicked me out of the house. Can you believe that?"

"Well, you said she was filing for divorce. I wouldn't imagine you would still live together."

"She won't try to work it out. She won't see a marriage counselor. It's like she went to that place, and she got brainwashed or something."

"I'm sorry." *Was that the right thing to say?* "But do you think doing a hit piece is going to make it better?"

"It will make me feel better. And perhaps she'll lose some business. Perhaps some other woman won't be subjected to whatever the hell they do there."

She looked up to the ceiling, then blurted out, "I don't think I can write a hit piece."

"*What?* But you *hate* the woods. You said so yourself. You were loathing this assignment. You threatened to quit your job!" he said loudly.

"I know, but—"

"No. I don't want to hear any buts. I want you to trash the place. When you get back, you have one week!"

There was nothing but silence, and she put her phone down. Then she picked it up again. Kimberly answered immediately.

"Hey, stranger!"

"Hey, Kim. You got a minute?"

"A quick minute. I've got a lunch date. A *real* lunch date."

"Oh, yeah? Who with?"

"His name is Aaron. I met him at happy hour yesterday."

"Great. I can't wait to hear about him." She took a deep breath. "So, you know that I love it here, right?"

"Yes, you've been body snatched."

She smiled. "Well, I failed to tell you—because you'll think I'm crazy—but Kenni and I have been, well, seeing each other."

"Seeing each other?"

"Having sex."

"Oh my god! Why haven't you told me?"

"I was embarrassed. But I'm not anymore because she's fantastic and I really like her. I mean, I hated her at first. Well, not hate, but you know what I mean."

"So, you're having a little summer fling with the camp counselor! How fun!"

"Right. And I cannot, in good conscience, write a hit piece. It would not be true."

"So don't."

"Turnbull just called me. He expects the article when I get back." She sat down on her bed. "What am I going to do?"

"Did he threaten to fire you?"

"Not exactly. But he wasn't happy with me."

"Then write the article truthfully and give it to him."

"But he wants a hit piece!"

"Isn't that illegal?"

"No. The article would be my opinion based on my experience here, even if I lied and trashed the place. It's only my opinion. You know, I could say they have you climb fucking trees without safety gear or they throw you off a cliff without rappelling lessons. Both are technically true."

"You said the rappelling thing was a farce."

"It was. But I didn't know it at the time, and it scared the shit out of me. Anyway, that's not the point. I could write things like that and turn it into a hit piece. It would be easy." She lay back on the bed and stared at the ceiling. "But I don't want to. I can't. Because it's not like that."

"Then write it truthfully. If he gets pissed, he gets pissed. I'm sorry, Joni, but I've really got to run. Call me tonight if you want to talk some more."

She smiled. "Yeah, I haven't really been sleeping here at the lodge. I sneak back in before the alarm goes off each morning. It makes me feel really naughty."

"I'm glad you're having fun. I look forward to hearing all about it. Can't wait to see you again."

"You, too. Have fun at lunch."

She rolled to her side on the bed, her eyes closed. What was she going to do? Would he actually fire her if she refused to write the article like he wanted? She opened her eyes. Maybe he *would* fire her. Then she would have no excuse for not moving back to the East Coast. It was something she probably should have done years ago.

She sat up with a sigh. Yes. Then why hadn't she? She'd been in Denver eight years already. She barely kept up with any of her old friends from New York. Why would she move back? Well, it wasn't like she'd embraced living in Denver. Or Colorado, for that matter. Still, she never seriously contemplated moving. She liked her job, and she liked her friends.

Yet here she was, probably going to get fired from that job. She wondered if she and Kenni had not become involved, would she still be opposed to writing the hit piece? She'd like to think so, yes.

She got up. She couldn't contemplate all that now. She would be late for lunch if she didn't hurry. And afterward, they'd tackle the obstacle course again. And maybe this time, she'd make it over the damn water tank.

CHAPTER THIRTY-SEVEN

Joni walked with her team to the obstacle course, absently listening as Sarah Beth and Erin discussed hair color. While Erin's nearly black hair was grating at first, she was used to it now. She was surprised, then, when Erin announced that she was going to cut it off very short when she got back home and would allow her now-natural gray to show.

"I started coloring my hair when I spotted my first gray strand. I freaked out. I think I was thirty-one at the time," Erin said.

"Is this your natural color?" Joni asked, knowing full well it was not.

"Of course not. But the last four years or so, this is the only color that will cover the damn gray up. I even tried going blond once and I looked hideous."

"Why cut it?" Christine asked. "I mean, I think I really am going to cut mine, but yours is already kinda short."

"No, I mean *really* short. Like take it all off. I think it'll be cleansing," Erin said. "Then I'll let the gray grow out and decide on a style then." She laughed. "Besides, that'll *really* piss off my husband." Her smile faded as quickly. "He probably wouldn't even notice. His mistress is quite attractive."

"I'd divorce his ass," Christine said. She fingered her own hair. "Maybe I should do the same. I think it *would* be cleansing."

"I'm not cutting mine!" Sarah Beth said with a laugh. "My face is way too round to go any shorter than I am."

They all turned to look at her then. Joni stared back at them, shaking her head. "No. I'm not cutting mine either."

"I bet Kenni would like it short."

"Like I care what she would prefer," she said as dryly as she could manage.

Christine laughed. "Joni, Joni, Joni. Do you really think we don't know that you've been sneaking back to your room in the mornings?"

She was certain her face turned bright red, and she couldn't even muster up a protest. "You do?"

"We do. I was in the bathroom yesterday morning when you came slinking by. And I also saw you this morning too."

"Damn."

"Oh, I think it's wonderful. You two make a cute couple. And the sex must agree with you. You haven't been quite as noxious as before."

Again, she felt a hot blush on her face, but she feigned indignation. "Noxious?"

"Well, your language, at least."

Sarah Beth moved closer to her. "So, what is it that you do?"

"Oh my god! This again? No!"

Sarah Beth laughed. "Just teasing. Christine explained it to me."

"Oh, my god," she muttered. She held her hand up. "Just... don't. Just don't...*ever*!"

They were all still laughing quietly when they got to the obstacle course. Joni looked at Christine and gave her the best glare she could manage. Christine smiled and blew her a kiss, deflating whatever anger she'd tried to amass.

"Okay, ladies. We're still not going to do a timed run, so there is no competition in that regard. However, if some of you make it across the water—and we hope that you do today—then whichever team has the most success gets the win."

"That leaves us out," Erin said quietly.

"I don't know, Joni was pretty close yesterday," Sarah Beth said.

"So were a couple from Team Four," Joni reminded them. She gathered them all together in a circle. "You just have to concentrate. Mind over matter. Don't let go of that fucking bar until you get across the water!" *Good god, I'm giving a pep talk!* "We can do this!"

"You want to run it in teams or stagger everyone?" Kenni asked the group.

"Make Joni go first!" someone called.

Joni narrowed her eyes. "Who said that?" she asked Christine quietly.

"I think it was Britney. Team Four."

"God, I hate them."

"Joni? Want to go first?" Kenni asked.

"Want to or *have* to?" she countered.

Kenni smiled at her. "Come on. If you make it across, then you put the pressure on everyone else."

"Yeah, right."

But she went forward, making the mistake of looking into Kenni's dark eyes. God, but the look there almost made her swoon. She quickly grabbed the rope hanging over the stumps. Who knew having really good sex would turn her into a big mushball?

Kenni gave her a subtle wink. "You ready?"

Joni nodded. "I'm going to make it across today."

"That's too bad," she said quietly. "Because I love the wet T-shirt look you've had."

Joni stared at her. "You did not just say that."

"I did." Then she stepped away from her. "Okay, let her rip."

Joni shook herself, trying to get her concentration back. She'd gotten quite good with the stumps and the moving balance beams. So good, in fact, that she didn't really need the rope for guidance any longer. She scampered across both obstacles without incident then crawled under the mesh in record time. When she got to the death pit, she didn't even pause to think about it. She simply grabbed the bar and sailed over it, landing gracefully beyond it. She didn't stop to congratulate herself. She went on to the rope bridge, slowing a bit so that she wouldn't miss a step and lose her footing.

But then the water loomed. It was rippling gently from the breeze, and she only gave it a quick glance. Kenni came up beside her as she was about to climb on the platform.

"You can do this. You can fucking do this!"

Joni grinned. "Yeah. I can fucking do this!"

She squeezed the bar so tightly her knuckles were turning white. She took a deep breath, then pushed off. *Hold on! Hold on!* She felt her hands loosening. *Don't you fucking let go!* It felt like minutes passed instead of seconds. She could see the water below her and it seemed to be getting closer. But no! The ground was getting closer, and she heard the enthusiastic yells and cheers from the group as her feet landed, not in the water, but on the straw that was placed around the water tank. She had a good six inches to spare!

"You did it!"

"Oh my god! I fucking did it!" she yelled excitedly. Without thinking, she flung herself into Kenni's arms, unmindful of the others as she kissed her. "I did it!"

Kenni, too, seemed to forget where they were. She pulled her into a tight hug, then returned her kiss. "Way to go!"

Their eyes held, then they separated. She wondered if she looked as embarrassed as Kenni did.

"All right! Joni made it across on her first try." She clapped several times. "Great job! Who wants to go next?"

"Are we all going to be kissing like that if we make it across?" Christine asked, causing all the others to laugh heartily.

Kenni sported a blush, and Joni narrowed her eyes at Christine. "No. You may not kiss her." This caused everyone to laugh again.

"No kissing," Kenni said, seeming to have recovered. "Joni was just overcome with excitement, I guess."

"What was your excuse?" Joni shot back.

Kenni laughed good-naturedly, then pointed at the group. "Marsha. Give it a try."

Joni moved away from the others and sat down, leaning against a ponderosa pine. She took a deep breath, allowing herself some time to reflect on what had happened. She was proud of herself, yes. It was indeed mind over matter, because she knew she wasn't really strong enough to hold her bodyweight for that long. So yes, she was proud. Probably the proudest she'd ever been of herself. She looked up into the sky, not sure how that made her feel. Did she feel happy or sad? Hell, what did that say about her life thus far if running a damn obstacle course—and succeeding—was her proudest moment?

She realized she was still smiling, though, so no, she didn't feel sad. She *did* feel happy. She turned her attention to the others, watching as they ran the course. This time, she was actually— genuinely—rooting for them to make it across the water too. Even Team Four. She wanted all the others to feel as good about themselves as she did right now. She felt like she'd accomplished something, and she wanted them to have that too.

She shook her head but continued to smile.

My god, what is wrong with you?

CHAPTER THIRTY-EIGHT

Kenni ran her fingers lazily across Joni's stomach, then higher, caressing her breasts. Joni had claimed her breasts were nonexistent, and yes, they were small. But she'd found they were very sensitive. She gently touched a nipple, hearing Joni nearly purr with pleasure.

"You drive me crazy."

Kenni smiled. "Still?"

Joni opened her eyes. "I'm sorry I kissed you in front of the others."

Kenni shook her head. "I was as excited as you were."

Joni rolled to her side, leaning up on an elbow. "Can you believe only four of us made it across the water?" Joni laughed. "And Sarah Beth? Who in the hell would have thought she'd make it!"

"It was a good day, huh?"

Joni nodded. "It was a great day." She lay back down and sighed. "But I need to talk to you."

Kenni stilled her hand. "Okay."

Joni entwined their fingers and squeezed them slightly. "You know why I'm here, right?"

"Oh, yeah. You're doing an article on the place."

"Yes."

Joni seemed very nervous, and she wasn't sure what to make of it. She leaned over and kissed her, then propped up against the pillows. "What's wrong?"

Joni scooted up higher too, leaning next to her, their bare shoulders touching. "Do you remember Charlotte Turnbull?"

She frowned. "Charlotte?"

"She was in your September group last year."

Kenni nodded. "Okay, yeah. Charlotte. Yes, I remember her."

"She's my boss's wife."

"Okay. And?"

Joni turned toward her and looped an arm across her stomach. "And when she got back from here, she was different, and she eventually filed for divorce."

Kenni nodded. "I seem to remember her being very unhappy in her marriage. I'm not surprised, I guess."

Joni sighed. "Yeah. And that's the problem."

"What do you mean?"

Joni chewed on her lower lip nervously, then finally looked up and met her eyes. "I...I have a confession to make."

She nodded. "Okay."

Another sigh. "Well, my boss is obviously upset about the divorce and all. He blames you for it."

"Me?"

"Yes. And he gave me this assignment because he knows I hate the woods, the outdoors. He knew I would hate it here." Joni squeezed her hand. "And he wants me to write, well, basically a hit piece."

Kenni stared at her, trying to read her eyes. "I see. And sleeping with me is...what? Research?"

"No! That has nothing to do with it." Joni sat up. "Even if we weren't sleeping together, I still wouldn't write a hit piece. I can't. Because everything you intended this place to be...it is. I told you once that I hadn't changed. That when I left here, I would go back to who I was. And at the time, I think I believed that."

"And now?"

Joni met her gaze. "I'm different. I'm not the same person I was when I got here. And in three short weeks, I've changed. I…I love the stuff we do now. I love hiking and being outdoors. I love the challenges and the freaking obstacle courses. I love being a part of a team. All things I thought I would hate. And I'll admit, when I first got here, I *did* hate it all. You stole my wine! I thought it would be easy to write the hit piece that he wanted." She smiled. "My plan was to hang out a few days, write the article, and escape."

"So why didn't you?"

Joni laughed. "For one thing, you had us doing all these crazy things from dawn to dusk, there wasn't time. Not to mention I was exhausted each evening." Her smile faded. "Okay. So, tell me what you're thinking."

Kenni shrugged. "I don't know, really. I had actually forgotten the reason you were here."

"To be honest, so did I."

"Why are you telling me this?"

"Because he called me today. I told him that I loved it here. I told him I couldn't do the article that he wanted." Joni gave a heavy sigh. "I'm probably going to lose my job, but I'm going to write an honest article. Of course, I doubt he would publish it if it's positive." She curled back down beside her. "I wanted to tell you because I was feeling guilty. And maybe if we hadn't become friends and hadn't been getting naked together, I wouldn't have told you. But regardless of our relationship, I still wouldn't have written a hit piece."

"I don't guess it matters. You wouldn't be the first person to write one."

"Yes, you told me. I don't understand why. Everything about your program is so positive. I mean, when you really listen to the others talk, you can hear—see—the changes in them. Sarah Beth was depressed when she got here, hating her life. Now?" Joni laughed. "Did you *see* the dance she was doing when she cleared the water?"

"Yeah, she was quite excited. But this place isn't for everyone. Even all the women here now, there are probably three or four of them who don't get the concept of what we're teaching, and they are most likely wondering why the hell they're here."

"I guess since you don't have counseling sessions and the like, I can see why someone might think this is a weight loss clinic or something." Joni sat up quickly. "I've lost six pounds! Darla says my muscle mass has increased too." She then flexed her arms, showing off her biceps. "Look! You can actually see a muscle there!"

Kenni smiled affectionately at her, then leaned closer to kiss her. "Impressive."

Joni smiled against her lips, then drew out the kiss a little longer. "Enough talking. Time is short."

Yes, indeed. A little over a week left, then Joni would leave with the others. The joy she'd felt this month would fade, no doubt. Flying away as if it had never been there. Then she'd be alone again, forced to put on a happy face for the next group of ladies who would come through her door. Unfortunately, there wouldn't be another Joni James in the bunch.

CHAPTER THIRTY-NINE

"Tell me something about yourself," Joni requested. They were on a hike down to Mirror Lake, and she and Kenni were walking together at the back of the group.

"Let's see." Kenni seemed to be thoroughly considering the question. "I was a fat kid."

"Fat?"

"Yep. Really fat. And I was bullied."

"Oh, no," she said, squeezing her arm. "That's awful."

Kenni shrugged. "Happens to a lot of people."

"Well, you're obviously not overweight now. What happened?"

"My mother put me on a diet." She laughed. "Everyone in the family was on a diet then, because she threw out everything that had sugar in it. She stopped making starches. No potatoes, rice, pasta. Just veggies and protein."

"Is that why you do that here?"

"It had some influence, yes. I was a carb and sugar addict, I'll admit. That's why I avoid those things now. But when we started this, I wanted to be able to change our clients' body compositions and removing carbs is the fastest way."

"So, you lost weight and were no longer bullied?"

"I was a bit of an introvert anyway, so I didn't mind not having a lot of friends. When I was suddenly a normal size, yeah, some of the same ones who made fun of me wanted to be friends then."

"I hope you told them to kiss your ass!"

Kenni laughed. "Not in so many words. Now, tell me something about you."

"I don't have anything as dramatic as that." She thought back over all her quirks and habits, trying to decide which one to share. "You already know I cuss like a sailor, and I love wine."

"Do you still miss it?"

She sighed. "A little, yes. Probably more from habit. You know, get home from work, pour a glass of wine, relax. The first few nights here, I thought how nice it would have been to be able to sit on the deck and watch the stars and sip wine." She held her hand up. "Anyway, I love Hallmark Christmas movies. Like I'm addicted to them. Actually, I like all Hallmark movies, as cheesy as they are."

"Really? I would have never guessed."

"I know. I don't seem like I'm that romantic, do I? But I love them. They give me the warm fuzzies."

"Okay, I can picture you curled in the corner of your sofa, a blanket over you, a glass of wine, all the lights out...watching a romantic Christmas movie."

Joni turned to look at her, then bumped her shoulder playfully. "Perfect. Except you forgot my Christmas tree with its blinking lights."

Yes, that was the scene on many a night, wasn't it? Only thinking about those nights now made her lonely. She leaned closer to Kenni again.

"Are you sick of me coming over every night?"

Kenni looked at her and smiled. "I was kinda hoping you'd come over every night until you leave."

"Good. I was kinda hoping the same thing."

CHAPTER FORTY

Kenni sat on one of the benches on the gym deck. All of the women were milling about, waiting their turn to get weighed and measured. Both Jenn and Mindy were helping Karla, so it was going fairly quickly. This was the last full day. Tomorrow, after breakfast, she would give her final speech to everyone, then they would do a formal checkout and a survey, then the ladies would begin leaving, back to their lives and families.

As she'd told Joni the other night, it wasn't for everyone. She could pick out the ones who were only going through the motions. Inevitably, those women were on the losing teams. Team Five and Team Four, since the beginning, had been fighting for the top spot. And all four women on each team seemed to be invested wholly in their mission. She smiled, thinking of Joni's words last night. "I want to kick their ass tomorrow!" Team Five had a one-win advantage over Team Four. They would run the obstacle course this afternoon. If Team Four won, then they'd be tied and she would have to come up with another challenge to break the tie. At this point, it was only for bragging rights as all of the perks for winning each day had been doled out. Of course, if Team Four won, she would owe Jenn an additional thousand bucks.

Her smile faded. Yes, everyone would leave tomorrow. Joni would leave tomorrow, too. They had stopped trying to be discreet about their affair. Everyone already knew, so she didn't see the point. They showed up together at six each morning for breakfast, and Joni went with her each evening after dinner. While they didn't talk about Joni's impending departure, she knew it was foremost on both their minds. She thought—

"You daydreaming?"

She turned, finding Sky watching her. She smiled at her and nodded. "I guess."

Sky came over and sat down beside her. "This was a good group. Most everyone was engaged."

"Yes. I can think of only a couple who probably wished they'd never come."

Sky nudged her. "You seem to have had an exceptionally good time."

She laughed. "Is that what we're calling it?"

Sky smiled. "I like Joni. She's been good for you."

"You think so?"

"Yes. Loosened you up, that's for sure. I think it's been good for all of us to mix up our routine like we did. I've known you a lot of years now, and this was the most spontaneous you've ever been."

"I know. You're probably right. We should mix things up more. Even though we didn't stick to my normally rigid schedule, things still ran smoothly."

"Well, we did get off schedule. You never did make it to the fourth obstacle course."

"That was intentional. I still had three ladies who couldn't make it over the water. I didn't want to shake their confidence by attempting something even harder. And I think you were probably right. We should have made the water tank only ten feet long instead of twelve. I think I'm going to try to modify that by next year."

"I don't know. It's pretty exciting to see them make it across. Ten might not be enough of a challenge."

Joni came out of the gym, a big smile on her face. "Guess what? I have officially lost eight pounds of body fat and gained four pounds of muscle!" She lifted up her T-shirt, exposing her belly. "And I've lost an inch and a half off my waist!"

"Great job!" Sky said as she stood. "I guess I should see if they need help."

"Will we have a scavenger hunt before lunch?" Joni asked Sky.

"Not today, no. Yesterday was the last one."

Joni looked disappointed. "They were fun. And I can now identify like five different pinecones," she said with a laugh.

"You probably thought they were fun because your team won all of them this week!"

Sky walked off and Joni took her spot on the bench. She bumped her shoulder affectionately. "Whatcha doing?"

"Just hanging out." She met her eyes. "Thinking."

Joni sighed. "About me leaving?"

"Yes. I'm going to miss you."

Joni nodded. "I know. I'm going to miss you, too. I'm going to miss a lot of things, but I'll especially miss you."

"Going to miss climbing trees?"

"Yes. And hiking. And running the obstacle courses." She pressed against her shoulder harder. "Making love." Joni turned to face her. "You know, we could maybe try to get together sometime."

"I won't have a day off until October," Kenni reminded her.

"God, that's two months."

"Yeah, but maybe we could plan a date for early October."

"A date?"

"Yeah. Maybe I'll pop up to Denver. You can take me out to dinner or something."

Joni frowned at her. "What about Santa Fe?"

"I've been mulling over the idea of staying up here for the winter."

"Up here? Won't you get snowed in or something?"

She nodded. "Yes. The road to Tin Cup will be impassable by January. It depends on the weather and spring storms, of course, but my Jeep might make it down from here by mid-to late-March."

Joni studied her. "Why stay here? Alone."

She held her gaze. "I think I'd rather be here alone than to be in Santa Fe alone. This at least feels like home."

"You told me once that you didn't like to be alone."

"I don't. But I'm quite used to it."

The deck was filling up and there was chatter all around them. This discussion wasn't something she wanted to have here. Joni seemed to sense that as well.

"I can see it now. By February you'll be stark raving mad and will spend your time designing out-of-this-world tortures for the obstacle courses," Joni teased. "Pity the first group of women who come next year!"

CHAPTER FORTY-ONE

Joni didn't want to take the time for talking or sleeping, but she couldn't keep her eyes open any longer. She finally rolled away from Kenni with a contented sigh.

"I think you're the best kisser ever," she murmured. "Like I could just kiss you for hours."

"I think you did."

Joni smiled. "I think I've had more sex in these last two weeks then I've had in my entire life."

Kenni laughed quietly. "I guess I could say the same."

Joni opened her eyes, finding Kenni watching her. "Are you really going to stay here alone this winter?"

"I don't know for sure. I have a couple of months to make up my mind."

"But what'll you do?"

Kenni propped up the pillow and lay back. "Like I said, I'm alone anyway. Why not stay here?"

Joni shook her head. "Those are just words, Kenni. What's the *real* reason?"

Kenni looked away from her, staring at the far wall. Joni knew she wasn't actually seeing the wall. It was like she was trying to look *through* the wall. She leaned up on her elbow and touched Kenni's stomach, rubbing lightly across her skin, her fingers tracing the tattoo on the hollow of her hip—a tiny hummingbird over an arched rainbow.

"Tell me."

"Santa Fe isn't really home, and I don't have friends there. Not really." Kenni turned to look at her again. "I...I get depressed."

"Depressed?"

"Depressed. Lonely. Questioning my existence."

"It'll be different up here?" she asked gently.

Kenni gave a half-hearted smile. "Well, like you said, I can devise a new obstacle course or something."

Joni didn't return her smile. "Why don't you have friends there? You're very likeable. Pleasant. Everyone here likes you. Your staff appears to love you. Are you different when you get away from here?"

"Like I'm out of my comfort zone?"

Joni nodded. "Is this your safe place?"

Kenni met her gaze and nodded. "Yes. Although that loneliness never really goes away. It's just hidden when I'm up here."

"Hidden? Meaning you've got so much to keep you busy, there's no time to dwell on it?"

"Yes."

"And when everyone leaves, and you don't have all this to keep you busy?"

"This is familiar. Home. I can still take hikes. I can still get out. Truthfully, I've wanted to stay up here before during the winter, I just haven't dared. Because once the snow comes in earnest, there's no getting off the mountain if I change my mind." Kenni took her hand and entwined their fingers.

"Why do you dare this year?"

"Are you worried about me?"

"I am."

"Don't be. I'll be fine."

She didn't know why she was worried. When she left here tomorrow, their brief affair would come to an end. Whether Kenni was getting along fine or not, she wouldn't know. Because she would be back in her real life, and Kenni would start a new month with new women. Now that she'd been here, she understood the purpose of it all, but she wondered how many of those women really knew what they were hoping to gain by spending a month up here.

"What are you thinking?"

She looked up, meeting Kenni's gaze. "Lots of things. I'm going to miss being here. Miss the daily routine. And I'll miss my team. We've exchanged phone numbers, and we might keep in touch, just to see how everyone's getting on." She paused, then smiled. "And I can't believe I'm saying this, but I'm going to miss all this nature stuff. I'm going to miss being on the mountain, being outside." She laughed. "My friend Kimberly says I've been body snatched."

"'The mountains are calling, and I must go,'" Kenni said quietly. "John Muir's words."

"Who is that?"

"He was a naturalist. A conservationist. And in Denver, you're not far from the foothills. Lots of hiking. You should get out. Go into the mountains."

"Maybe."

Kenni leaned over and kissed her. "I'm going to miss you being here. Not just here, in my bed, although I'll certainly miss that. But our friendship. Our talks. I'll miss that."

"I know. It was a short month, wasn't it?"

"The shortest. Maybe in October, we'll talk. Maybe we can have a weekend or something." Kenni pulled the covers up. "We should get some sleep now. It's nearly two."

"I don't want to sleep." She curled next to her. "I'll miss it here, Kenni…but god, I'm going to miss *you*."

Their kiss wasn't hard and furious. No, it was slow and dreamy, and she felt her body melting once again. She heard the soft moan she uttered, and it made her want more. She rolled onto her back, pulling Kenni on top of her. She didn't care what time it was. Didn't care that they'd have to get up in a few short hours. She couldn't stop kissing, couldn't stop touching.

Couldn't stop loving.

CHAPTER FORTY-TWO

Joni was surprised by the tight hug she got from Sarah Beth. She hugged her back just as fiercely.

"Gonna miss you and your potty mouth," Sarah Beth said. "Thank you for being my friend."

"Oh, you're going to make me cry," she accused as she hugged her again. "Thanks for being *my* friend. And a great teammate."

Christine and Erin came over too. Christine wasn't shy about hugging her either. Then she laughed. "You and Kenni were late getting to breakfast."

She was proud of herself for keeping a blush off her face. "Yeah, we had a rather lengthy goodbye."

The other three women laughed.

"It must have been all-night lengthy," Erin teased. "Neither of you look like you've slept at all."

This time a blush did light her face. "Okay," she said quickly. "Moving right along. I'll expect a text from you all to let me know your progress. And of course pictures if either you or Christine cut your hair."

"I'm definitely going to," Erin insisted as she fingered hers. "I have some thinking to do on the drive back, too. I'm ready to make a change, ready to file for divorce. He can have his young mistress if he wants. I don't think I want to spend the rest of my life with a man who doesn't love me." She smiled. "And I can admit that I no longer love him. Life is short, as Kenni says. I'm sixty-two. Still young enough to get out there…and maybe I'll meet someone. If not, I'll be perfectly fine alone."

Christine nodded and hugged Erin. "I hope to have your courage. Because living in a loveless marriage sucks, I know."

"Then get the fuck out!" Joni blurted without thinking. "I mean, yeah, what Erin said…life is too short."

Christine stared at her. "What about you? What changes are you planning to make?"

"Well, for one, I'm no longer going to shun the outdoors. Like, I might join a hiking club or something crazy like that." She turned to Sarah Beth. "What about you?"

"The first thing I'm going to do when I get home is find a yoga class. I definitely want to continue that." She smiled. "I feel so much better about myself than I did when I got here. It was time and money well spent."

"I agree," Erin said. "I'm going to miss you all. Let's try to keep in touch."

Joni watched them walk away, then turned around, looking for Kenni. Yes, they'd said their goodbyes earlier, but she still wasn't going to drive away without seeing her one last time. She saw other teams giving goodbye hugs too, and she spotted Team Four doing a big group hug. She rolled her eyes.

"Yeah, we still beat your ass," she murmured.

She finally saw Kenni talking to Sky. She went over, smiling at them both. "I'm going to miss your scavenger hunts, Sky. They were really fun."

"I seem to remember you calling them stupid on that first day," Kenni reminded her.

"I thought *everything* was stupid on the first day," she said with a laugh.

"Well, I'm glad you enjoyed them," Sky said. "I have fun setting them up too." She touched her shoulder. "It was great having you here, Joni." She smiled at her. "I'll let you two have some privacy."

Joni nodded her thanks, then turned to Kenni. Kenni gave her a brief smile.

"All packed?" Kenni asked.

"Yes. The others just left."

"Yes, I saw. Come on. I'll walk you to your Jeep."

She fell into step beside her. "When do your new guests start arriving?"

"Any time after one."

"Wow. How do you get all the rooms cleaned in time?"

Kenni pointed to three white vans parked near the lodge. "The cleaning crew. There are twelve of them. They can get a bed stripped and remade within ten minutes."

Joni leaned against her as they walked. "Have I told you that this has been the best month ever?"

"Really? And on that first day, you thought it was going to be the worst," Kenni said with a laugh.

Joni finally linked arms with her and pulled her closer as they walked. God, she was going to miss this woman. Whoever would have thought? Because, yes, she came up here thinking it would be the worst month of her life.

"Actually, I had planned to escape after the first few days, remember?"

"Yeah, but I had you sucked in by then. Brainwashed, you know."

"Something like that."

Kenni smiled at her. "It won't be the same without you here. I'm going to have to find me a new guinea pig."

"Well, I hope you don't sleep with her!"

"Never."

They paused beside her rental. There were only a few others still there. She noticed Anna and Britney from Team Four still chatting beside one of their cars.

"Have you decided about the article?"

Joni raised an eyebrow. "I'm not doing a hit piece, Kenni, if that's worrying you. I'm hoping that once he reads it and realizes that you weren't the one to ruin his marriage, he'll publish it." She shrugged. "Or he may trash it."

"I'm not really worried. I trust you."

She nodded and sighed. "So…if you're ever in Denver and need a dinner date or something…"

"Yeah. And if you ever venture out this way again, give me a call."

They'd discussed this already last night. Kenni wouldn't have any free time until October. Two long months away. And even then, Kenni still wasn't sure if she would head down to Santa Fe for the winter or stay put and ride it out here. If she stayed here, maybe they could see each other in October. But what about her? Well, she didn't know what direction her life would take from here on out. She supposed she'd think about it on the long drive back home.

Unmindful of anyone watching, she slipped into Kenni's arms and held her tightly. She could feel Kenni relax against her in that familiar way she had. She closed her eyes, then turned her head, blindly finding Kenni's mouth. Seconds passed—or was it minutes?—before they pulled apart.

She smiled, then touched Kenni's cheek with her hand. "Goodbye, Kenni. Thank you for…well, everything." She grinned. "Some things more than others."

"Take care, Joni."

She nodded and got inside the Jeep. Kenni took a few steps away, then folded her arms, waiting—watching—as she drove away. Joni impatiently wiped at the tears that started to fall.

Damn. Why in the hell am I crying?

CHAPTER FORTY-THREE

"I cried. I cried when I left. Can you believe it?"

Kimberly sipped from the wine she'd poured. "No, I can't. I mean, I know you said you loved it there, but still, I figured you'd be anxious to get home."

"I thought I would be too."

"You look great, though. I guess that place agreed with you."

Joni laughed. "Yeah, and I don't think it was only because of the sex. Who knew being in the fuc...I mean the *damn* outdoors for a month would have this effect."

"Damn? What's wrong with you?"

She smiled. "I'm trying not to say fuck so much."

"Why?"

She shrugged. "I don't know. Maybe if I was more Zen...or you know, like yin and yang or something, then I wouldn't be so prone to say fuck all the time."

Kimberly stared at her, eyebrows raised. "Zen? Yin and yang? Who *are* you?"

She groaned. "I don't even *know* anymore. I really don't. Am I that person who was out there?" she asked, pointing out the window of her apartment. "Is that me? I felt really good out there. But now I'm back home, back in the city. Is this me? Do I get back to my old self? I don't fucking know!" she said with a laugh.

"And what about Kenni?"

"What about her?" She pointed to the window again. "She's out there. I do miss her, though. A lot."

Kimberly tilted her head as she watched her. "Did you fall in love with her?"

Joni's eyes widened. "Oh my god, no! I only knew her for a month. You don't fall in love in a *month*."

"Well, did you make plans to see each other again? You know, it's not that far."

She sighed. "Not really. She's got clients there until October. After that, depending on where she goes for the winter, she said we might talk and maybe grab a weekend or something." She paused, remembering the goodbye kiss they'd shared. It had seemed so final, and she supposed it was. "We had an affair. It was great, and I think we both thoroughly enjoyed it. But it's over. Back to real life. So, I guess to answer my own question, this is who I am. Here. Not out there." She picked up her wineglass and took a sip. "God, I did miss this, though."

Kim pointed at the breakfast bar. "Did you stock up on wine when you got back or are those the bottles she confiscated?"

She laughed. "I would have forgotten about them, but Kenni had them boxed up for me." Her smile faded quickly. "I don't want to go to the office tomorrow. He's going to grill me about the place. And I've got to start on that damn article."

"Have you decided how you're going to write it?"

"I'm going to write a truthful article. It's the only thing I can do. And if he gets pissed, he gets pissed."

"Do you think he'll fire you?"

"I'm trying not to think about that."

CHAPTER FORTY-FOUR

Kenni had almost skipped her usual evening walk, but she knew she needed to get back to her routine. She was in a funk, as Sky had told her twice already. And yeah, she was. She couldn't seem to get her spark—her mojo—back. They had twenty new ladies, yet she still looked around, as if Joni would be among them. There were no F-bombs being dropped, no daggers being shot her way, no threats to kick her ass. This group of ladies seemed a little more meek and mild, more subdued. They were only on day four, but there wasn't the open competition and dislike between teams like it had been with Teams Four and Five.

She turned her flashlight off and leaned against a tree, staring overhead. It didn't take much to picture Joni doing a double fist pump and high-fiving her teammates when they'd won the obstacle course run on the last day. Sarah Beth and Christine had been dancing, and even Erin, the most reserved of the team, had done a little jig.

She slid down the tree to the ground, feeling a now familiar sense of sadness settle on her shoulders. She had known she would miss Joni, sure. She didn't know there'd be this profound feeling of loss hovering around her. She felt kinda empty inside and this, of course, reminded her of how she felt when her family was killed. It reinforced her desire to not get involved with anyone. Not that her affair with Joni constituted involvement. Yet, she had let her inside, hadn't she? It was amazing how close they'd gotten in such a short time. She knew it wasn't one-sided. She knew that by the way Joni had made love to her that last night. And by the tears she'd seen as Joni drove away.

She took a deep breath, trying to find some contentment again in the things she used to love. Like now, being in the forest at night. She closed her eyes, listening for familiar sounds. No owls called this evening, though. It seemed eerily quiet, reminding her of how alone she was.

She got up and clicked on the flashlight, resuming her walk. Through the trees she could see the lodge. Her gaze lifted to the third floor, but there were no lights on.

As she maneuvered through the trees, she pushed Joni from her mind. Instead, she thought about tomorrow's activities. Was it too soon to climb the big tree? She smiled. The *fucking* big tree.

CHAPTER FORTY-FIVE

Joni had avoided Turnbull at every turn this week as she painstakingly wrote and rewrote the article. She was embarrassed to admit that she'd shed tears while writing it. She would never divulge that to anyone, not even Kimberly. It was now finished. But she hesitated to send it on. It was as she wanted it, and she was proud of it. Yet she hesitated to send it to him. He would be shocked, she knew. He would demand she rewrite it. Hell, he might even fire her on the spot.

She stared at the screen, seeing "submit" staring her in the face. With a deep breath, she clicked on it, sending it on its way.

"Christ," she murmured. "He's going to be *so* pissed."

Well, she couldn't worry about it. She slammed her laptop closed and stood. It was a happy hour Thursday, and she was meeting the gang at Louie's Bar and Grill. Actually, she'd been meeting someone every day for something. She knew she was simply trying to stay busy. If her friends wondered about her sudden neediness, they didn't say anything. She assumed that most thought she'd missed going out for dinner and drinks and was making up for lost time.

That wasn't it at all. Kimberly was the only one who knew about her affair with Kenni. Not that she was embarrassed by it or anything. She just didn't want to talk about it, same as she tried not to think about it. Of course, writing the article brought everything to the forefront and it was still fresh in her mind. The whole month was still fresh, not just the affair.

She smiled as she walked to the elevator. She hadn't admitted this to anyone, not even Kim, but she'd had more fun in the last month than she'd ever had in her life. It hadn't been hyperbole when she'd told Kenni it was the best month ever. Because it really had been the best.

Those thoughts chased the smile from her face. What did that say about her life? What did that say about her?

As soon as the elevator doors opened, her phone rang. She fished it from her shoulder bag, cringing. It was her boss. She took a deep breath before answering.

"Hi, this is Joni," she said pleasantly, hoping she didn't sound as nervous as she felt.

"It's me. Got your article."

"Yes, sir. Have you had a chance to read it?"

"I skimmed it."

There was only silence, and she swallowed, wondering what he expected her to say. She decided to say nothing. He had called her. So, she waited patiently for the elevator to get to the ground floor, sighing with relief as a quiet ding sounded before the doors opened. She smiled at two men who were waiting to get on.

"I take it this is not a draft?" he finally asked.

"No. It's my account of how the month went."

"Your assignment was to trash the place," he said matter-of-factly.

"I know. But I couldn't in good conscience write the hit piece you wanted. Because the place is not like that. There is no brainwashing. There's no counseling. There's no man-bashing."

"Then what the hell is it?"

"If you'll read the article, you'll see that they use physical activity to, well, as the website promises, to empower you and, well, liberate you."

"Liberate? What the hell does that mean?"

"It means that some women, in their lives and in their marriages, don't have free will. Or don't exercise free will." She paused in the lobby before going outside. "The activities and challenges that we did, well, it instills confidence. And I could see the difference in almost everyone who was there. Including myself."

Again, there was silence, and she waited for his reply.

"This is what you want me to publish?"

"Yes."

"Okay, then. It's a little lengthy so I'll have to tweak it to make it fit. Thanks, Joni."

She stared at the phone after he had disconnected. Where was the yelling? Where were the demands that she rewrite it?

"Weird. Very weird."

CHAPTER FORTY-SIX

"Thanks for meeting me for lunch," Joni said before dipping a chip into the salsa. "I know Sundays are your laundry day."

"The main reason I hate Sundays," Kimberly said. "But you must have known I would not pass up margaritas and Mexican food." Kim too scooped up some salsa.

"Wait a minute. What about this new guy you met? You never said how your lunch date went with him."

Kim waved her hand in the air. "Not good. First of all, he didn't pick up the tab."

"Strike one," she said with a laugh.

"And two, he talked about himself nonstop. In fact, I don't think he asked me a single question about my life."

"So kinda full of himself?"

"Very. He was cute, though, so I almost overlooked all that. But no, I found myself drifting away as he was droning on and on about something. I couldn't actually see myself going on a second date with him. Thank god it was lunch and not dinner."

"Did he ask for a second date?"

"He did. I've ignored his text and calls."

"You're ghosting him? Why not just tell him?"

"Tell him what? That he's an obnoxious bore?" She held her hand up. "And I know we're over thirty and I should be able to say no to a date rather than ghost them, but I didn't want to deal with it."

"I guess I don't blame you."

"So, what's going on with you?"

She ate another chip. "What do you mean?"

"I do believe that you have been on lunch dates and dinner dates every single day that you've been back and not a one of them was a *real* date."

She sighed. "I didn't want to be alone."

"Why don't you just call her?"

"What good would that do?" She held her hand up, much like Kim had done. "I don't want to talk about her."

"Okay. So, what about your article?"

"Oh my god! Get this! I turned in my article and Turnbull did not blow a gasket. There was no yelling, and he didn't even raise his voice. He just reminded me that I was supposed to trash the place. But I guess he's going to publish it." She smiled. "And when you read it, you're going to want to book a stay there. It's *that* good."

"Well, I've been to the website, and I know how much they charge. I don't see that happening."

"I know. And I keep thinking since I didn't trash the place, Turnbull is going to start docking my salary to pay him back."

Kim took a large swallow of the margarita, then leaned her elbows on the table. "So," she said dramatically. "Let's talk about you and dating."

"Dating?"

"Yes. Because Laura met someone, and she told me she'd be perfect for you."

Joni rolled her eyes. "If I had a dollar for every time someone told me that."

"Right. But she texted me a picture." Kimberly pulled out her phone, flipping through texts until she found it. "Here."

Joni took the phone, staring back at an attractive woman. Her hair was blond and barely brushed the tops of her shoulders. Her makeup was subtle, nothing glaring, although she could have done without the red lipstick. She flicked her gaze back to Kim and shook her head.

"Nothing. I'm getting nothing."

"What do you mean nothing? She's cute!"

"Meh."

"Meh?" Kim took the phone from her, then held it up as if Joni had not seen the picture. "She's like the poster child of who you date. She's thirty-four. She has no baggage. She's single and has been for ten months or so. She's a loan officer at a bank." She smiled. "You never know, that could come in handy someday."

Joni laughed, but still shook her head. "You're right. She's exactly my type. But I'm not ready to date."

Kim put her phone down. "And you know why? Because you're in love with someone else."

"I told you, I'm not in love with her," she said firmly. "For one thing, I don't even know what it feels like to be in love. But I'm pretty sure it takes longer than a month."

"Says who? Who made up dating rules? Why does there have to be a time limit?"

"Why are you pushing this so hard?"

"Because you're terribly unhappy, and you have been since you got back. You try to hide it, but we've been friends too long."

Joni met her gaze, and she was shocked to feel tears threatening. "You're right. I'm fucking miserable."

Kimberly smiled at her. "I see you still haven't quite worked out that Zen stuff you were talking about."

She dabbed at her eyes with the napkin. "I think about her like every second of every day."

"Then call her."

"I'm not going to call her. It'll just prolong it. I need to get over her and get on with my life." She pointed at the phone. "And maybe you're right. Maybe I *should* go on a date."

Kim leaned on her elbow and rested her chin in her palm. "If you're not in love with her, then what is there to get over?"

She had no answer, of course. What *was* it she was trying to get over? Why was she not interested in dating? Why had she started dressing differently? Why did she barely bother with makeup?

"I've changed, haven't I?"

Kim smiled sweetly at her. "You have, yes."

"I'm sorry."

Kim waved her apology away. "Don't be sorry. I love you regardless."

The tears she'd barely been holding at bay fell now in earnest. "Damn you," she murmured.

CHAPTER FORTY-SEVEN

Kenni fingered the mouse, absently moving the cursor back and forth, yet afraid to click on the link. She'd signed up for alerts for *Mountain Life Magazine* to let her know when the new online edition was published. She didn't know if Joni's article would be in this one or not. Perhaps it was too soon. She was feeling anxious, though, so she clicked on the link. A colorful mountain scene popped up and she scanned the titles of the various articles. She caught her breath when she saw *Lyon's Den Retreat for Women. Good or Bad?*

She hesitated only a few seconds before opening the article. She didn't know why she was so curious to read Joni's depiction of her month here. She glanced at the title again, seeing *By Joni James* printed neatly beneath it.

Driving up the rocky and bouncy gravel road that takes you into the Lyon's Den, I wasn't sure what to expect. Was I driving into Heaven or Hell?

She smiled at that, then frowned sharply at the next sentence. *It didn't take me long to realize that it was indeed Hell.*

Kenni frowned, her eyebrows drawn together as she skimmed the article quickly, words and phrases jumping out at her. *Boot camp experience. Extreme physical activities demanded of you. Cliff rappelling without any training or lessons. Regimented. No down time. Worked to exhaustion each day. Mental health deteriorated. Dangerous conditions.*

She leaned back, her eyes wide as she read another sentence. *I can't believe this place is still in business. How is it that no one has sued them yet?*

"Well, I'll be goddamned," she murmured. She got up and went to the door of her cabin, needing some fresh air. Sure, Joni had warned her that her boss had wanted a hit piece. She'd also said that she wouldn't write one. She'd said that she'd loved it here. What changed? Or had nothing changed? Had Joni been lying all along? Had she been using her? She swallowed. Yeah, it sure felt like it.

She walked outside, going off the deck. She moved into the trees as dusk was about to settle over the forest. She felt like she'd had a blow to the chest. Or maybe a punch in the gut. It wasn't the article itself. She didn't care about that. She doubted any of her clients read *Mountain Life Magazine*. No, it wasn't the article. It was Joni. How could she pretend to love it here, pretend to have affection for her, have sex with her...then completely trash her life's work?

Yeah. That stung. She had trusted Joni. She'd let her guard down. She'd let Joni get inside. And for what? So she could use her, then rip her heart out and toss it aside?

She again tried to swallow the lump in her throat and was unable to. She felt like crying, something she hadn't done in a very long time. Instead of going back to her cabin, she walked on, finding the path she used to link up with the main trail. She didn't have her flashlight, but she didn't care. With luck, she'd get lost and fall off the cliff or something.

She searched her mind for some comforting quote, something to convince herself that it would all be okay. That *she* would be okay. She took a deep breath as she moved among the trees—the sights, the smells, the sounds as familiar to her as her own face.

She nodded, finally thinking of a quote by John Burroughs. She said the words out loud, letting them sink in.

"'I go to nature to be soothed and healed, and to put my senses in order.'"

She nodded again. Yes. She would be fine. To hell with Joni James. She wouldn't give her another thought.

CHAPTER FORTY-EIGHT

Joni stared at her screen. "Oh my god." Her eyes widened. "Oh...my...god." She scanned the article, then stood quickly, nearly knocking her chair over. "Oh, my fucking god," she said sharply. Without thinking, she opened her door and marched purposefully to Turnbull's office. She ignored Janet, his secretary, and barged in without knocking.

"How could you?" she demanded.

His smile was more of a smirk. "I assume you mean the article."

"Of course I mean the goddamn article! Take it down now!"

"Joni, you're not the boss here. You don't dictate what gets published."

"But that's not my article!"

"Of course it is. You sent it to me over a month ago," he reminded her.

She threw her arms up. "It's not the *real* article!" she yelled. "How could you?"

He stood. "You need to calm down, Ms. James. You provided me with two articles. Granted, the first one was a little bare, but

I was able to add some of your content from the second article to flesh it out. But they *are* your words, Joni."

She stared at him, unable to even think clearly much less make a compelling argument. Yes, they were her words. All of them. She couldn't deny that. Before she did something to totally embarrass herself—like jumping over the desk and punching him in the face—she spun on her heels and fled his office. Back in her own, she slammed her door and leaned against it, her mind reeling.

What were the chances that Kenni had read it? Did she even subscribe to *Mountain Life*? No. But she wouldn't have to subscribe, she reminded herself. She would be allowed three free articles. She took a deep breath. Maybe she hadn't read it. But she needed to call her, to warn her, to explain what had happened.

She glanced at the clock on her laptop. After twelve. Were they at lunch? Was Kenni in her office? Were they still on a scavenger hunt? She quickly pulled up the website, finding the office number. Her hand was trembling as she called, her cell phone heavy in her hand.

"Lyon's Den. How may I help you?"

Her heart thudded in her chest at the sound of Kenni's voice. She pushed down her nervousness. "Hey. It's me. Joni."

There was unexpected silence. No joy at hearing her voice. No exuberant greeting.

"If you're calling to apologize, don't bother."

"Oh shit. So, you read it already?"

"Of course, I read it. Great job, Joni. You had me fooled. You had us all fooled."

"Kenni, no. I can explain. I—"

"No need. I don't really care anymore. And please don't ever call me again."

Joni jumped as Kenni literally slammed the phone down. She dropped her own phone on her desk and stared dumbly at the wall. Tears stung her eyes, and her chest felt heavy. No, not her chest. Her heart hurt. She rubbed between her breasts, wondering at this ache she felt.

Now what was she going to do?

CHAPTER FORTY-NINE

Joni parked in the circle drive, staring at the huge mansion in front of her. She should have called first, of course, but she had no way of getting Charlotte Turnbull's number and she certainly couldn't have asked Turnbull for it. But given the way her luck was running today, Charlotte probably wouldn't even be at home.

She took a deep breath, then walked up the stone steps onto the huge front porch. She looked around, thinking porch was far too tame a word to use for this. Before she could ring the doorbell, a voice sounded out of the speaker on the side of the door.

"Yes, who is it, please?"

She looked around, wondering where the camera was. "It's... well, it's Joni James. I work for *Mountain Life Magazine*. I was hoping to visit with Mrs. Turnbull."

"One moment, please."

She nodded. *Where's the fucking camera?* She found nothing. Even the doorbell appeared to be unadulterated. A few moments later, the front door opened. A young woman smartly dressed in black trousers and a black blouse smiled at her.

"She will see you, Ms. James. Come this way, please."

"Thank you."

She looked around at the mostly white interior. Even the marble floors were white with only a few streaks of black mixed in. Unfortunately, she did not get a tour of the house. She was led to a room not far from the entryway.

"Thank you, Carla."

"Yes, ma'am."

Joni stood there, hardly recognizing Charlotte Turnbull. The dull blond hair that was usually held in place by massive amounts of hairspray had been cut short and left natural. It was a soft brown color, and it feathered to the sides, making her look much younger than Joni knew her to be. She finally moved, going closer.

"I don't know if you remember me. Joni James," she said, offering her hand in greeting.

Charlotte shook it firmly, then motioned to the leather sofa. "Yes. Even though I only see you at the annual office Christmas party, I do remember you. Please, have a seat."

"Thank you for seeing me. I'm sure you're wondering what I'm doing here." Joni smiled. "I'm actually wondering that myself."

"Well, let's don't beat around the bush then. I assume it has something to do with the magazine."

She nodded. "Sort of. Mostly. Mr. Turnbull published the wrong article of mine—an inflammatory article that was written before I'd actually done research. The tone of the article is what he requested, but it wasn't my view."

"I don't think I'm following you."

She sighed. "No, I don't suppose you are." She stood and began pacing. "He wanted me to spend a month at the Lyon's Den, like you did."

"Lyon's Den?" Charlottle smiled. "What a wonderful experience that was for me. But he loathed the place. Why would he want to publish an article about it?"

"Like I said. Inflammatory. A hit piece."

Her eyes widened. "I see."

"He blames them for your divorce."

Again, her eyes widened. "He told you? I'm surprised. He's tried to keep it a secret as he's convinced I'll change my mind. I think when I had his clothes packed and left outside for him, he got the message."

She nodded. "Yes, he mentioned he was living in an apartment."

"Again, I'm shocked that he would tell someone."

"He was angry, and I think he wanted me to understand why he wanted me to write the hit piece in the first place. Regardless, I didn't fancy spending a month in the wilderness." She smiled quickly. "I hate the outdoors. Or rather I did. And he knows that I don't do things like that. He sent me there, knowing I would hate the place. I was to write a hit piece on it. Revenge, I suppose. Something to get back at you or Kenni."

"I would like to think you're joking, but I know Paul. He does have a bit of a vindictive nature. Yes, he blamed the retreat for me changing and for the divorce. He never thought to blame himself."

Joni nodded. "He was convinced they did man-bashing or brainwashing or something."

"It's not like that at all."

"Yes, I know. I spent all of July there. And I absolutely loved it."

Charlotte nodded. "And then you couldn't write the type of article that he wanted."

"Exactly. Because it would be a lie. I wrote a truthful article, one that was very flattering actually. That was the article that I thought he would publish. Instead, he published the article I had written before I even went there."

"Again, I don't follow you. You wrote another article?"

"Sorry. Because I didn't want to go, I simply went to the website, read some of the testimonials, read some of the reviews, and faked all the rest to write the hit piece that he wanted. He wanted me to trash them, to ruin them. The article I wrote was… well, I killed the place, like he wanted."

She nodded. "And when you went against his wishes for your real article, he published your original piece, the one that was a fabrication."

"A fabrication, yes. Completely made-up. Oh, he took some bits and pieces of the new one, trying to make it legitimate, I guess." She moved to sit again. "I came here today hoping you might have some influence on him…hoping to get the article pulled offline."

She was surprised by the rather sneaky smile Charlotte gave her. "Joni, *I* own the magazine, not Paul."

"You? But he always—"

"The magazine is still a family-owned business, started by my grandfather in the 1960s. My maiden name is Ashford."

She raised an eyebrow. "The hotels?"

"Yes. The first modern hotel was in Las Vegas, back in the midcentury. They had a casino there too. But the Ashford wealth came in the late 1800s when the railway came to Denver. Our first hotel was built near Union Station." She waved her hand. "Ancient history. The main thing is Paul isn't upset at Lyon's Den because I'm divorcing him. He's upset that he's out of the family business and, thus, the money."

"I don't understand."

"My marriage was arranged by my father. I'm the only child, and he didn't think I could handle the family fortune without some guidance. Paul was an investment broker at the time, and he worked for the company who handled my family's estate. I balked at first. We dated, but I wasn't remotely in love with him. My father, however, was very persuasive." She gave a sad smile. "I simply got tired of arguing with him. At least my father had the good sense to draw up a prenuptial agreement. I don't know if he did it in case of divorce or if he was worried that I would die and then Paul would have control of everything."

"Wow."

Charlotte nodded. "Yes, that would describe it and not necessarily in a good way. Both of my parents have passed away. I lost my mother last summer. That's really what spurred me to go to Lyon's Den. I was miserable in my life, miserable in my marriage. Going through the motions, as they say. I heard about it from one of my so-called friends at the country club. She hadn't gone to it—she thought the concept was absurd—but a friend of hers had been raving about it to her. So I looked into it. It was the best decision I ever made."

Joni nodded. "Yes. Mr. Turnbull says you've changed. I can see it too."

Charlotte smiled at her. "I absolutely loved the retreat. Kenni was such a wonderful hostess and teacher. So subtle in her messages."

"Yes. Yes, she was."

"It completely changed my life, obviously."

"I know what you mean. I had such fun there, I didn't want to leave," Joni agreed.

"Oh, I know. I felt very safe there. I didn't want to leave either. I met some wonderful women, and we continue to keep in touch. But I learned so much about myself, and I knew without a doubt that I wanted to make some major changes in my life." She smiled. "Still, it was hard to leave there."

Joni nodded. Yes, she knew all too well how hard it had been to leave.

"Not that any of this is your concern—or your business," Charlotte said bluntly. "But it feels good to say some of these things out loud to someone. My marriage was over long ago, Joni. Twenty years, maybe more, so making that change was easy. Like so many, you just keep on, pretending you're happy. At first, I told myself that it wasn't so bad. Paul was a handsome man, and I could do a lot worse. I put on a happy face. And on the outside, I was. My friends, the ladies I played tennis with and did brunch and wine and cheese parties and all that," she said with a wave of her hand. "They never knew I was unhappy in my life. And it wasn't until I went to the retreat that I saw myself in so many others there. I also saw myself in the ladies that I socialized with here. I was two different people. I wouldn't say I changed while there. I would rather think that my true authentic self finally came out. Paul says I've changed drastically, of course. While that's true, it's simply that I've shed my skin, so to speak. Like I unzipped a bodysuit and climbed out of it."

"Excellent analogy. I changed up there too. But I feel, like you, that who I am now is who I always was. It was hiding beneath all these false layers that I believed to be true."

"Exactly!" Charlotte folded her hands together. "Now, let's talk about this article you want me to pull."

"I'm assuming you haven't read it."

"No, no. I rarely even look at the magazine now. I never liked the direction Paul took it, but I didn't bother myself with it. I was far too busy doing important things like champagne brunch and lengthy lunches with the ladies. How sad my life was." She held her hand up. "No need to go over all that again." She stood and moved to her desk. "Let's take a look at the article."

Joni stood behind her as she opened the laptop that was on the desk. Charlotte quickly pulled up the magazine's site and Joni pointed to the title of the article. She couldn't bear to read through it again, so she glanced around the room as Charlotte silently read it.

The walls here were dark, a stark contrast to the white in the entryway. Drapes were pulled open, revealing a manicured landscape outside with colorful flowers and shrubs. She caught a glimpse of water in a pool that was partially hidden by a stone wall. Beyond that, she could see the silhouettes of the mountains far in the distance. That made her—

"This is absolutely rubbish!"

She brought her gaze back to the laptop, nodded. "Yes, I know."

Charlotte picked up the phone that sat on her desk. Joni took a step away, almost feeling the anger seeping from her.

"Patrick, this is Charlotte Turnbull. There is an article on the site by Joni James." Charlotte scrolled back up, reading the title. "*Lyon's Den Retreat for Women. Good or Bad?* Pull it immediately. Kill it."

Joni tilted her head, trying to listen, but all she heard was a mumbled voice.

"Whose name is on your paycheck, Patrick?" Charlotte nodded. "I will deal with Paul. Remove it *now*."

Charlotte spun her chair around, and Joni took another step away from her, wondering if she was going to get yelled at. Or worse, fired.

"You were right. That was a total fabrication. Your mention of rappelling was taken from the real article, I assume. I don't believe that is on their website at all."

Joni nodded, then she smiled hesitantly. "That rappelling exercise scared the sh…crap out of me."

Charlotte laughed. "Yes, it scared the shit out of me too!"

Joni relaxed. "It was like Kenni said, we trusted her, we trusted ourselves. Oh, and what about the water obstacle? I was the first one to make it across!"

Charlotte groaned. "I was one of the last ones. I was so excited when I finally conquered that I nearly fell in anyway!"

They smiled at each other, apparently both of them thinking back to their time at Lyon's Den. Joni held her hand out.

"Thank you, Mrs. Turnbull."

"Please call me Charlotte." She squeezed her hand in a more friendly shake. "I'm going back to Ashford as soon as the divorce is final."

"What about the magazine? Will Mr. Turnbull continue to run it?"

"Absolutely not! Not after this, certainly. I hadn't decided what to do with it, but Paul will not be involved. I have an appointment with my attorney on Thursday to discuss it." She turned to a small device on the desk and punched a button. A few seconds later, the screen lit up and Carla's face appeared.

"Yes, ma'am?"

"Please come to escort Ms. James out."

"Yes, ma'am."

Charlotte turned back to her. "I'm wondering if Kenni reads this magazine. I would hate for her to have stumbled upon the article."

"I already called her. Yes, she read it."

"Oh, my. How did she take it?"

"Not very well," she said truthfully. "I tried to explain, but…"

"Perhaps I should call her then," Charlotte suggested. "I feel awful about it."

Not as awful as I feel. But she shook her head. "I'm not sure that would help. You see, Kenni and I…well, we had a little more of a personal relationship. And she took the article as, well, a stab in the back, I guess."

Charlotte eyed her. "Personal?"

"Well…"

Then Charlotte smiled. "You mean a romantic relationship?"

"Yes."

Charlotte nodded. "Okay, then I guess I should probably stay out of it."

There was a light knock on the door, then it opened. Carla smiled at her and waited. Joni nodded, then turned to Charlotte once more.

"I can't thank you enough. I really appreciate it."

"And I appreciate you bringing this to my attention, Joni. I'll be in the office one day next week, I imagine. I'll be sure to stop by and see you."

"Thank you. I'd like that."

She nodded and smiled at Carla, following her back to the front door, and then made her escape outside. Well, that went far better than she had expected. She sighed, though. Kenni had already read the article. She was upset and she'd hung up on her.

Yeah. And she told her not to call her again. *Ever* again, she'd said.

A wave of sadness fell over her, but she stopped it in its tracks. Instead, she turned her head, looking west toward the mountains. They were but hulking shapes in the distance, but she felt the pull of them. She closed her eyes and held her face up, letting the sun's rays kiss her skin. One of Kenni's many quotes came to her.

The mountains are calling, and I must go.

She opened her eyes and gazed again at the mountains. Yes. She'd spent only a month there and yes, it had felt like home. But was it the mountains, or was it Kenni?

CHAPTER FIFTY

Kenni found she had little patience for the obstacle courses. This group of women were slow to catch on, and there was no one among them to show them how. She scanned their faces now as they all looked back at her expectantly. No, she had no guinea pig in this group. No Joni, her mind screamed, but she pushed that away and forced a smile to her face.

"Surely someone wants to start," she said with feigned enthusiasm. "How about Gail?"

Jenn came forward. "Why don't we split everyone up into teams?" she suggested. "Let's start with Team One. Run it like yesterday, but try to pick up the pace a little."

The women then gathered into teams with only a few mumbled words. Kenni looked at Jenn with raised eyebrows. Jenn nodded at her.

"Yes, I miss Joni too. She seemed to move things along."

Kenni shook her head. "I never said I missed her."

Jenn rolled her eyes. "You've been a bear. Yes, you miss her." She held her hand up. "And yes, I heard about the article from Sky. I went out to read it, but it wasn't there."

"What do you mean it wasn't there?"

Jenn shrugged. "It wasn't there. I guess they took it down. But you need to snap out of this. You haven't been your usual charming self, and most of the women here are scared of you."

She ran a hand through her hair, finally nodding. "You're right. I'm sorry. I can't seem to focus."

Jenn put an arm around her shoulder. "Call her. Talk it out. Then get your mind back here with us, instead of with her."

She watched Jenn walk away, noting that Jenn was basically taking over the running of the course. Kenni let her. This group was into the third week, and they hadn't even mastered the second obstacle course. She wouldn't dare do the rappelling exercise with them yet.

She walked to the back of the group, making herself smile at them, noting some wouldn't meet her eyes. Christ, were they really scared of her? She moved to the back of the group, absently watching them. Her mind, however, drifted to Joni, as it often did.

What did Jenn mean that the article wasn't there? Had Joni taken it down? If so, why? Guilt, perhaps?

It didn't matter. The affair was in the past and she was over it. She decided she would go down to Santa Fe for the winter after all. She wasn't going to be a hermit. She would call up some of the people she knew there. Hell, maybe she would start dating. She nodded. Yeah. That's what she'd do.

She'd start dating.

CHAPTER FIFTY-ONE

Joni glanced up as Darlene rushed into her office and closed the door. She raised her eyebrows questioningly at her.

"Are you busy?"

Joni looked at the screen and shrugged. "Going over new restaurants. My next exciting assignment," she said dryly.

Darlene came closer and leaned down on her desk. Her voice was quiet. "I heard a rumor."

"Oh, yeah?"

"I heard from Janet, who heard from David…who heard from Patrick that Mrs. Turnbull killed your article."

Joni nearly growled. "Not my article. Well, not my *real* article. And yes, she killed it. At my request," she added, not caring if the office gossip chain brought that back to Turnbull or not.

"Well, something else is going on. Janet says Mr. Turnbull has been holed up in his office all morning, and it sounds like he's packing."

"Packing?"

"Yeah. Like, you know, packing up his office."

"Ah. Like maybe he got fired or something?"

Darlene stood up straighter. "Fired? He owns the magazine. Who could fire him?"

Joni stared at her, waiting. Darlene's eyes widened.

"Mrs. Turnbull?"

Joni smiled.

"Then the rumors are true? They're divorcing?"

"Is that the rumor?"

Darlene pointed a finger at her. "You know, don't you?"

Joni was saved by her office phone ringing. It was Janet. "This is Joni."

"Yes, Joni. Mrs. Turnbull is here and would like to see you. May I send her back?"

Joni glanced quickly at Darlene. "Yes. Of course." Then she motioned to the door. "You have to leave. Mrs. Turnbull is coming."

"Here?" Darlene ran to the door and jerked it open. "We need to have lunch and talk!"

Joni waited only a few moments before Charlotte Turnbull came in. She had a friendly smile on her face, and Joni returned it.

"Charlotte, good to see you again."

"Well, I promised I would stop by." She closed the door before sitting down. "Are rumors going around? I could hear whispering."

Joni laughed. "Yes. Lots of speculation, I'm sure."

"My attorney and I met with Paul yesterday. He's leaving. He'll be out by noon." She folded her hands together. "I've decided to take over. I want to move the magazine back to what it was originally intended to be. More about the mountains and less about Denver."

"I think that's an excellent idea."

Charlotte nodded. "I spent the last several days going back over past editions. I went back two years, I think. Dreadful stuff. I see that Paul had you doing reviews on restaurants."

"The only benefit to that assignment was getting to eat for free at all the best places," she said with a laugh.

"Well, a waste of your talent. I loved the article you sent me. It captured the true essence of Lyon's Den."

"You had a chance to read it?" Charlotte had called her two days ago, asking her to send the real article over to her.

"I did. And I instructed Patrick to publish it. It's probably up by now."

"Oh, that's great, Charlotte. Thank you." She paused. "I know it's none of my business, but how did things go with Mr. Turnbull?"

"About as I expected. He threatened legal action to keep control of the magazine." She waved a hand in the air. "Not going to happen. My father was very explicit about that. As my attorney said, he doesn't have a prayer. Now, I have a question for you. How would you feel about moving up to the front office?"

"The front office?"

"Be my assistant. My right hand. Help me change directions. Let's get the 'mountain' back in *Mountain Life Magazine*."

She didn't even have to consider the offer. She nodded readily. "Of course. How could I turn that down?"

"Thank you, Joni. I know we don't really know each other, but I feel that I can trust you. Now, I know assignments have already been made for next month's deadline, but I'd like you to do a follow-up on Lyon's Den."

She stared at her. "A follow-up?"

"Yes. Not necessarily about the retreat itself, but more about *you*."

"Me?"

"Yes. What your expectations were when you went, how you changed, how your outlook on life has changed. Things like that. What are you doing differently now that you weren't doing before? How have people's perceptions of you changed? Or your perceptions of them. I would like our magazine to have a more personal feel to it. Most of our articles come across as reporting or news items. I'd like to shift that."

Joni nodded slowly. "Okay. I...I can do that, sure."

Charlotte smiled broadly. "Great! Then give Kenni a call and see about going out to visit."

Her eyes widened. "You want to book another stay there?"

"No, no. Just pop out there for a few days, reacquaint yourself with it all. See how you *feel*, Joni. Write me something from the heart. And if you want, you can interview me and add a little of what my experience was, to give another perspective." She smiled again. "Give her a call."

She stared at her, wondering if she should tell Charlotte that Kenni had slammed the phone down and told her not to call again. *Ever*, she reminded herself.

"Well, you know I told you that Kenni had read the article. She wasn't particularly happy with me. I'm not sure she would welcome me back there."

Charlotte stood, still smiling. "Call Sky then. Work something out."

Joni stared at the empty space in the doorway long after Charlotte had left. Call Sky? Would Sky help her? Kenni was her boss. Kenni was her friend. Would she go behind her back like that? She slid her gaze over to her office phone, feeling a wave of anxiety hit her.

She would be lying if she said she didn't think about calling every single day. But Kenni's sharp tone, her clipped words... the slamming of the phone. All things that were still fresh in her mind. With a sigh, she picked up the phone.

It wasn't Sky who answered, though.

CHAPTER FIFTY-TWO

Kenni normally answered the office phone without ever glancing at the Caller ID. She did this time, though, and she hesitated. Then she summoned up her most professional tone. "Lyon's Den Retreat. May I help you?"

"Please don't hang up on me."

Joni's quiet words, her soft, familiar voice washed over her. "Okay."

"Please let me explain."

"I told you, you don't—"

"I do. Look, that wasn't my article." Joni paused. "Okay, well, yes, it was, but I didn't write it like that." Another pause. "Okay, technically, I *did* write it like that, but—"

"You're not really helping your case here, Joni."

"Look, I wrote that article before I came there because I didn't *want* to come there. He wanted a hit piece, and I thought, hell, I can write a hit piece. I don't have to go to the stupid fucking retreat to write one, you know."

The smile hit Kenni's face before she realized it, and she quickly chased it away.

"And?" she managed.

"So, I wrote the article by looking at the pictures on your website and reading reviews and all that. I gave it to him, thinking that would get me off the hook. But no. He made me go anyway. And as you know, I loved it there. I wrote a real article when I got back. I thought that was the one he was going to publish. But all he did was take my original one and added bits and pieces from the new one. I had no idea he would do that. I'm so sorry, Kenni. I don't how else to explain it to you."

"I see."

"Have you read the new article?"

"No."

"You should. It's—"

"Okay. I might," she said a bit more curtly than she intended.

"I…I miss you. I miss—"

"Don't do this, Joni. It's over and done with."

"I'm so sorry, Kenni. Please—"

"Thank you for calling. Goodbye, Joni." She waited, hearing Joni's gentle breathing. She closed her eyes, wondering why she was being so cold to her. Well, she knew why, didn't she?

"Okay. Goodbye, Kenni."

She put the phone down, feeling nearly overwhelmed with sadness. Yes, she missed Joni too. She didn't *want* to miss her, but she did. Joni's explanation was pretty much what she assumed had happened. Then why was she being so standoffish? Why was she not accepting the olive branch Joni had extended?

Because she enjoyed being miserable, apparently. She stood up and went to the window, staring out into the trees. She missed her. But what good would it do to make amends? She needed to get over their affair, push it from her mind like she'd been doing, and get on with her life. Joni James had no part in it. A fling that ended as quickly as it had begun—she didn't need to make it into more than it was.

"Let it go," she murmured.

CHAPTER FIFTY-THREE

"I've never seen you like this."

Joni burrowed deeper into the corner of her sofa and pulled the blanket up to her chin. "I needed some quiet time."

"For three days?" Kimberly sat down on the opposite side, shoving her feet away. "You got a promotion at work. Why aren't you excited about that?"

"I am."

"You have a funny way of showing it."

Joni sighed. "She wants me to go back there."

"Where? Who?"

"Charlotte Turnbull, my new boss. She wants me to go back to Lyon's Den."

"Good lord! For another *month*?"

"No. Just a few days or whatever. She wants a follow-up article."

"That's great. Then maybe you and Kenni—"

"I called her. She didn't hang up on me this time and she let me explain what happened."

"Good. And?"

"And nothing. She was very businesslike. Very cold. And her goodbye was final."

"Oh, I'm sorry, Joni."

She held up a hand. "I don't want to talk about it. Even thinking about it makes me want to cry."

"What are you going to do?"

"Oh, Kim, I don't know. I thought maybe I'd *pretend* to go back there. I can write a follow-up article without actually being there, you know."

Kim laughed. "Really? You would think you'd have learned your lesson from the first time."

"This is completely different. I just have this fear that Charlotte is going to call there or something. If she finds out I didn't go, I'll probably lose my job."

Kim rubbed her legs affectionately. "Not to continue to harp on this, but I think you should go. I think you and Kenni need to talk this out and clear the air."

"We have."

"You have not."

"Oh, Kim. What's that going to accomplish? The article hurt her, I'm sure. She said that I had them all fooled, so I'm certain she thinks I was lying to her and I used her. I know that's what she's thinking. And anyway, I can't go up there unannounced. There's a locked gate. I couldn't get on the property even if I wanted to."

"You could call—"

"I thought you weren't going to harp on it?"

"Well, I am. Because you're being stubborn," Kim accused.

"Stubborn? I am not. I fucking called her. She was not receptive to my apology. End of story."

"It is not the end of the story. You're in love with the woman. Did you tell her that?"

"Oh, for god's sake! I'm *not* in love with her. Will you get that out of your mind!"

Kimberly raised her hands questioningly. "Then what is all this for? Why are you moping around, refusing to go out, hiding in your apartment watching Hallmark movies?"

"Because I don't know whether I'm pissed off or if I want to cry!" She leaned her head back. "Okay, I'm maybe mostly pissed off right now. I cried last night."

Kim squeezed her leg. "I'm sorry."

"I mean, I apologized! This whole thing wasn't even my fault to begin with! Granted, I shouldn't have written that first article, but I hadn't even fucking met her yet! Now it's like she acts like there was nothing between us. It's over and done with, she said." She tossed the blanket off. Oh, she was on a roll now. "She fucking hung up on me! Can you believe that? Slammed the phone down! Told me not to call her again. Ever!"

"Okay," Kim said slowly. "Yes, let's go with pissed off then."

Joni shook her head, then laughed. "I'm sorry. I didn't mean to yell. But yeah, I'm pissed off!"

"Do you really think she's still that angry about it all?"

Joni sighed. "I don't know. Maybe. Or maybe she's using this as an excuse to gracefully end whatever it was we had going on." She pulled the blanket back again. "She's got some…some issues. I told you about her family."

"Yes. Tragic."

"I think she's afraid of letting someone get too close. And anyway, what can I offer her? I'm here in Denver. She's up there in the mountains. She doesn't have a single day off from May through September. It's crazy to even think about having some kind of a relationship."

"So, you have thought about it then?"

"Of course. I…I like her. I had a crazy good time with her." She sighed. "I miss her."

Kimberly smiled at her and patted her leg. "Then call. Go see her. That's where you want to be. Up there with her. So go."

She closed her eyes, picturing Kenni's face. It had been almost a month since she'd been there, but she could still see her clearly. Yes, she wanted to go. Yes, she wanted to be up there in the mountains with Kenni. Even now, with her eyes closed, she could smell the forest. So yes, she would call Sky. If she had to use Charlotte Turnbull's assignment as an excuse, she would, but she *had* to see Kenni.

A ding on her phone told her she had a text, and she reached for it blindly. It was a group text, and she automatically smiled as she saw Sarah Beth's, Christine's, and Erin's names. She tapped on it, then nearly screamed as she saw a picture of Erin.

"Oh my god! She fucking did it!"

"Who? What?"

"Erin. From my team. She cut her hair off!" She held the phone up so Kim could see.

"Wow. That's like a military cut."

"Yeah. I love it. She went gray at an early age, so she'd always colored it. It was jet black. She said it was the only color that would cover the gray. She said she was going to cut it off and let it grow back naturally." She was still smiling, realizing that some of her sadness had left her. She quickly texted Erin back. *I fucking love it! Christine? Are you next?*

CHAPTER FIFTY-FOUR

Sky's voice was cheerful and familiar, and Joni felt her apprehension fade almost immediately. In fact, she actually smiled.

"Sky…it's Joni. Joni James from—"

"Joni! Of course! How are you?"

She paused. How was she? She answered truthfully. "Kinda fucking miserable."

Sky laughed. "Well, I know someone else who is pretty miserable too. And I'm so glad you called."

"You are?"

"Yes. In fact, Jenn and I were talking last night, and we debated whether to contact you or not."

"About Kenni?"

"Yes. Would it be…well, weird if we asked you to come back and see her?"

"Oh my god! That's why I was calling." She paused. "But…did you read the article?"

"Yes. And Kenni explained what happened. In fact, I read the new article that is out there now. Very nice. The first one was a hatchet job."

"Yes, I know. I'm sorry."

"No need to apologize. As I said, Kenni explained it. But, Joni, she's not herself. There's no spark anymore. She's…I hate to say it, but she's in a really depressive state. She's in a funk, and she can't seem to pull herself out. Jenn mostly calls her a bear. We thought maybe you could come see her."

"I was calling for that very reason. I want to see her. But I think she's a little pissed at me, judging by our last two phone calls."

"She was hurt, yes. Her words to me were that she felt like you'd used her and betrayed her trust."

"I figured that, but that's not how it was," she insisted.

"I know. I saw you two together, saw the way you looked at each other. I think she's just running scared."

"Scared?"

"Well, not to scare *you*, but I think she realized that she was falling in love with you. And then the article…"

Joni squeezed her eyes shut. *In love? Was it true?*

"Does that shock you?"

She took a deep breath. "I'm not sure." Then she smiled. "Yes. I think I fell a little bit in love too," she finally admitted.

"I know you did. So? Can you come?"

"Can you sneak me in there?"

She heard the rustling of papers before Sky spoke. "No. That's impossible. The gate is locked. It has an alarm. Kenni would know if it opened."

"Shit. What can I do then? Hike up?"

Sky laughed. "Missed all that hiking, did you?"

She smiled. "Yes, actually I have. I've missed a lot of things there."

"Okay. Well, this is what we thought. September first, the new group of women will come."

Joni's eyes widened. "And the gate will be open."

"Yes."

She smiled. "And I can drive right up to the lodge."

"Yes. Come about three thirty. Most everyone will already be there. It'll be easier for you to hide among them."

"Hide?"

"Yes. I don't want her to have the chance to run or plan her escape. No warning. I'll let Jenn know you're coming. And we'll let the rest of the staff know that day too."

"You think she'll be mad?"

"I don't care. I just want my cheerful Kenni back. I think you can do that."

"I hope so. Thank you, Sky. I guess I'll see you in a few days then."

"Look forward to it. Bye, Joni."

Okay, so that was almost too easy. But would Kenni be mad? No, she didn't think so. Kenni was using the article as an excuse to push her away...and keep her away. Kenni most likely thought her heart was safer that way. Because yes, they had both fallen a little in love. She could see it plainly now. The last few nights together, the way they touched. The lingering glances. The drawn-out goodbye kisses that neither wanted to end. And god, she'd cried like a baby when she'd driven away.

With a lightness she hadn't felt in a very long time, she quickly shot Charlotte an email, letting her know she'd be gone. Then she packed her laptop and anything else she thought she might need. She picked her keys up from her desk and went to the door, looking around once more before closing and locking her office.

She stopped at Janet's desk. "I'm off on assignment. I sent Mrs. Turnbull an email with the particulars. I'll be back in a few days. Maybe a week."

"Okay, sure. See you then."

She didn't know why, but she felt free as soon as she stepped outside into the sunshine. She let her gaze travel to the mountains on the horizon. She suddenly couldn't wait to get back up there.

The mountains are calling, and I must go.

CHAPTER FIFTY-FIVE

As Joni parked her rented Jeep among all the luxurious SUVs at the lodge, she had an unexpected sense of déjà vu. Perhaps because she had pulled up next to the same tree as before. A tree she now knew was an Engleman spruce. Or maybe it was because of the tiny gray birds foraging there—mountain chickadees. Or the fresh mountain air and familiar smells. Or maybe it was simply being back here, at a place that had transformed her into a completely different woman.

She stood next to the Jeep, contemplating taking her luggage with her or leaving it hidden. She decided it would be presumptuous to come with luggage in hand. For all she knew, Kenni might very well kick her out of camp and send her right back down the mountain.

So she left it all, going toward the lodge instead. A handful of ladies were milling about, and she spotted five of them in a group, making introductions. After glancing around and seeing no familiar faces, she headed in that direction. She couldn't help but smile at the looks on their faces. Some were nervous, some skeptical, some excited.

Before she got there, however, she spotted Sky standing near the front door. She stopped in her tracks, fearing Kenni would be there with her. Sky noticed her and waved her over. She was greeted with a tight hug.

"You made it! Good!"

"Yes." Then she looked behind Sky. "Is she around?"

"In her office."

"Her office? Doesn't she usually greet everyone?"

"Yes. Like I said, she's been in a funk. Come on. I'll sneak you into the dining room from the back deck."

"Do the others know I'm here?"

"Yes. I told them all last night. They're so excited. Especially Jenn."

Sky linked arms with her, and they hurried around the side of the lodge. Everything was so familiar—the woods where they'd done most of the scavenger hunts, the deck, the big bell. She found it hard to believe that it had been a month since she'd been there.

"It feels so good to be back here," she said to Sky. "It's almost like I never left."

Sky smiled at her. "Left part of your heart here, huh?"

"Yes. Yes, I did. And I was afraid to admit it."

"Well, I'm certainly glad you're here. If anyone can get Kenni back into the light, it's you." Sky paused at the back door, looking inside before going in. "All clear. Come on. How about you sit at your normal spot?"

She smiled at that suggestion. "Trying to push her over the edge?"

Sky laughed. "Just trying to get my Kenni back."

There were twelve or thirteen women in the room, some sitting quietly and others chatting. Joni didn't know if she should integrate herself with them or simply take a seat and ignore them. Before she could decide, the main door opened, and more women came in. Sky motioned her to sit, and she did. She quickly counted the ladies there and all twenty were inside already. She murmured hello to those who sat at her table. They all had name tags on, and she saw them glance at her chest. She touched the spot where she would have normally placed her name.

"I'm Joni," she said. "I forgot my name tag."

"Oh. Well, I bet Sky would bring you one."

Joni smiled at the woman—Gretta—and shook her head. "I'll get it later."

As the tables filled up, Joni felt her nervousness grow. Kenni would most likely be shocked to find her there, yes. But she really didn't think that Kenni would refuse to see her, refuse to talk. Still, she was nervous, and she folded her hands together in her lap, squeezing her fingers tightly each time the door opened.

Jenn spotted her and winked. Karla came in and glanced her way, telling evidence that Sky had told them where she was. She returned Karla's smile, then scooted her chair back a little, giving her a clear view of the door. She couldn't shake her nervousness, though, and she thought this was a very bad idea to spring this on Kenni like they were. Especially with an audience.

No. She should have gone to Kenni's office, she should have let her know that she was there. She was about to get up when the door opened again.

Her breath lodged in her chest.

CHAPTER FIFTY-SIX

The pep talk Kenni had given herself—with help from Jenn—had faded as four o'clock approached. A new group was assembled, and they were—according to Sky—eager to get started. She only wished *she* was. She hardly remembered muddling through the last week. She had done the ladies a disservice, she knew. Hell, she had even contemplated refunding them a portion of their payment. She needed to snap out of this…this *funk*, as Sky and Jenn called it.

So, she practiced smiling several times before opening the door and going into the dining hall. Mostly quiet conversations were going on, and she looked at Sky and nodded, trying to tell her she was okay. She walked to the front of the tables, smiling at all the women gathered there.

"Welcome to Lyon's Den," she started. "I'm Kendall Lyon. Most everyone calls me Kenni. We're very happy to have you here. Before we go over everything, let me introduce you to my staff."

As she often did, her gaze traveled to Table Five, as if thinking one of these times Joni would be sitting there like she used to.

She stared, blinking several times. She was certain that her heart had stopped beating. She looked away, then back, but the image remained. Christ, was she hallucinating?

She shook her head as if to clear it, then turned to Sky. "Most of you...have been in contact with...with Sky," she stammered. "She's...she's my right hand."

She looked back to Table Five, and yes, the image was still there. God, she'd lost her damn mind. She had finally snapped.

"Sky...um...Sky is...she..."

Sky stepped next to Kenni and waved at everyone. "Hello! I'm Sky Reynolds. So happy to have you all here." She clapped. "I do a lot of things, but I'm famous for my scavenger hunts. I can't wait to get started."

Kenni swallowed, wondering what was wrong with her. She felt like she was about to have a panic attack. She pulled Sky closer.

"Please handle it. I need some air."

She didn't wait for a reply. She went back out through the door and into the lobby. She looked around frantically, half expecting to see Joni hiding in every corner. Was she seeing ghosts now? Had she totally lost her grip on reality?

She bolted out the front door, still not sure where to go, where to run to. She blindly walked around the side of the lodge, heading to the quiet sitting area. She hadn't been there since Joni had left. That's because she could still see them on the bench, could still feel the thrill of their first kiss.

She stood near the bench now, her gaze darting around. God, she needed to get her head on straight. She had lost control. She took several deep breaths. Maybe over the winter, she would see a therapist. Maybe she needed some counseling. Or maybe this was a sign. Maybe she should call Joni. Maybe she needed to go see her. She shook her head. No. She'd call her, she decided. She would call and maybe they could talk and—

She heard a twig snap behind her, and she jerked around, letting out a loud gasp as the ghost stood there. She took a step backward, wondering if she should scream for help or run back to the lodge.

"Are you okay?"

Kenni tilted her head. "What are...*who* are you?"

"Oh my god! It's been a month and you've already forgotten me?"

"Joni?" she asked hesitantly.

Joni frowned. "Do you have amnesia or something?"

Kenni reached her hand out slowly and noticed that it was shaking. She poked Joni's shoulder. "Am I dreaming?"

"What's wrong with you? Are you okay?"

She took a step away, slowly shaking her head again, trying to clear it. "I...I thought I was hallucinating." Then she held a hand up. "Wait a minute. What are you doing here?"

Joni chewed her lower lip before answering. "Well, I'm kinda on assignment."

"Again? Really?"

"Really. Charlotte Turnbull kicked her husband—my boss— out of his office and sent me here to do a follow-up on the article."

"You've got to be kidding."

"I'm not."

"Okay. How long are you planning to stay?"

"I'm not sure."

Kenni nodded. "And where are you going to sleep? I didn't see your name on the roster, so I don't guess you booked a room."

Joni held her gaze. "I'm going to sleep with you. In your bed."

Kenni swallowed. "You are?"

"I am."

"We should...we should probably talk, don't you think?"

"Probably, yes. But it's been a fucking stressful month. Leaving here, leaving you, then all the crap with the article." She took a step closer. "I went to Charlotte, and she got the first article killed, pulled it from the site. And she got my real article up. But then she fired her husband and took over the magazine...and then she gives me this assignment to see you, to write a follow-up. Not a follow-up on Lyon's Den. A follow-up on *me*."

Kenni didn't move as Joni took another step toward her.

"I missed you."

Kenni nodded. "Yes."

Joni smiled a little. "Yes, you *know* I missed you, or yes, you missed me too?"

"I missed you too."

"You're not going to kick me out of camp, are you?"

"I guess not, no."

Joni came closer still. "Good. And I didn't even sneak any wine in this time."

Kenni finally smiled, because here she stood, feeling her heart beating with joy again simply because Joni had walked back into her life. Joni took the final step to reach her, and she stood still, barely breathing as Joni pressed close to her.

"I missed your kisses," Joni said quietly. "Can I please have one?"

"One will lead to two."

Joni smiled. "That's what I'm hoping. I vote we skip dinner."

"I'm not making a very good impression on my new clients."

"Tomorrow will be better. I'll help you on the obstacle course. I can't wait to run it again."

Kenni touched her face. "You're really here."

"Kiss me."

Kenni did, moving the few inches necessary to touch her lips. That spark she'd been missing ignited a fire in her, and she moaned into the kiss, pulling Joni flush against her. The last miserable month faded away, taking her loneliness along with it.

"God, I love the way you kiss me," Joni murmured.

"Let's go to my cabin. I want more than a few kisses."

"Then let's hurry."

CHAPTER FIFTY-SEVEN

Joni collapsed on top of Kenni, unable to hold herself up any longer. She burrowed against her neck with a contented sigh.

"God, I've missed this."

Kenni ran her hands over her back. "You mean you haven't slept with anyone?"

Joni lifted her head, looking into Kenni's eyes. Her question was asked casually, but the look in her eyes was a bit more wary. "Would it have bothered you if I had?"

"Yes," Kenni said without hesitation.

Joni leaned down and kissed her, then rolled to the side. "I haven't even been on a date. I didn't want to." She touched Kenni's hip, tracing a finger over the hummingbird tattoo. "I got a promotion."

"Oh, yeah?"

She sighed. "I should be excited about it, but I'm not sure. Charlotte moved me to the 'front office' as she called it. The magazine had evolved into more about Denver and less about mountain life. She wants to change it."

"Why aren't you excited?"

"I don't know. Something feels off." She moved her hand higher, across Kenni's stomach now. "I was scared to come here. I thought, you know, that you would tell me to leave. That you would still be mad at me."

"Joni, I wasn't ever really *mad* at you."

"You hung up on me!"

Kenni smiled. "Yes. I was taking out some frustration, and you know, having old-fashioned desk phones still allows you to properly slam them down."

"You weren't mad? Then what? Hurt?"

"Okay, I'll admit, the article pissed me off. The thought that you had written those words, yeah, that hurt. I thought you'd been lying to me the whole time. That you'd used me."

"Used you for what? Sex? It wasn't like I pried information out of you. You shut me down several times, if you recall."

"I opened myself to you and let you inside. I didn't consider the consequences, I guess."

Joni leaned up on an elbow, trying to read her eyes. "Consequences?"

"Like now. You're back in my bed. I feel, I don't know, whole again. Happy. But there are still consequences."

"Such as?"

"Such as you'll be leaving again. This is temporary. What's really changed?"

"And when I leave, you'll turn into a bear again?"

Kenni frowned. "A bear?"

Shit! Joni sighed. "Okay, so I may have spoken to Sky. She said you've been a bear. Or that Jenn calls you that."

"She knew you were coming?"

"Yes, and please don't be mad at her. They were worried about you."

"She called and asked you to come?"

"No. I called her. You know, my assignment."

"That's real?"

Joni smiled. "It's real. Though I would have come even if it wasn't." She moved closer to Kenni, resting her head on her shoulder. "I was mad at you."

"Me?"

"Yes. For hanging up on me. For not letting me explain. For thinking that I'd trash this place when you know I loved it so."

"Yes. I was mean to you. I'm sorry."

Joni smiled and kissed her shoulder. "Mean? Is that what you want to call it?"

Kenni snaked an arm around her and pulled her back on top of her. "So, what are we going to do, Ms. James?"

"I want to stay here for a few days and hike with you, and play with you, and climb the fucking big tree. I want to talk and snuggle and make love."

"And then what?"

Joni closed her eyes for a moment, picturing all that. Then she opened them, meeting Kenni's gaze. "Then I'm going to scare you by telling you that I'm falling in love with you."

Kenni's eyes darkened, but she didn't pull away. "Are you?"

"Yes."

Kenni's eyes gentled and a slow smile formed. "You think that'll scare me?"

"Haven't you been hiding your heart all these years? You don't want to love anyone, and you don't want them to love you."

Kenni nodded. "I thought that, yes. This month without you told me that that was a foolish way to live life. My loneliness was magnified. I was…yeah, a bear."

Joni leaned down to kiss her. "And you are *so* not a bear." Then she smiled against her lips. "Maybe a teddy bear." She pulled back again. "You're falling in love too, aren't you?"

Kenni flipped them over, now resting on top of her. "I don't know what this is. My heart springs to life when I'm around you. I smile more, I laugh more."

Joni had thought she needed to hear the words. She hadn't wanted to be the only one baring her soul—her heart. She decided she didn't need to hear them, though. Kenni's eyes told her everything. The contented smile on her face told her more. So, she simply returned the smile and brought a hand up, urging Kenni down for a kiss. A long, slow kiss that had her moaning and wanting more. She spread her thighs, letting Kenni settle there.

Yes, she was falling in love—madly.

CHAPTER FIFTY-EIGHT

Kenni stood next to Jenn as Joni got ready to run the obstacle course. The group of twenty ladies had been listening to Joni's every word as she gave them a brief tutorial on it. As some of the women voiced skepticism that they could make it, Joni laughed.

"When I first did this, I thought they were trying to kill us! But you'll soon learn this is baby stuff. Wait until you have to climb the fucking big tree!"

She and Jenn both laughed outright, although it was mostly nervous laughter coming from the group. Jenn leaned closer to her.

"Joni's a natural at this. Have you considered hiring her?"

Kenni frowned. "Hiring her?"

"Have you forgotten I'm getting married?"

"No. I just preferred to pretend you weren't. But Joni's got a job in Denver."

"Yes, I know. She also loves it here." Then she nudged her with her shoulder. "She's also good for you. She's here one day and you're already back to your old self."

"Maybe it was the one *night* that she was here."

Jenn laughed. "No doubt. But you should consider it."

Kenni's gaze followed Joni's progress, and as Joni stopped at the first balance log, she turned to the group.

"This one doesn't move, so don't be afraid of it. The second one over there does move. Use this rope to help you balance." She hopped off and went to the moving ladder. "Now this was a bitch the first time I did it. Don't fight it. Just climb right up."

Kenni nodded. Yes, Joni was a natural. She realized that since Joni had once been one of those women, she had a different perspective on how to run the course. She wasn't doing it from a coach's point of view, but rather from a client's. She ran the rest of the course, giving little hints at each turn. Kenni was impressed by how gracefully Joni climbed the mesh wall and tumbled over the top.

When she came from behind the wall, Joni was smiling broadly. "How fun!" She clapped her hands. "Who wants to try it?" Then she turned to her and Jenn, smiling a bit sheepishly. "Sorry. I guess I'm not really running this show, am I?"

Kenni laughed. "You're doing great. Why don't you pick someone to go first."

Joni walked by them, her voice quiet. "My own guinea pig. How nice."

Kenni smiled back at her. "You can't sleep with her."

Joni laughed delightfully as she moved to stand in front of the women. "Darla? You want to give it a try?"

"Okay. It looked easy enough."

"You're going to love it. Let's go!"

Kenni couldn't take her eyes off Joni. Her hair was windblown and natural. She looked comfortable in her hiking shorts and boots. Her hazel eyes were a vibrant green today, and the smile on her face never wavered. Kenni was mesmerized by her, just as she'd been since the first day she'd met her. And yes, she was falling in love. Honestly, she was probably way past the falling part, wasn't she? And yes, Joni was right. It did scare her. So much so that she hadn't dared to utter the words to Joni.

Now? Now the words wanted to come out. She was nearly bursting with the need to say them out loud. So, she did.

"I'm in love with her."

Jenn leaned closer to her. "I know."

She glanced at Jenn. "You think I should tell her?"

Jenn shook her head. "You, my friend, are a lost cause. Of *course* you should tell her!"

* * *

"That was fun," Joni said as they hiked back to the lodge. They were at the back of the group, and she smiled, listening to the chatter of the women as they discussed the obstacle course. "I tried to tell everyone to remember this day because by the end of the month when they run it for the last time, they'll be so much better. Most won't recall being this clumsy and out of sync. I know I didn't."

Kenni nodded. "You did good with them."

She bumped her shoulder. "I sort of took over. I'm sorry, but I was having so much fun."

"No, no. It was good. Since you were once one of them, they could relate better to you, I think, rather than me or Jenn."

"Maybe."

"You know, I've got a job opening," Kenni said rather casually.

She looked at her with raised eyebrows. "What do you mean?"

"Jenn's getting married, remember?"

"Oh, yeah. I'd forgotten. This is her last month."

"Yes. Gonna have to hire someone to replace her."

Joni suddenly felt nervous. "Are you...are you suggesting *me*?"

Kenni smiled at her. "I am."

"Oh, Kenni. I don't know anything about all that stuff. Jenn is—"

"You managed the whole running of the obstacle course without much help from me or Jenn."

"But..."

"I know. Long shot. You already have a job that I assume you love. But I thought...well..."

Joni linked her arm through Kenni's as they walked, then leaned closer. "Are you serious?"

Kenni met her gaze. "I don't want you to leave."

She stopped walking, halting Kenni's movement as well. "Why?" she asked quietly. "Why don't you want me to leave?" She saw Kenni swallow before answering.

"I don't want you to leave because…because, yes, you were right."

Joni held her gaze. "Right about what?"

"I…I *am* in love with you."

She smiled at her and leaned closer, kissing her gently. "I know. You told me last night." At Kenni's frown, she clarified, "With your eyes, your touch. You can't hide that, Kenni, even though you tried to."

"So, I'm busted, huh?"

Joni kissed her quickly. "You're busted." She linked their arms again and started walking. "So, about this job…you're serious?"

"Very. But you just got a promotion."

Yes, she had gotten a promotion. Charlotte wanted her to help move the magazine in a different direction. Is that what she wanted? Would she and Kenni be able to maintain their relationship long-distance? Or would she feel suffocated in the city now?

"Too much to think about?"

Joni shook her head. "No. Because I love it up here." The group had gotten far ahead of them, and she stopped walking again. "It's a surprise offer, yes. Because, Kenni, you know I'm not qualified. I can't teach them all the things Jenn taught us."

Kenni pulled her off the trail and fingered the limb of a tree. "What tree is this?"

"It's a Douglas fir," she said without much thought.

"Famous for what?"

She smiled. "Mice hiding in the cones."

"And what fucking big tree will we climb?"

"A hundred-year-old ponderosa," she said easily. "Their lifespan is five hundred."

Kenni smiled at her. "See? You know things. You can teach."

Joni stared at her. "What about us?"

"What do you mean?"

"Will there be like…too much togetherness and you'll get sick of me?"

Kenni smiled. "Just like Jenn, you'll take part of the group on hikes, and I'll take the others. We won't be together all the time. And you'll have your own team to mentor. I know you thrive on competition. It isn't only limited to the teams. The team leaders are involved too."

"How so?"

"The winning team's leader gets a thousand bucks as a bonus for the month."

Joni laughed. "Oh, hell yeah." She tapped her shoulder. "Because I'm going to beat your ass!"

They embraced then. Tight. Hard. Their kiss didn't last long because they were both smiling too much to kiss. They held hands as they continued along the trail, lightly swinging them as they walked. She felt nearly giddy. She didn't have to leave here if she didn't want to. She decided she would call Charlotte this evening. Despite her new job offer, she did want to write the follow-up article. And maybe Charlotte would let her contribute other pieces from time to time. If she felt inspired to write, that is. But she didn't want to think about that now.

"I vote we skip dinner."

Kenni laughed. "We skipped dinner yesterday."

"Okay, then let's get Wanda to make us a plate, and we'll take it home with us."

Kenni stopped and pulled her closer. "Home. Yes, I like that."

"You know what else?"

"What?"

"I think it would be really fun to get snowed in here this winter. You know, with you."

Kenni touched her cheek gently. "You want to stay?"

"I want to stay wherever you stay."

Kenni smiled and leaned closer, giving her one of those sweet, slow kisses that melted her bones. When Kenni pulled away, her eyes were dark with desire.

"I vote we skip dinner."

Joni laughed and tugged her along. "What a brilliant idea. Wish I'd thought of it!"

Bella Books, Inc.

Happy Endings Live Here.

P.O. Box 10543

Tallahassee, FL 32302

Phone: (800) 729-4992

www.BellaBooks.com

More Titles from Bella Books

Hunter's Revenge – Gerri Hill
978-1-64247-447-3 | 276 pgs | paperback: $18.95 | eBook: $9.99
Tori Hunter is back! Don't miss this final chapter in the acclaimed Tori Hunter series.

Integrity – E. J. Noyes
978-1-64247-465-7 | 28 pgs | paperback: $19.95 | eBook: $9.99
It was supposed to be an ordinary workday...

The Order – TJ O'Shea
978-1-64247-378-0 | 396 pgs | paperback: $19.95 | eBook: $9.99
For two women the battle between new love and old loyalty may prove more dangerous than the war they're trying to survive.

Under the Stars with You – Jaime Clevenger
978-1-64247-439-8 | 302 pgs | paperback: $19.95 | eBook: $9.99
Sometimes believing in love is the first step. And sometimes it's all about trusting the stars.

The Missing Piece – Kat Jackson
978-1-64247-445-9 | 250 pgs | paperback: $18.95 | eBook: $9.99
Renee's world collides with possibility and the past, setting off a tidal wave of changes she could have never predicted.

An Acquired Taste – Cheri Ritz
978-1-64247-462-6 | 206 pgs | paperback: $17.95 | eBook: $9.99
Can Elle and Ashley stand the heat in the *Celebrity Cook Off* kitchen?